MARRIAGE TO A MISTER

MEDDLESOME MATCHMAKERS
BOOK ONE

ANNE CHERIE

EDITED BY
BECKY SLEMONS

COVER DESIGN BY
QUIRKY BIRD COVERS

Marriage to a Mister

MEDDLESOME MATCHMAKERS BOOK ONE

ANNE CHERIE

To Randy, simply because
you are everything.

UPCOMING BOOKS
BY ANNE CHERIE

MEDDLESOME MATCHMAKERS SERIES

Marriage to a Mister

Running from Rakes

Capturing the Captain

Victory over the Viscount

AMERICANS IN LONDON SERIES

The Americans in London Series is a three-book spin-off of the Meddlesome Matchmakers Series and follows three siblings as they find love across the pond.

CELESTIAL COURTSHIP SERIES

The Celestial Courtship series is a four-book cozy fantasy romance set in a historic world torn apart by old magic, old traditions, and even older rivalries.

1

THE DEVOTED DAUGHTER

Lady Fleur Osborne watched as fine white powder slid off the spoon and into the glass. The drink foamed and crackled, misting her hand as it reacted violently when she began to stir.

"To see you standing there mixing that awful drink, one would think you were trying to poison someone."

Fleur looked up to see the cook, Mrs. Davis, canter into the kitchen with a bag of flour in one arm and jar of spice in the other.

"With the way my father feels this morning, he may very well wish it were poison," said Fleur.

"Morning? It's past noon just, not a bite of breakfast. Sent back both trays I sent to the library. Yelled at poor Mary, he did, before she ran off crying who knows where." Cook slammed the sack of flour down onto the table, and a plume of white engulfed them both. "Oh! Forgive me, milady."

Fleur laughed between coughs, waving her hand to

clear the air. "It's fine, Mrs. Davis, and you know my father's temperament as well as anyone, especially when he's been out all night with the earl."

She ran her hands over her dark hair, careful not to disturb the curls her lady's maid so painstakingly set that morning, but frowned when a few loosened and fell. Looking down, she sighed at the state of her mint green day dress and patted herself to remove the dusting of flour.

Once righted, Fleur placed the drink onto a small tray, nearly dropping it when a loud noise from above stairs echoed. Muffled shouts and booming footsteps preceded the slamming of the front door. She glanced upwards towards the ceiling, beyond which, her father sat in his library.

Fleur winced. "Oh, dear."

"There goes another," said Mrs. Davis, shaking her head as she waved her hands in the air, more flour flinging from her fingers. "You'd think your father would agree to one o' them matches. At this rate, he'll have refused every suitable man in London. Old and young!"

Fleur blinked hard, still feeling the flour on her face and long lashes. Her cheeks puffed, and she blew out the air, sending a tendril of hair flying, wondering if this time the suitor offered for her or her younger sister Julia.

"I'm certain my father has his reasons," said Fleur, smiling at Mrs. Davis. "He must be aware of some fault or other failing to turn them away so decidedly, and seeing how we young ladies are not to know half of what the men in this town do or say when we are not present; I'll have to trust in his judgment."

Mrs. Davis looked her straight in the eye with a mischievous grin, one that said she knew precisely what the young men were about.

Fleur decided a change of subject was in order. "Can you believe we leave for the country in only two days? Oh, how I have missed Norfield."

"Always so eager to return to Hampshire, you are," Mrs. Davis said, still cleaning flour off the table tops. "One would think you did not like all these fancy balls and invitations to parties."

Fleur could not help but laugh. It was a well-known fact to those who knew her best that she disliked town life, even more so during the season.

"You know me only too well, Mrs. Davis. I live for the town life, every night another ball or musicale. Every day another visitor with news of who will marry whom or, more importantly, who refused whom. It isn't monotonous at all," said Fleur with a theatrical wave of her hand while the tray and drink in the other rattled dangerously.

Cook laughed. "That will be enough dramatics for one day, milady, run along with you now and take that to your father, but be mindful, he's bound to be in a foul mood."

Fleur nodded and made her way out of the kitchen, up the small staircase and onto the main floor towards the library. She tried not think of the ball that evening, where she and Julia would be food for the hounds, once they found out — and they always found out — that her father had yet again refused another gentleman's offer.

It did not help that she was three and twenty, her fourth season winding to a close. An utter disgrace some would call her in hushed tones meant for no-one, and yet everyone, to hear. Having failed her only duty as a daughter of the *ton* it seemed her saving grace was not that she was considered comely, her fine blue eyes and dark raven hair attracted many a suitor on their own merits, she knew. But no, her grace fell to her connections and dowry. Both of which, in her case, were considerable.

Being the daughter of a duke had not saved her, however, from the gossip and melee of the marriage mart. It seemed to only increase their interest in her failed offers. Her father, well-known for rejecting every match to cross his doorstep, did not seem to sympathize with her plight. His only concern was her health and happiness, and in his mind, there was not one man in all of England that could secure it. Unless that man was named Viscount Ravenbrook, heir to the Blackburn Earldom and son to his oldest friend, the Earl of Blackburn.

Yet to her, he was only Edward. The boy who kept a watchful eye on her and her sister while they played with his younger brother, Evan. The boy she had not talked to properly since she was sixteen, the boy who was now a man, though she could not see it, and she wasn't altogether sure she wanted to.

She huffed again, trying to move another stray tendril of hair from her face, her hands full with the tray. She stopped halfway across the hall when she heard yet another commotion coming from the direction of the front entryway.

"What now?" she murmured to herself.

Hurrying across the hall, she saw Lord Blackburn arguing with the new footman, who was failing at refusing the earl entry.

"I don't care what his grace said. You will admit me at once. Never in my life have I been treated thusly in this home!" The earl punctuated his words with a thump of his cane and a wave of his hand. "I told you before I have important business with the duke, the outcome of which depends greatly upon every minute I stand here waiting."

Fleur's eyes widened at the urgency of the earl's words and she scurried forward to the door. "Lord Blackburn, do come inside, please." She turned to the footman, her hair swinging in her face once more. "Mr. Craigs, Lord Blackburn is a very close family friend, and if he comes to us with such urgency there must be a reason, please allow him entry, no matter if my father has instructed for no visitors."

Craigs hesitated, but, unwilling to refuse the lady of the house, he stepped aside.

Lord Blackburn entered slowly, eyeing the young man as he removed his hat and gloves, handing them over to him roughly, his demeanor decidedly cross.

"Craigs is it? New are you? Where is old Bradly?" He asked, looking around as if to find him hiding somewhere.

Craigs quickly nodded, unsure if he should answer the rapid-pace questioning.

Fleur felt pity for the poor man who gained Lord Blackburn's censure and ire and moved to distract him. "Why don't I take you to my father? He's in the library, though I'm afraid he is feeling quite ill."

"I can only imagine, my dear, after last night's festivities," the earl agreed, noting for the first time the flour that clung to her face.

"What happened here?" he asked, motioning to her hair while his stern expression softened into a smile.

Fleur sighed. "Just a small mishap in the kitchens."

Lord Blackburn laughed and took the tray from her grasp, then offered his arm before walking towards the library.

Fleur looked at him, noting that he also looked a little pale and wondered what important business could provoke such urgency. "Lady Blackburn is well, I trust? Julia and I both look forward to seeing her tonight."

"Not to worry — my lady is very well, though anxious for this evening. Lady Brockhurst is one of her dearest friends, so she is, of course, excited about seeing everyone. Balls are a nuisance at best, but she insists we make an appearance to what seems like every fête of the season. It's all so very tiresome."

Fleur laughed at his words, his overly put-upon countenance enacted to cheer her, though deep down she could not help but agree. The whirl of the season was exhausting, and as tonight was the last ball they would attend before leaving, she felt her decay into spinsterhood exceedingly.

Spinster.

It really was a dirty little word bandied about by men and old matrons to frighten poor girls into marriage with threats of poverty and loneliness. It was a compelling argument for a looming bleak existence that took her breath away with fright of being forever alone, a finality so large it felt like it would swallow her entire future.

It wasn't that she did not appreciate her father's attention and devotion of turning away men he found unsuitable. She knew she had no intention of marrying any of the suitors that offered for her, so her father could not be faulted, but after four long years was it really so difficult to find someone she could talk with? Someone she could perhaps laugh with? She had that once, she remembered, and she feared it ruined her, not able to forget those feelings or his memory.

They arrived at the library, and Lord Blackburn stopped and turned to her. "You're fretting, my dear."

Fleur looked him in the eye, trying to reassure him with a smile. "Forgive me, my lord, for my inattentive company. I have much on my mind before we away to the country."

"Why don't you run along to Lady Julia? I'll deliver this

to your father," he said, punctuating his words with a lift of the drink tray. "And tell your sister that Lady Blackburn insists you both join her tonight in our carriage."

Fleur's spirits lifted in an instant. It had been too long since she had a moment to speak with Lady Blackburn, and they would not see her again 'til next season.

"Please convey to her our acceptance, my lord. We shall look forward to it."

The earl agreed and raised the tray to her once again, a nod to goodbyes, and with a new spring in her step, she made her way upstairs to find Julia. At least she would enjoy tonight, and then perhaps tomorrow she would tell her father she no longer wished to take part in the season, that this would be her last.

The thought of making such a declaration soured her mood, but Fleur was determined to find happiness of her own making. She must, or she feared it would follow and haunt her. After all, she had a doting father, a sister who adored her, and a cousin who would see mountains moved to ensure her happiness, not to mention her friends. Could she really ask for more? Truly ask for more? She doubted anyone could be so loved and remain unhappy, and she refused to think herself so selfish that she could not see the light for the clouds.

2

MATCHMAKING FATHERS

Julian Osborne, the Duke of Norfield, sat in his library, his head in his hands and elbows propped upon his desk. His eyes pinched closed against the glare of the sun as it reflected on polished wood walls. He willed the throbbing to cease, he even demanded it, but his body refused him.

He groaned in defeat, laying his head upon his desk, deciding he would benefit from a swift beheading when Baines laid the rest of the day's correspondence in front of him.

"Your letters, your grace."

Julian raised his head, his dignity insisting upon it. "What was I thinking? Letting in that foppish Hamilton. He was in absolute hysterics! I cannot fathom what on earth made him think Lady Fleur was engaged. Damned fool, as if he stood a chance with either of my daughters after those rumors of him and that actress."

"I believe the young gentleman will not return anytime soon, you were less than subtle with your censure."

"Not the calm and patient whelp I once was, eh,

Baines?" Julian asked, raising his hand to smooth down his neatly trimmed beard.

"I would never say so, your grace," said Baines with a long, amused look.

Julian grinned and tugged on his shirt sleeves to straighten his appearance. "No, I suppose you wouldn't, lest you find yourself out on your ear."

"After forty years of loyal service, I doubt you would do something so cruel to this old man."

"Old man," Julian whispered. "Are we really so old, Baines?"

"I'm afraid so, your grace."

Julian could not fault his answer. His own hair was not so dark as it once was, the grey at his temples and beard glistening in the sunlight, the fine lines around his dark eyes increasing as he smiled at the man who had been his valet, and then his steward, his strongest ally since he inherited his duties at the age of fourteen.

"You're getting mischievous in your declining years, Baines. Shall I alert Lady Julia that she has another cohort in the household?"

"I would never presume to give a duke, especially the Duke of Norfield, any sort of mischief, your grace. As to the other, please spare both you and I the trouble. Lady Julia has many spies and compatriots in the household. I do not wish to be added to her ranks."

Julian laughed, running his fingers through his hair before rubbing his eyes. "It's true, instead of using her come-out to find herself a husband, my youngest has been devious as ever, purposely ignoring the entire production of these seasons. At this rate, she'll never find a husband."

"Was not it you, your grace, who turned down at least two of her suiters in the last week alone?" Baines asked.

"And that is two less than you've rejected for Lady Fleur if my count is correct. The young men about town are beginning to call you 'The Tyrant'."

"The Tyrant?" Julian shouted, whipping his head to meet Baines' eyes and regretting the action instantly when his head swam, and his stomach churned. He supposed he had been a little harsh on the last boy, but really, the man was an idiot. Rambling on and on like that, daring to weep like a child. How could he ever entrust such a man to take over the care of his precious daughter?

"If having a name such as 'The Tyrant' scares unsuitable young men away from my daughters, so be it. I'll not allow them to marry fortune hunters or useless, brainless young men that can neither provide for nor protect them."

"Wasn't the last gentleman heir to the Bransford Earldom? I dare say he would have been able to provide for Lady Fleur admirably even if he is prone to occasional hysterics."

"No, no, he would never do, besides, Lord Blackburn would never let me live it down if I acquired a dandy for a son-in-law."

Baines raised his brow and cleared his throat; an action Julian knew to mean he did not agree. "If you say so, your grace," he replied, simply.

Feeling his headache worsen, he gently returned his head to the desk, basking in relief from the cool wood against his brow when an insistent knock came at the door followed by the blustering entrance of his friend Charles Woolf, the Earl of Blackburn.

"Norfield!" boomed the earl, followed by the crash of a slamming door. "We need to... what the devil are you doing?"

Julian raised his head hastily. It would not do to look

like he had been drooling on his desk only moments before. "What does it look like I'm doing?" he asked, trying to keep his head still, his voice low and menacing. Which was harder than it looked when it was all he could do not to ask Charles why he was carrying a serving tray. "I'm resting. What do you want?"

"Resting? I'm absolutely aghast that you could rest at a time like this. And did you know your new man tried to put me off at the door? Fleur had to come to my rescue when he wouldn't allow me entry." The earl motioned widely with the tray, and the drink overflowed the glass.

Baines made his way forward from the corner of the room, taking the drink from the earl before he could spill again and set it upon the desk in front of the duke.

Julian gave him a thankful look and waved him off, gently dismissing him.

His gaze found Charles as Baines left the room. "Blackburn, you are rambling again. As for the other, that's what servants do. They follow orders," said Julian, his sarcasm evident. "Orders like, 'I do not wish to be disturbed' or 'Let anyone in at your own peril'."

"Do not wish to be disturbed?" Charles raked his hand through his slightly long, blonde yet graying hair. "Do you expect me to wait around all day while your man finds out if you're home when I know damned well you are? At a time like this?"

The duke gave a low chuckle and watched his friend drop himself uninvited into the chair across from him. It was true that Charles never waited for anything, especially something as tedious as being announced, though decorum and manners dictated it be so no matter how long they had known one another.

"I'll have a word with Craigs. Now, shouldn't you still

be at home, listening to Lady Blackburn scold you for coming home in the wee hours?" Julian asked. "You really overdid it at White's last night. I haven't seen you drink that much since we celebrated old Barnby's marriage, and that was twenty-five years ago or more. We really must stop celebrating his birthdays — they always end in a week of misery to my head."

"I don't know whether you realize it, but you're the one that looks the very devil, and it's already past noon," said Charles. "It was certainly you who was foxed last night, but we have not the time for this. Why aren't you more distressed? I feel positively ill at what we've done."

"Blackburn, stop acting like an old scold," Julian interrupted with a scowl, perplexed and annoyed at his friend's alarm. "If I wanted someone to nag me to death, I would have remarried long ago. Tell me what this is about."

Charles stood from his chair, his jaw slack and his eyes wide. "You dog, you don't remember," he stated, as he begun to pace the floor. "You don't remember, and Maddie is furious — with the both of us I might add, not only me. She's had Edward and I up since before the breakfast hour coming up with a plan to mend this... this chaos! And you know she's right, it's the only plan that makes any sense. Our children must marry and quickly. Should we start the banns this Sunday? Or wait 'til the house party? That may be better," Charles muttered to himself.

"Banns?" Julian asked in a shamefully high-pitched voice before swallowing hard. "Charles, I have come to think of your penchant for babbling as an endearing quality over the years, but make sense. I haven't the slightest idea of what you are referring to. Sit down, be quiet, and let me think."

Julian held Charles' defiant gaze as he looked his

friend straight in the eye. When he broke, he picked up the glass before him and downed the drink in one swift gulp, feeling dread creep upon him instead of relief from the soda tonic.

He hurriedly tried to recall the night before. There was brandy, talks of dowries, brandy, discussions of grandchildren, and again, the cursed brandy. He remembered his friends cheering and congratulating them, shaking their hands and passing around more celebratory drinks as they all talked of a wedding.

Oh hell, thought the duke, his dark eyes widening and snapping to Charles' blue.

"Figured it out, have you?" Charles asked flatly, miffed at being ordered into the chair, a chair he was standing next to and most assuredly not sitting in.

Julian groaned and laid his head back upon his desk with a hard crack, not even minding the dull throb as it intensified. It seemed — in their unfortunately drunken state the night before — the duke and the earl discussed a betrothal between their children. No, discussed was too mild. Announced was a better word. They had announced a marriage between their households to God and anyone else who would listen.

"It cannot be that dreadful," he said, looking up at Charles, hoping against hope his memory served him ill. "Who will have remembered? We were all jug-bitten. Furthermore, not one of our friends care for such news, so will they even remember?"

Charles glared. "You and I both know some of our friends are nosier than a maiden aunt, and you can rest assured that they will remember. Besides, more than just our room was privy to our drunken antics. The entire club heard."

Julian snorted. "How would you know? You could not possibly —"

Charles removed his gloves one at a time, throwing them down on Julian's desk with a slap before sitting. "I know, dear friend, because my wife came into my bedchamber this morning and boxed me about the ears whilst I was still sleeping — a terrible way to wake, mind you — and told me that whilst she'd been out that morning she was congratulated by no fewer than three people asking when the happy occasion was to be held and which of our children were to be married. My wife, being the clever woman she is, escaped without confirming any of the story, only conveying an announcement would be made soon. She instantaneously knew we'd done something foolish and came home to confront me. I confessed to the whole damned thing."

Julian hung his head and blinked. "This is what young Hamilton was talking about this morning when he ran here in a panic. Why he thought Fleur was betrothed. Good God, you're right. It must be all over London." Julian thought back to his encounter with the boy. His repeated questions on if Fleur was betrothed and to whom. "Charles, no one knows which one of your sons is supposedly marrying one of my daughters. Now that I think about it, Hamilton seemed to be unsure."

"Hamilton? Was he here? I hope you refused him seeing as we already have a disaster on our hands."

Julian nodded, his mouth a grim line as he wondered what they were to do. Two sons and two daughters, none of whom were attached, though two must form a rushed betrothal.

Julian could not believe his own idiocy. He'd spent years — *years* — shooing away men he deemed inappropriate for his daughters — men he knew they did not love — and in one reckless move he sealed one of their fates to be matched in a loveless pairing.

He closed his eyes and knew within himself that wasn't altogether true. At one time Fleur did love one of the earl's sons, he was sure of it, but that had been many years ago when she was but a girl.

The earl had two children, the eldest being Edward Woolf, Viscount Ravenbrook. A very good catch and at the age of thirty, he would make a fine husband for either of his daughters as Charles' heir. He was, by all accounts, Julian's preferred choice in both situation and temperament, but unfortunately, the earl did have one other son.

Evander Woolf, a standoffish and stubborn man with a name that suited none other so well as he. He was six and twenty, also of good marrying age, but in the duke's eyes, he was quite ... unsuitable. Yes, definitely unsuitable. The man was practically a recluse since the days they would visit Blackburn Hall. He refused the military commission his father had offered and practically disappeared. Julian heard he speculated wildly in new, and quite frankly, dangerous and unsound investments.

Evander – Evan, as they called him – had been Fleur's playmate as a child. Many summers had they spent at Blackburn Hall only to return again for Christmas, especially after the passing of his own beloved wife. His daughters retreated into the arms of Lady Blackburn in their grief, and Charles was there to comfort and distract him during his own time of sorrow. It was almost as if they never left, only returning home to see to Norfield's needs during the spring and fall.

He knew during their time together Fleur and Evan had formed an attachment to one another, but he found out too late just how deep it ran. Not until he and Charles pushed the boy by trying to match Fleur with his elder brother did he discover the depth of their feelings. Once known he would have agreed to the match, if only Evan would take a respectable position in the military, or even the church would do. Either would secure his daughter's future, but he refused them outright.

Evan reacted by leaving Blackburn Hall, fleeing back to university, breaking Fleur's heart in one cruel move after a vicious quarrel Julian wished he had never witnessed or entered into. She was but sixteen when they parted, and they had not met each other since.

She had cried for days, been melancholy for months, and when she finally emerged from her sorrow he had sworn to himself he'd not return to Blackburn Hall. He would not put his daughter in the middle of those memories, not when he had fled Norfield for so many years to forget his own. And damn Evan for not agreeing

For a moment Julian became unnerved, angry that Charles and Madeleine may try to pair Fleur and Evan, try to right past wrongs. He could not find it within himself to forgive the boy, not for his cruel words, or for his leaving not only Fleur but them all, and for what? His reckless business adventures? How was that more important than Fleur's security and happiness?

He calmed when he recalled that Charles said Maddie had spoken to Edward that morning, nothing about Evan.

Julian breathed a sigh of relief. "What did Maddie say?"

"She said we were both old fools and —"

"Not that. I can imagine what she would have said on that subject, but what does she think we should do? How are we to address this?"

"A marriage between the families. We cannot recant,

not when it was us doing the announcing. Anything else would be a scandal of the first order, and the *ton* would shout with mirth and drag both your girls through speculation and gossip. They would be merciless."

Julian's face drained of all color, the reality of what they had done settling in. "God help us."

"Yes." Charles agreed, pulling out his golden watch from his fob pocket, checking the time. "Maddie thinks the marriage should be between Edward and Fleur, as they are the eldest. Not to mention I have not seen that younger son of mine since the season began months ago — he comes and goes as he pleases. She's already spoken to Edward, and he is coming here to address Fleur within the hour if you are amenable. And Julian, you must be."

Julian nodded, feeling as though the sense and order that ruled his life had run away from him. "How many times will we cause our children grief? Why do they have to pay for our assumptions and our mistakes?"

Charles bowed his head, knowing Julian talked about the past as much as he did the present. "We can only hope Edward and Fleur will grow to love one another. They already do to some extent, you know this, having been raised together should make the transition a little easier, one would think."

Julian grasped the letter opener on his desk, his knuckles turning white. "How does your son feel about the betrothal?"

Charles paused. "He was very accepting."

"Not exactly a confession of love, is it?" Julian asked, his jaw tight.

"He wouldn't want to see your girls come to harm any more than myself or Maddie."

"We tried pairing them off before, Charles, and look what happened."

"There is always Evan," Charles said slowly and carefully.

Julian's eyes hardened, his voice rough. "No."

"It's been seven years and we pushed him to far — "

"I said, no. If he had shown himself when Fleur made her debut into society I would have considered it. I know she held some hope that he would. In the end he let her down once again."

Charles nodded, not willing to bring up the old argument of his younger son, knowing Julian would never relent, not after everything. "Then try not to worry. Maddie has thought of everything, brilliant as she is. Within the last few hours, she planned a house party and sent off invitations. Everything has been arranged and instructions sent to the staff at Blackburn Hall. The two can be married at the end of the gathering in a quiet ceremony surrounded by family and a few friends. They will have time to come to know one another, Julian. After all, the banns still have to be called."

The duke nodded — it was a good plan, considering the circumstances. "I suppose we must announce the betrothal tonight. Everyone's tongues will be wagging. I am curious, though, what would you have done had I refused your plan?"

Charles huffed but made no move to answer. Julian suspected he had none.

"You said Ravenbrook would be here within the hour?"

"Yes, of course. The sooner, the better I think. We should not delay, don't you agree?"

"I do, but I must speak to Fleur immediately and at least

give her some time to prepare herself," Julian said while turning, if possible, a shade more puce.

"Do you think she will take it badly?" Charles asked, sinking further down into his chair at Julian's glare to such an obtuse question. He rubbed his face in frustration. "Edward will be here any minute."

"The more reason for you to get out of that chair and delay him so I can speak to my daughter," Julian said through gritted teeth. "Tell him to come back in a few hours, or better yet tell him the whole thing is off! Sod the plan and sod the entire British aristocracy," he shouted, anger settling in. "Besides, this is entirely your fault, Charles. Who in their right mind speaks about such matters of import when they're drunk at a birthday celebration? Of course we made a scene."

"You must see sense, Julian! The last thing we want is for Lady Fleur to feel cornered, but they must marry —." The earl was interrupted by a sharp knock at the door, followed by Craigs walking in with the tray. A small card was placed on top to announce the visitor, Viscount Ravenbrook.

"He is here," stated Charles.

"There really is nothing to be done," said Julian, standing from his chair and looking towards the door.

"Have your man show my son in here while you prepare your daughter. Having a minute's notice is better than having none at all. Really it's more than some fathers give their poor daughters."

"Those fathers ought to be shot," Julian seethed, though he was no longer certain he was any better. "Right, I'll have your son see her in the drawing room after we have spoken. I don't foresee any difficulties — Fleur is a reasonable girl and I think she will see sense in the match. They have at the very least considered one another with all the hints we have dropped over the years. It won't be too much of shock to her, will it? And they have grown up considerably since then, so perhaps they will see each other differently now?"

"You're stalling, Julian," said Charles, his voice soft.

Julian nodded and left the comfort of his library. He wanted what was best for his girls, so why was he always making these careless mistakes? He did not know, but he would see her happy, and he felt she had more of a chance to be content with Edward than she did with other suitors who were veritable strangers compared to Ravenbrook.

Feeling somewhat better about the situation, he made his way upstairs, hoping all the while his youngest would not be with Fleur when he tried to explain the situation. If his headache was terrible now, he didn't want to think how he would feel after that confrontation.

3
A LOVE REQUITED

Evan Woolf stood by his mahogany desk in his small library and shuffled through his papers, a smug smile on his face.

He decided he was feeling rather content, and for Evan, that was saying something. Having only reviewed his latest investment a moment before, his spirits lifted at the good news from his solicitor. Though mostly he lent his high spirits to the thought of telling Nathan that he'd been right, because that meant that Nathan had been wrong.

How delicious, he thought, smirk still in place.

He picked up the letters again, ready to reread the pleasing news when he heard a knock on his front door.

"Damn," he said, throwing the papers down with a great smack and moving to the window to see who had arrived uninvited. Unable to see, he shrugged and left the unknown person to knock.

He walked around the desk to sit down and start his day's correspondence when the knocking became more rapid and forceful. Only one person in all of England could knock in that persistent manner, Nathan Carter.

Smiling again, he bounded from his library to the front entryway and shooed his cook away from the door. "I will answer, Eliza," he said, swinging open the door as she shook her head in what he knew was great displeasure at having to tend to the door at all.

Nathan stood in the doorway, straight-faced and impatient. "I've been knocking for ages, what have you been doing?" He walked inside, tripping over a fraying carpet, his blonde hair falling into his eyes. Evan nodded to Eliza her dismissal, who then harrumphed and went back to her kitchen.

"I've been working, Nathan. It's that thing people do in order to earn a living or satisfy one's need for growth. Not that you'd understand."

Nathan looked around trying to find a place to set his belongings. Every surface was filled with papers and books, so he settled for throwing his hat and cane in the corner of the entryway before turning to a mirror and righting his hair.

"And why wouldn't I understand?" Nathan asked, his preening finished. "I have my own interests too."

Evan shook his head. "You'll definitely be interested in this, come and have a look," he said, walking back towards his library.

Nathan groaned and moved carefully through the mountains of books that had crawled their way out of the library doors and into the hallway, piled high on the floor.

"When are you going to organize all this?" he asked, waving his hand around and stepping over a growing hill of science tombs.

"When I have the time, I suppose," said Evan, already in the library, having maneuvered the piles with ease.

"You do realize if you hired some help they would take

care of this for you, along with answering the door," Nathan said slowly and deliberately. "I'm sure Eliza would appreciate it as well," he added when Eliza came in with a tray and slammed it on the small table in the corner.

"Hello, Eliza," Nathan said cheerfully.

She grunted once more, and Evan looked toward her. "She doesn't mind, do you, Eliza? Besides I'm only one person and hardly any trouble at all."

Eliza mumbled what Nathan heard as *No trouble at all, indeed,* and flew out of the room. It was frightfully amusing to him. "So what is it that you wanted to show me?"

Nathan watched Evan as he shuffled through paper after paper and mumbled. "Sometime today perhaps?"

"Here it is!" Evan boomed. "Look at this, look at it," he said as he shoved the letter in Nathan's face, so he had only the choice to take it. "I told you, didn't I? The cylinder press was bound to be the only way for the print world to succeed in mass production. We can now print eight hundred times faster than with the older models. John Walter has agreed to purchase, you know, and others will follow suit once they see his production speeds."

Nathan's face soured as he read over the letter. "John Walter, as in *The Times,* John Walter? Well, congratulations, you'll now be rich as Croesus, not that you weren't doing well before."

"Says the man with a trust bigger than my entire portion. Some of us need to produce and not just exist."

Nathan shrugged.

Evan gave up and walked over to his chair, moving papers he had slung around moments before into messy little piles. "So, what brings you here? If it's about tonight's ball I've already conveyed my regrets to the hostess *and* my mother. I don't know why she insists her friends invite me. I haven't said yes once in all these years."

Nathan clucked in disbelief. "Because she hopes you'll relent and come, you idiot, but that's not why I'm here. I received this early this morning." Nathan reached into his pocket and removed an invitation. He waved it around before sliding it back into his coat.

"Ah, yes, that," said Evan, his face drawn and clearly annoyed. "I was planning on visiting my mother this afternoon to convey my regrets to that invite in person and also bid them farewell. A house party? Can you imagine? And not a word of it until this very morning. If I hadn't had such good news along with the invitation, I'd be in a very foul mood.

"There can be no doubt on that subject," said Nathan, smiling and shaking his head.

Evan looked over to Nathan, curious. "I assume you will refuse? In fact, you can join me to visit my mother and hand her your regrets as well. She is always happy to see you, though I can't imagine why," he said, smiling and dodging a piece of random paper Nathan flung at him. "I do have business to attend to beforehand, so keep that in mind. If you accompany me this time you can't complain as you did the last."

Nathan looked at him wearily. "My answer depends greatly on your destination."

Evan smiled. "My solicitors."

Nathan pulled a face. "Last time, you told me it would only take a moment and then we were there for two entire hours."

Evan shook his head, remembering how Nathan had sulked around his solicitor's office, trying to occupy himself, when he accidentally kicked a cabinet, sending a framed portrait of the man's wife crashing to the ground, breaking to pieces.

Evan laughed at his thoughts. "To this day when I visit, he moves that portrait as if I'm about to attack it."

Nathan smirked. "He should not have left it perched so precariously on the edge then."

"If you'd rather not go you could speak to my mother tonight, that is if you're attending the Brockhurst's Ball."

"I have been invited," said Nathan. "Shocking, seeing how I'm only the son of a lowly baron and the second son at that."

"Yes, but you are very rich. It acquits you of all flaws, didn't you know?" asked Evan laughing. He walked over to his chair before lifting the coat he had perched on the arm. He shrugged into the ill-fitted superfine one arm at a time, the brown tones of his over and waist coats warring with one another. "Are you joining me, or not?"

Nathan sighed. "I suppose, but only if you truly will be there for a moment."

"Would I lead you astray?" asked Evan, smirking.

They made their way outside, and Evan practically cantered down the lane, with Nathan trying to keep pace. He knew his business would take a bit longer that he admitted, but watching Nathan squirm from acute idleness was one of his favorite pastimes since university, but more than that, he was happy to spend the day with his friend.

———

LADY FLEUR OSBORNE sat in the family's private upstairs parlor and wished. She wished for patience with her knitting as the wool slid from her fingers and needles for the third time that morning. She wished for rain that afternoon, hoping she would not have to honor her acceptance of taking a drive in Mr. Hamilton's new phaeton. But most of all, she wished she could stay home that evening, though she did look forward to seeing her friends one final time.

She had finally managed to move the fallen stitches back onto her needles with a feeling of accomplishment when a loud *bang!* made her startle, and all her hard work unraveled as it fell to the floor. Pursing her lips, she swung around in her chair towards the door, knowing she would find her sister there.

"Julia Osborne!" she shouted, then took a deep breath to calm her nerves while her sister looked startled as she.

"Good heavens, why are you shouting?" asked Julia, hand clutched to her heart, her eyes challenging.

Fleur's brows knitted as she turned back to the tangled maze on the floor. "Why is it that every time you open a door it sounds like a pistol echoing thru the house? How many times must I ask you to show some restraint?"

Julia tapped her chin in feigned thought as she hummed. "At least once more?"

Fleur pursed her lips again, this time failing to hide a smile. "A lady walks calmly and gracefully into a room; she does not go charging in like a... oh, what's the use? Honestly, you're nineteen now and well out into society. I should not have to remind you like a child."

Julia sighed and walked further into the room, her blue muslin swaying, matching the light hue of her eyes, her dark chestnut hair shining. She settled on the arm of the wingback situated next to the window. "Shouldn't you give me up for lost?" she asked, leaning towards the window and moving the curtain slightly so she could look out onto the busy streets of Mayfair.

"No doubt I should, and stop staring out of the window.

What if someone sees you?" Fleur asked as she leaned down and picked her matted wool up off of the floor.

"Oh, it's Mr. Trentham. Look at him, standing in the streets smiling like the world's biggest fool." Fleur watched in horror as Julia raised her hand and wiggled her fingers, acknowledging him from the window.

Speechless, Fleur opened and closed her mouth trying to form words that would not come. She stood, her forgotten knitting crashing to the floor once more and rushed over to her sister's side. "Come away from the window at once. What will he think of us?" She hissed, trying not to look out of the window herself.

Julia turned towards her sister. "What is there to think? He saw me, nodded, and I greeted him cordially."

Fleur laughed, her mouth hanging open in disbelief. "Julia, you cannot casually wave at young men from windows. Do you want people to think you're acting in a flirtatious manner?" she asked, running her hands down her dress, smoothing nonexistent wrinkles in her embarrassment.

Julia shook her head, removing her hand from the curtains, allowing the sheer fabric to fall closed. "Fleur, you can be such a goose sometimes. Nothing I did was even a little flirtatious."

Fleur, frowned, unable to understand how Julia could think waving at men from second story windows was not flirtatious. "Well, at the very least staring at people is impertinent. What is Mr. Trentham to think of us?"

"As I said before, he wouldn't think anything — all he ever does is smile like he has not one thought in his pretty little head. Besides if it's rude of me to stare out of the window, wouldn't it be doubly rude of him to stare in?"

"You're unimaginable sometimes, Julia. You really are,"

said Fleur, refusing to argue further. "Did you come here for a reason? Or did you just want to pester me?" She walked back to her chair, woefully eyeing her knitting. When she bent once more to pick it up, she tried in dismay to make sense of the emerald tangle. "Oh, dear."

"Why do you insist on doing something that frustrates you so?"

"Because I find it relaxing..." Fleur pulled a random string, only to make the knot tighter, "... usually."

Julia laughed. "Did you hear the commotion this morning? He's done it again."

"By the sound of it," said Fleur. "I've just left Lord Blackburn with him in the library. Perhaps he will soothe Papa's nerves."

Julia snorted. "Unlikely. How many does that make this season?"

Fleur counted in her head, surprised by the number. "Four? No, five."

"Six, between the pair of us. We'll be laughed at again." Julia sighed, resigned to the situation, so common it had become. "No matter, since we're leaving soon. Prudence and I are making one last trip to Hatchard's before we are to away. Are you sure you wouldn't rather join us?"

"You know I agreed to accompany Mr. Hamilton on the row this afternoon." Fleur's fingers caught in the knotted mass. "This is impossible."

Julia frowned. "I can't imagine a more tedious activity than riding about with Mr. Hamilton as he goes on and on about the virtues of his new phaeton. I'd rather untangle that wool you're holding."

Fleur grinned before she could stop herself. "Julia, that is very rude."

"It is also very true," she countered. "Well, then, I must

be off. Since I can't convince you to come with us, enjoy your afternoon of conversation, if you can squeeze a word in edgewise."

Julia slid off the side of the armchair and floated from the room. Fleur wondered if her sister would ever mature, though she knew she would miss Julia's vitality and free spirit if she did, having helped raise her after the death of their mother.

When Julia was born it was true, she had lost something that day, something precious, her beloved mother, but she had gained something just as dear to her. First, a sister she was able to love and spoil, then almost a daughter she could dote upon, and last a best friend and companion.

Fleur set down her wool and reached for her tea. Raising it to her lips, she frowned into it as she tasted the dregs that signaled the end of her cup. Just as she was about to rise to ring for another pot, she heard a slight knock, and when she looked up she saw her father hovering in the doorway looking uncertain ... and quite ill.

She rushed to him. "Papa? You look positively green," she said as she ushered him into a chair for fear he would fall over. "Is your head still bothering you? Should I send for the doctor?"

"No, no, nothing is the matter with me, my dear, it's just your father is an old fool," he said as his eyes darted around. "Where is Julia? I haven't seen her all morning."

"She's in her room readying herself for an outing with Prudence. Why? Are you hiding from her?" She asked, a smile slowly forming on her face.

"Hiding? I'm doing nothing of the sort. I was merely inquiring."

"Of course, Papa," she agreed, much too readily.

Julian cleared his throat and took Fleur's hand in his own, leading her down into the chair next to him. He did not let go. "Fleur, I must speak with you about a matter quite serious. You see myself and the earl... that is to say... we were hoping that you might feel inclined..."

He trailed off, and Fleur worried, for she had never seen her father so uncertain. "Papa, whatever it is you have to say it can't be so unpleasant as all that," she said, her smile gentle. "Now, what is it?"

"Tell me, my dear, what are your thoughts toward Lord Blackburn's son?"

Fleur stiffened and held her breath — her heart came to an abrupt stop before it thumped in her chest again, reminding her of the need for air. She took a slow, steadying breath.

"Which son, Papa? Lord Blackburn has two if you recall."

Julian grimaced. "Of course I meant the elder boy, Edward."

Fleur tried to calm her racing suspicions, though she had an inkling of where the conversation was headed. "My thoughts, on the viscount?"

Julian nodded and rubbed her hand. "Yes, my dear, go on."

"I don't know that I can rightly say. We don't move in the same circles, as you know."

"Just in general then," Julian waved his hand around. "We spent nearly every summer and Christmas at Blackburn Hall until you were sixteen. You must have some sense of your feelings."

"I... of course I remember him from when we were children, but he would always sit away from the rest of us while we played together, watching over us. He was so much older — practically a man even then. We must have seemed awfully silly to him while we played our childish games."

Fleur remembered thinking how lonely she felt when she would see him, sitting off all by himself, usually with his nose stuck in a book, removed but always observing them from afar, making sure they didn't breed too much mischief. The only time he would join them was when he would read aloud to them, or when Evan would beg him to be the bowler in a game of cricket. He doted on his younger brother terribly and nearly always gave into him, the same as she did with Julia.

"I've seen him on several occasions, but we never converse." Fleur couldn't help but think that he still looked like that quiet little boy when she saw him at parties. "He seems almost... shy. The same as when we were young, she stated, uncertain. "I haven't spoken to him properly in years, Papa, and when we were young he hardly spoke even then."

Julian nodded, agreeing with her appraisal. "Lord Ravenbrook is a bit bookish, and he takes his responsibilities as Ravenbrook very seriously, but he is not grim, not like... well, that is neither here nor there, what I mean to say is he isn't a dull sort of man."

Fleur knew to whom he was comparing Edward. She remembered the younger brother – she always would. Evan had been there her entire life, until one day he was just ... gone, his comforting and constant presence in her life unexpectedly ripped away from her.

Fleur shook her head, determined to clear the painful thoughts away. That was the past, and Evan was no longer a part of her life.

Julian reached up slowly and gently tapped her on the forehead. "Fleur, you're frowning."

She looked into her father's dark eyes, brow furrowed as much as her own. "Perhaps you should tell me what this is about."

Julian cleared his throat. "Last night... no, I should go further back. For so long Charles and I have dreamed of intimately connecting our families. We had hope that you and Edward would come to care for one another, come to an understanding."

Fleur nodded. She had always known — she'd have been a fool not to — she just had expectations of her own. Expectations that were somehow the same, but very different.

"It was our hope that perhaps this would happen naturally as time passed, but you never grew close in the way we had hoped and then, well..."

Julian cleared his throat again. "Last night, Lord Blackburn and I discussed the matter of you and Ravenbrook and how wonderful a match you would make. We discussed the matter fully, even foolishly making plans. A few of the other fellows may have overheard us,"

"May have?" Fleur asked, skeptically.

"We were a bit loud in our enthusiasm."

"I see," she said. And she did.

Julian ran his hands thru his hair, ruining the neat part. "This morning, Lady Blackburn was out in town, and people started congratulating her on the upcoming nuptials and pressing for details."

Fleur pulled her hands from her fathers and grasped them tightly together. "That must have come as quite the shock. What did she say?"

"Only that it was to be a surprise and the families would make an announcement soon."

Fleur leaned back into her chair. "Oh."

"Forgive me, Fleur. I don't know how things got so out of hand. You know as well as I how tongues will wag. I have no defense... I... the earl and I do feel it's best that you marry straightaway, but you must know this. I need for you to understand this above all else. You don't have to marry him. You don't have to marry anybody. I will tell the entire British Empire to jump off The Tower if it would please you."

Fleur tried to muster a small smile, shaky and watery as it was. "And seal Julia's fate as spinster along with my own? You know they always blame the woman in these matters. It would somehow be my fault, and then poor Viscount Ravenbrook would be humiliated and I would be a jilt."

"Edward could use some excitement in his life. The boy is too predictable by half."

Fleur laughed and shook her head. "Is this how you intend to convince me to marry him? Didn't you just say he wasn't dull?"

Julian grinned and shrugged his shoulders, unable to say more.

"I have been doing some thinking of my own, Papa, and please believe my sincerity when I say I am a bit weary of the whole thing. The dances, the parties, and being on the 'marriage mart'. I'm three and twenty and have no real marriage prospects, not one person who has come to you for my hand would I have accepted, and I thank you for turning them away, but I do want children and a life of my own. And yes, I have always known you wished I would come to care for Edward in that way. He is a good man."

Julian anxiously bit his lip. "What are you saying, Fleur? Are you saying, yes? That you will have him?"

She looked downward to her hands. They were white from her own grip, but she released them and blood seemed to flow once more, small tingles running through her fingers. She could not stop herself from thinking of Evan, of that moment when all her hopes of a future with love came crashing down around her, when the man she'd come to care for more than anyone had told her he hoped she never stood in his line of sight again.

She looked up into her father's eyes, he patiently waiting for her response, and she hesitating. She always hesitated, and in that moment it irritated her. She knew it was time to let that part of her life go — she had to if she was ever to move on. She thought it was time to take her life into her own hands, and take a chance.

"I will do it, Papa, I will marry him," she said. A small shiver ran down her spine at the finality of her agreement. "I assume this is to be rushed?"

Julian's shoulders relaxed slightly, and she knew he was relieved. "Yes, my dear, but do set your mind at ease. Once you accept him, you will have time. Lady Blackburn has arranged for a house party at Blackburn Hall to begin in a few days' time. The banns will give you a few weeks to familiarize yourselves with one another again."

Fleur breathed a sigh of relief of her own. "And when am I to expect him?"

"Well, actually, I was hoping... that is to say —"

"Please don't start that again, Papa."

"He is here, right at this very moment. He is waiting in my library with his father and expects to wait upon you down in the drawing room any moment."

Fleur stiffened and stared at her Father with wide eyes,

"Oh... oh my... you... he's here? Now? I'm not even dressed to receive —"

"Nonsense. He will think you are lovely, my dear," said Julian, saying the only thing he could in such a situation.

She pressed her hands down her skirts, her nervous habit revealing itself once more. "But what am I to say to him?"

"You say yes."

Exasperated, Fleur gave him a quelling look, and he at least had the decency to look cowed before standing to leave.

He walked towards the door but stopped halfway, turning to look at her. "Fleur, I just need to say this once more, and then I'll leave it. You know you can refuse him, and I will not be angry, don't you? This situation is entirely of my own making, and I only hope one day you can forgive me."

Fleur rushed forward and hugged him, laying her head on his chest, comfort rushing through her as he wrapped his strong arms around her. "There is nothing to forgive, Papa, honestly. I know you only want what is best for me." She looked up at him and tried to smile, but her lip trembled a little. "I just need a moment to gather myself and then I'll be down."

Julian nodded and walked out the door. Marriage. It was supposed to be such a happy occasion for a young woman, but he felt as if he'd cheated her out of something great. A greatness only a man and woman truly in love, a love requited, could ever achieve.

4
EVERY GIRL'S DREAM

She watched her father leave and a shaky breath she hadn't even known she was holding left her. Marriage, she was to be married to Edward. Her mind boggled.

She shook her head and moved across the room to stand before a gilded mirror, one she chose on a shopping excursion two years prior when her father asked her to remake the rooms. She stared, her eyes focusing and unfocusing, her own blue eyes staring back at her. *What would he think?* She wondered. Did he know? Would he even care?

She suddenly had a great fear that he would come to the ball, of seeing him again that very evening but pushed it away. It had been seven years since they had parted, and even though she would marry his brother, that didn't mean she would see him anytime soon.

"He won't come," she told herself. "He never does."

She reached up to touch her reflection and thought of him, what once was a nasty habit she had tried so hard to break now came all too easily.

She remembered their past as if it was only a moment

ago. Especially the moments she made him laugh – Evan having a surly disposition even then – made those moments even more precious to her. And though sometimes they would quarrel, they always would forgive one another.

She remembered a particular time Evan had promised to teach her to play cricket and had sworn her to secrecy as he knew they would both be reprimanded if found out, and predictably someone had, and that someone was Edward. Evan was furious and reacted as he always did.

Edward had scolded Evan gently for his tantrum of blaming Fleur for revealing their secret and Evan, hurt at his brother's disappointment in him, had left them standing there.

She still to this day could remember how rigid his back was as he ran from them. She had wanted to cry, to call out to him, but Edward had comforted her, asking her if Evan ever stayed mad at her for long. And he was right, by that night Evan was with her again, laughing, as they read each other silly lyrics from songs they had found in the music room. She was only six years of age then, but she remembered it so clearly.

Fleur heard the clock chime and looked over at the time, knowing she should leave to receive Lord Ravenbrook. At that moment it was so very clear how different the two brothers were. One gentle but firm, the other impatient and coarse. She shook her head and gazed at her reflection one last time, pushing her hair around, postponing the inevitable.

Could she marry Edward and be happy? He was very amiable and unquestioningly handsome, but could she live with him as his wife for the rest of her life? He would treat her well, she knew, he always had, but was contentment and polite affection enough to ensure they could have a life-time together?

She blew a puff of air out at herself and firmly slapped her cheeks. "Of course you can marry him, you silly girl," she said to herself. "He's kind and handsome, he's every girl's dream."

She walked through the door toward Edward, but it was the lonely image of Evan as he ran away from her that day that held her thoughts.

"He's just not your dream," she whispered to herself and closed the door.

———

EDWARD SAT in the duke's library with his father, wondering what he had gotten himself into. He was accosted by his mother at an hour that could not be held as decent for any unmarried gentleman during the season, and his mother had revealed a shocking plan.

It was all absolutely ridiculous, and absolutely necessary.

So there he sat, on time and waiting. The viscount hated to wait.

His father occasionally snuck glances his way, trying to calculate his mood, and it was starting to chafe his nerves. After all, the old codger had nothing to be nervous over, he wasn't the one who had to affiance himself to a woman he hadn't seen since her childhood, save for a few glances and nods across a crowded ballroom.

He remembered her as a child — a short but gangly thing with dark hair and the lightest, piercing blue eyes. He tried to remember the last time he saw her in his home at Blackburn Hall. It was Christmastime, he recalled, and they hadn't come to stay with them since. And although he didn't fully understand why, he had his suspicions, and they revolved around his brother.

Now his father had sealed his fate and hers with a night of drunken tomfoolery. It wasn't that he was opposed to marriage — he knew well enough that he was approaching one-and-thirty and would have to marry and set up his nursery. And though there wasn't anyone he was particularly attached to, he, the same as any man, would like the opportunity to choose his own bride, his own fate.

He knew that was no longer an option, so he would do his duty and marry the Duke of Norfield's daughter as required of him, and perhaps his mother might let him sleep until a decent hour after this affair was all said and done.

His nerves rankled once more when his father twitched and knocked into his elbow.

"Father, why do you look as if you're the one who will be proposing marriage? You watch me as if I'm about to run. I've already agreed to marry the lady, and I've no real objections, save for those any man has about being married."

Charles snorted. "It's only that Norfield didn't exactly have time to speak about all the arrangements to Lady Fleur."

Edward turned to his father. "What do you mean? Since when do fathers speak about marital contracts with their daughters? Besides, Norfield has been your closest friend for years. I don't see why such matters can't be attended to later, under the circumstances."

"What I mean by saying she has not been made aware of the arrangements is that she hasn't been made aware at all, of any of it," he explained while having the good grace to appear apologetic. "Norfield is with her right now, explaining—"

Edward rose halfway from his chair. "What! You can't be serious?"

"Shush, Edward, not so loud." Charles grabbed at his son's shoulder, trying to quiet his outburst.

"Not so loud?" Edward barked, then lowered his voice to an angry whisper. "Are you seriously suggesting to me that I'm here to ask a lady to marry me that has no prior idea that I was to arrive until this very moment? What have you been doing all morning?"

"What do you expect us to do? Reverse time? I spoke to Norfield about it as soon as I arrived and then he left to speak to his daughter."

"She must be completely astonished."

"I know it was not well planned," Charles explained lamely.

Edward stared at his father — no, more like glared. "Not well planned?"

Charles hummed and looked Edward over once more. "Edward, are you sure you are alright? It must have been a shock to you as well."

Edward ripped the spectacles from his face and rubbed the bridge of his nose. "I wish they hadn't taken my cane at the door. I'd wallop you with it."

"For shame! Threatening your own father!"

"You affianced me to a girl I used to carry around on my shoulders so she and Evan could pick plums in the back orchard."

"Here, use mine," said the earl, handing over a dark wood cane.

Edward smiled, relaxing back into the chair. "It's fine, Father. I'd have to marry soon as it is. At least I'm acquainted with Lady Fleur. And it's not as if you haven't made it painfully clear that you hoped we would suit. After all, you and Mother barely knew one another when you married, and you turned out just fine."

"Your mother and I, that was a different time. We may have had a quick engagement, but we loved each other and have since before we were married. Perhaps we were lucky in that way, but I cannot stress the importance of caring for your wife, Edward."

"Of course I care for her. I've known her since she was born."

"That's not what I meant."

Edward sighed. "I know what you meant. Does it make you feel better for me to say I look on her and Lady Julia as sisters? That I have never once considered her as a woman, the way a man should? I used to hold her when she was just a babe, for goodness sake. How would you feel?"

"Wretched. I do feel wretched. I suppose it is strange for you, and perhaps Evan would have been a better choice, however..."

"We both know his grace would never abide it, and Evan seems to be off hiding in that hole he calls a townhouse again. You know mother has written to him and insisted he attend tonight's ball, seeing as it's the last and we've not seen him for months, but he refused, as usual."

Charles grunted in agreement. "Perhaps it is fortuitous that he will not be there, considering the circumstances. I have every confidence that, after a fashion, Evan will come to regard Lady Fleur with the love of a brother."

Edward doubted that, but he didn't need to point out the truth for his father to know he was lying to himself. "I almost wish he would come, that he would grow a spine and have the power to stop this madness."

"We both know that will not happen, Edward, he has caused too much harm," the earl said. Looking away from his son, his mouth a grim line, he heard the jangle of the knob.

Julian stepped inside, looking like he had been kicked by a runaway mare.

"Well, what did she say?" Charles asked. "It cannot be good news. You look a fright."

"Everything is well," he answered. "She said she will receive you in the drawing room, Ravenbrook. Craigs is waiting to show you the way."

The viscount stood, nodding to his future father-in-law as he solemnly made his way through the threshold, looking very much a man going to his own funeral. The fathers shared a look, both secretly hoping Edward and Fleur would have more sense than they when it came time to secure their own children's happiness.

———

FLEUR SAT ALONE in the drawing room, wondering what to do with her hands. Should she fold them in her lap to keep her from picking at the embroidery of her dress? Should she ring the bell pull for tea? Should she use them to strangle her beloved father's neck for putting her in this position?

Fleur knew she would be married into an aristocratic match one day. She even wanted to be. She wanted a family and a husband to care for, but she had expected some warning, and she most assuredly didn't expect that day to be today.

She had imagined herself being content, located in the country on her husband's estate with children of her own to love. She wasn't so ignorant as to expect a love match —

those thoughts had long ago left her when her first two seasons crushed her idealistic expectations of love and devotion.

Influence and connections, that was the love of the *ton*.

Still, she knew her father had been patient, giving her four seasons in which to spread her wings. Yet, none of those men interested her. They were all too self-important or dependent on society, which in turn annoyed or intimidated her.

She only wanted a quiet life, a quiet, content life where she could be companions with her husband and have real involvement with her children without the interference of others.

You would settle for Edward, she thought, the shaming words finding her heart before she could push them away.

She tried to remember how Edward had greeted her when she last crossed his path at a recent engagement, but she could not, could not recall his face nor his manner above seeing him quietly standing in a corner amongst his own friends. She was sure they had not even conversed, not even to say hello.

Now she was waiting, dreading the conversation that loomed before her, the knock on the door that would change her future. These were some of the last moments she would spend being Lady Fleur Osborne. Now, she would be fiancée to Edward Woolf, or rather, Viscount Ravenbrook. Lady Fleur Ravenbrook, she let the title sit on her tongue but could not utter it. She would never be referred to as a Woolf, she mused, the bashful Fleur Osborne having a name like Woolf? Really, it was laughable.

Not that being a Woolf had ever crossed her mind before,

she thought, scolding herself instantly for thinking of Evan, when she was to marry his brother.

The small smile she had been able to conjure abruptly fell as the memories she had been trying to lock away came rushing towards her. She remembered the last time she and Evan truly spent time together, the time that began all of her hopes and dreams of them being together always.

"Will you write?" she had asked him as they walked the well traveled path to the pond.

Evan had frowned at her then, pausing to pick up small stones, sharing them with her one by one as they held them to skip on the water later. "Don't I always write to you?" he had asked.

Their walks were something they had done so many times before, to the point it had almost become routine. A small moment of peace that she looked forward to, but that day she had been distracted.

Evan was to leave for his first year of university the next morning, and even though she had seen him off to Eton every year before, it had seemed so much bigger that time, much more frightening to her.

She could not shed her feelings of dread that he would see a whole new world open to him, that he would not miss their small moments at Blackburn Hall, not want to return to her, a silly girl still under her governesses care, while he was entering adulthood. She felt their two years apart in age exceedingly.

"It feels so very different this time," she had told him.

He had grabbed her hand then, the shock of it causing the stones to fall and bounce on the ground.

"I will always return to you," he said as he squeezed her hand, a light touch that others might not have given any importance.

That moment had been her undoing — it was the day she realized she never wanted to be parted from him. The warmth of his hand on her own was familiar, yet it was almost as if she could *feel* his declaration as tangible as her own desperation. It seemed to awaken every dormant sense that he was not only her childhood friend but the man she was meant to share her life with.

Unable to respond as her own feelings overwhelmed her she had removed her hand from his own, the action waking them both out of their stupor, and he had walked her to the pond where they spoke of nothing, though it meant everything.

He departed the following morning.

For days she tried to persuade herself not to worry, for weeks she repeated his words in her mind, her own secret mantra. She held his promise close to her heart, and she was finally convinced he would honor it, and he had.

Evan wrote to her as he always did, nothing changed between them. Then he returned to Blackburn Hall that winter, altered, his manner affecting and cautious with her. It was then everything had started to go wrong.

Fleur wiped quickly at her eyes when she heard a small knock on the door, followed by Craigs bringing in the familiar tray with the small card that held the name of her soon-to-be betrothed. She stood to steady herself, as if to feel she was entering the battle ground.

She took a deep calming breath. "Show him in Mr. Craigs, and would you have Mary bring in the tray?" she managed to say without hesitation. She didn't even have time to be proud of herself before she saw Edward enter. All pretense of strength quickly left her in that moment.

I can't do this, she thought.

5

MARRIAGE OFFERS
& SWEAR WORDS

Edward walked into the room, doing everything he could to delay having to look at his intended. Once he could no longer use his surroundings as an excuse, he met her gaze. She looked like she would faint away any moment.

Her face was absolutely devoid of color, and the mint green muslin day dress she was wearing cast a sickly hue onto her skin. Alarm swept through him when he thought she might collapse into a fit of the vapors.

He rushed to her side. "Lady Fleur, please sit down," he said as he took her elbow and moved her to the closest chair.

"I'm supposed to be inviting you to sit down," she said in a small whisper.

Edward didn't know how to respond. She was so bewildered; she probably didn't even realize she had spoken aloud and would be frightfully embarrassed when she remembered.

The maid chose that moment to bustle in, setting down

the tea service between the chairs they now occupied. The movement seemed to wake Fleur out of her daze.

"Lord Ravenbrook, forgive me, where are my manners? Would you like a cup of tea?"

Edward watched as she lifted the teapot — it rattled dangerously as her hand trembled. Afraid that he would end up with a lap full of scalding tea, or worse, she, Edward took the pot and lowered it back down to the tray.

"Lady Fleur, thank you for your kind offer, but I have come here on a... very particular errand," he said, his own nerves rattling him. "I wonder if we could sit here and just talk for a moment?"

"By all means," she replied, a look of wide-eyed antici-pation, or more likely fright, upon her face.

"How have you been? We've not spoken of late," he asked, buying some time. "I trust you are well?"

"Very well, I thank you."

If anyone had told Edward before today that you could be deafened by actual silence he would have scoffed and cried nonsense, but not today.

"And your sister?"

"She is also... well, my lord."

He cleared his throat and cursed his own hesitance. *Go on,* he encouraged himself. "We seem to have found ourselves in a rather extraordinary position, Lady Fleur. I wonder if I should just get right down to it. Shall I?"

Fleur blinked then nodded.

"I was hoping... that is to say I..." Edward trailed off, obviously trying to gather his wits about him, feeling like a trapped fox ready to run any moment.

He swallowed and tried again. "Lady Fleur, it would be a privilege for you... I mean... not a privilege for *you,* but a privilege for *me*, that is to say... *damn*," he hissed, turning away from the look of shock in her eyes.

Edward sat completely still, wondering what to do. He couldn't remember there ever being a time where he had been so ineloquent, or to his own horror, swore in front of a lady, and for both to happen during his marriage proposal?

It was an unmitigated disaster.

He reached up and tore off his spectacles, rubbing his nose and thinking maybe if he could not see her clearly it would be easier. He immediately became alarmed when he heard a small sob.

Trying to think of the best way to start over and apologize, it occurred to him that he had never even seen a weeping woman, let alone been the cause for one, but as the sound became louder and less muffled, he realized that she wasn't crying at all, but rather, she was laughing.

Laughing at him.

If he weren't so overjoyed he didn't have a hysterical woman on his hands he would have had the mind to be a little insulted.

"You don't have to laugh at a poor man, Lady Fleur," he said, a slight smile on his face.

Fleur thought the expression rather suited him as she watched him reach up and push his spectacles back up upon his nose. He was still handsome as ever, with his long dark hair that fell past his shoulders, tied neatly at the nape of his neck with a ribbon, not at all fashionable for men of his age anymore, but she couldn't imagine him otherwise as he had always worn it so. And his eyes, they were such a dark brown she could almost imagine them black.

He is very attractive, she thought, *and tall*. His serious face was such a stark contrast to the bumbling mess he'd made of the marriage proposal that she started laughing again, color quickly returning to her face.

Edward took a deep breath. "Shall I try this again? I would be honored if you would give me the privilege of becoming my wife. There, that ought to do it don't you think?"

Fleur laughed again and nodded her head in acceptance. "I would be honored, my lord."

"Now that we have an understanding, not that it was unpleasant business at all," he said, causing her eyes to widen and another laugh to rock through her. "I believe my mother would like to informally announce our engagement tonight at Lady Brockhurst's ball if that is amenable to you?"

Fleur smiled. "Yes, of course."

There, that was better, Edward thought.

He stood to leave. "I do hope you will save the third set for me, and then we can adjourn to supper together?"

He watched as she took a deep breath. "I shall look forward to it."

"Then my mother shall convey the particulars to you — I'm sure you have much to speak about. Good day," he said with a polite bow before turning and making his way back outside of the drawing room.

Fleur slumped down into the chair. She felt happy that the worst was now over, for the next few hours at least. She was glad he didn't seem offended by her awkwardness, and his own gaffe made her feel like he understood her. No doubt her distress had been the cause of his, but he had behaved admirably.

On the other side of the door, Edward took a deep breath, not quite ready to face the bumbling matchmakers across the hall.

You, Edward Woolf, are a complete idiot.

He took his leave without informing his father and the duke of what was probably the worst proposal to have ever graced the halls of the House of Norfield. Yet, even with all of his self-reassurance that everything would be fine, he couldn't help think of what Evan would have to say about the whole affair.

———

NATHAN CLOSED the door to the solicitor's office with a firm pull, looking out onto the busy street with a frown. "I'll not believe another word you utter, Woolf. I waited for over an hour."

Evan laughed and walked towards his mother's residence. "Significantly shorter than the last, you should be grateful," he said, loudly enough for Nathan to hear him over the noise of the horse shod feet upon the street. "But let us not delay, we still have to convey our regrets to my mother."

Nathan clapped him on the shoulder. "I'm sorry to disappoint you, my friend, but I've already written to your mother, accepting her gracious invitation."

"What?" Evan exclaimed, stopping mid-stride. "Then why did you not say so this morning? Hell and damnation. Of all the tedious, odious things to agree to, a house party, Nathan?"

"Now, now, Evan, not in front of the peerage," Nathan mocked with great joy, looking around at the people who stopped to whisper at his outburst. "And how could I tell you, you wouldn't let me get a word in edgewise, with your gloating about the press —"

"You've ruined my best excuse to decline," shouted

Evan, interrupting Nathan. "Now I will have to accept and spend weeks fending off schemes of matchmaking and conversation."

Nathan gasped and clutched his heart. "Oh no, not conversation! Be sure to bring your broadsword, you may need protection."

Evan glowered as Nathan laughed. "I wonder who else received an invitation?" he asked while starting to walk once more.

"Really, Evan, you would think you would know. Perhaps if you visited home more often."

"Stop nagging," he said, harsh and short, unwilling to discuss the matter. "Surely you are curious too since you accepted."

"Let's see..." said Nathan, making a production of tapping his chin, knowing it would only irritate Evan further. "Oliver has received an invitation, and me of course."

"And how, pray tell, would you know the guest list? The invitations only arrived this morning."

"You'd be surprised what you can glean from the perils of conversation. I met Miss Phoebe Simmons on the road to your house and when I stopped to say hello I asked her if she was to return to the country or was to stay in town, and so she mentioned her invitation, then me my own. Evan, then we did this miraculous thing, we talked to one another. Now, if you ask me how *she* knew the particulars, that is anyone's guess. Women seem to know *everything*."

Evan glanced to Nathan and growled. "Who else then?"

Nathan's grin was wide, his mirth apparent. "Oh, you'll love this. Andrew Osborne was invited as well." He could see the annoyance in every inch of Evan's manner. He waited just a few more seconds, watching his friend work himself up into a full on fit, then he continued to wait until Evan opened his mouth to explode. "Of course the Captain can't make it, off fighting the good fight and all that."

"Thank God for that," Evan said, letting out a puff of air. "If he had agreed there wouldn't be any peace at Blackburn Hall between any of us. What was my mother thinking?"

"I was astonished as well, seeing as how you two despise one another. Though you were friends once, were you not?"

Evan nodded. "Yes, when we were children. He's the nephew of the Duke of Norfield, and he and his daughters spent many holidays at my father's country home. Sometimes Osborne would accompany them, though the last time I saw him..." Evan trailed off laughing. "The last time we argued I hid all his shoes in various places around the house, my favorite being inside a set of matching chamber pots."

Nathan blanched and shuddered. "No wonder he despises you."

Evan shrugged, smiling. "I was eight, and he was just as annoying as I was then."

"Perhaps it's time you made more of an effort, Evan. You're the only person of my acquaintance who rejects friendship and conversation at every turn, acting like everyone else who doesn't take your bleak line of thought should be in a ward. Perhaps it's time to stop shuttering yourself up in your library or that horrid country manor you just acquired."

Evan sidestepped a group of older ladies, nodding slightly to them before walking on. "The manor was a brilliant investment, in fact, I had planned to return there the day after tomorrow until all this house party nonsense interrupted my plans," said Evan. "But don't change the subject, there must be more. What about the ladies? This is all a damned matchmaking scheme, I tell you. Why else would she organize such an affair last minute? I know I rarely say it, Nathan, but I do look upon you like a brother, so I have to say, with utter devotion, that you and Oliver are both mad for accepting."

"Is that something you would say to a beloved brother?"

Evan shook his head. "You both should have run when you had the chance. My mother will be pushing the latest debutantes at your heads, mark my words."

"I'm not at all worried. All I'll have to do is give your dazzling mother one of my winning smiles and she'll let me get away with anything." Nathan laughed at Evan's disgusted look.

He growled between clenched teeth. "Your remarks about my mother are out of line, Carter, now tell me who else."

"Fine, if you insist. You're so dull sometimes. Both the Osborne girls, Lady Julia and, oh what is it, the elder girl, what is her name? Fleur, that's it, Lady Fleur." Nathan skidded to a stop, nearly bumping into Evan when the latter stopped dead cold in the middle of the sidewalk, staring directly ahead with his jaw clenched.

Evan slowly reached into his waistcoat pocket and felt the cool metal, smooth on one side, elaborately engraved on the other.

"Who else?" Evan asked, his voice rough, his eyes focused on something in the distance.

Nathan looked at him oddly but continued. "The Wilson girl, I've only met her once or twice, can't remember her first name, other than that, Miss Phoebe Simmons, of course, and Lady Charity Preston."

"Lady Charity?" Evan asked, surprised to hear the name. "You see, I warned you. It's all a damned matchmaking scheme. I'm going to refuse," he said and began to walk faster, not admitting to himself that the pace of his heart had also quickened at the mention of Fleur's name.

Nathan matched his stride. "You can't refuse your mother's invitation when your own friends will be in attendance."

"Use your head, Nathan, why else would my mother invite three unattached women with whom she has little acquaintance —"

"Most likely, I would think, because they are the friends of my betrothed," a slow deep voice cut in from behind, startling them both.

Evan and Nathan stopped walking and watched as Viscount Ravenbrook approached them. "Mr. Carter," he greeted with a polite nod. "On your way to Mother's, I take it?" he asked, addressing Evan.

Evan stared at Edward like he had lost his mind, asking his destination after giving such news, as if nothing important was revealed, it was unimaginable. "Betrothed? Since when? And to whom? *Has this entire day gone mad?*" he yelled in disbelief.

Not even showing a bit of surprise at his outburst, so used to Evan's moods as he was, Edward continued. "Lady Fleur," he answered, watching him carefully.

Evan stared disbelievingly up into his brother's dark eyes, unable to move. "Lady Fleur *Osborne?*"

Edward winced. "Yes."

Clenching his jaw, Evan turned abruptly and continued walking to his mother's house without so much as a word of disagreement or congratulations.

Nathan looked at his friend and then gave Edward a

quizzical look before he followed Evan and clapped him on the back. "Come now, Evan, don't be like that to the poor viscount," he said brightly. "Better him than you."

Evan shook free of Nathan and quickly ascended the steps of his parents' home. Once he reached the door, instead of knocking he quickly whipped around to face his brother. "When was this decided? I did not know you were courting the lady."

Edward reared back slightly when he saw the tight, angry look on his Evan's face. "I'm not, courting her, that is. It's a rather delicate situation, one I would prefer not to discuss here on the stoop," he said, looking around.

"I see," said Evan. "And the lady said yes? She must have, or you would not have called her your betrothed."

"She did, though it was a near thing. I admit it wasn't one of my finer moments."

"What do you mean?" Nathan asked when Evan failed to do so.

"I ended up..."

"Yes?" Evan asked impatiently.

"Well, I... I sort of swore at her," said Edward, wondering why he was telling his brother the embarrassing details.

"You swore at her? As you were proposing marriage?" Evan asked, a look of complete doubt on his face. "How is that possible? You don't even swear!"

"I became flustered. She was looking at me like she was about to faint, and before I knew it... it doesn't matter."

"Right, about to faint, was she?" Evan said, rolling his eyes skyward before turning and throwing open the door resulting in a loud slam on the wall, startling the poor butler.

"Mr. Woolf? My apologies, sir, I didn't hear the bell or I would have —"

"Calm yourself, Higgins, you know my little brother never rings when coming home," Edward said, inviting Nathan in before him.

"Higgins? Did I hear the door?" Lady Blackburn smiled and came rushing out of the side drawing room. "Edward? Evan? Why did no one tell me you had arrived, and with Mr. Carter here as well, really, where has Higgins run off to?"

"Mother," Edward leaned forward to kiss her cheek. "Don't be too hard on Higgins. Evan scared him off, as usual."

"Really, with the commotion you all were making, is it any wonder?" she asked. "I'd run too if I hadn't been married to the most maddening man in all of London for the last thirty-two years. As it is, I'm used to it."

Evan watched as his mother's ever-discerning gaze found him, and he felt himself shrink under her scrutiny. "Really Evan, look at the state of your coats," she scolded. "Do I need to speak to your valet?"

"You know I don't keep one," said Evan, tired of the same old argument.

She eyed him again, and he stood his ground. "It is most improper for a man of your stature not to keep a valet, or at the very least a butler."

"Father doesn't keep one," he protested.

"No, your father can't keep one, there's a difference," she said, thinking back to how Higgins disappeared each time Evan came for a visit. "Though I am beginning to notice a startling sense of familiarity about the situation."

Evan sighed, needing to escape. To think about the news his brother gave him, not trifling matters of his home or the state of his clothes. "Mother, as much as I love you,"

Evan said, punctuating his sentence with a kiss to her cheek. "I believe I can take care myself. I've been doing so for the past twenty years."

"Yes, and you look like it too," she chided. "At least let one of the servants take your coat to be pressed for this evening. I've no hope left in me that you actually had planned to change for tonight's ball?"

His patience waning, he tried to control his voice. "You know I have already declined the Brockhurst's invitation."

"Oh, but you must be there, Evan, the entire family will be there," she said, darting a look towards his brother, "Edward, you have some news of your own, do you not?" she asked nervously.

Evan watched his brother shift his stance and clear his throat. "Yes, Mother, she has accepted."

Madeleine closed her eyes and released a shuddering breath. "Evan, I really must insist on your attendance. I was hoping to have a moment to speak with you alone, but we're to announce your brother's engagement tonight."

Evan returned her look, hurt evident. "I don't understand... how any of this was decided without my knowledge."

Madeline reached for his hand. "Darling, you're never here —"

He pulled away from her, not letting her reach him. "I'll come to the ball, and do my duty to wish them joy, but I will excuse myself from the house party, if you don't mind?"

"Of course not," she whispered.

He saw her hand fall back to her side as he made his way up the stairs leaving them behind. He could hear his mother apologizing to Nathan for his rude behavior, her voice shaking. He knew he had been awful to his mother, but he couldn't bring himself to care, not right then. He needed a moment to think.

He had not seen Lady Fleur in years, but yet he felt like Edward had no right to offer for her. No right to be her husband, and he wondered why he should feel so betrayed and shocked to hear confirmations of what he always knew would come to pass.

The duke had always preferred Edward, him being the heir presumptive and he, being the spare. But no, he knew that was not the whole truth, and it was not fair of him. The duke had treated him with great fondness, until the terrible day he left. If only he had gone to the duke, explained his plans, his desires of a future he himself wanted for him and Fleur. Instead he acted out like a spoiled and frightened child.

He knew he must own to it, that he caused the rift between himself and the families by refusing a military career. He'd run angry and scared, and when his temper and his resentment of being cornered finally calmed into embarrassment and shame, he knew not how to return to them all. He still did not.

He remembered how he and Fleur would sit in the dark corner of the drawing room at night, chaperoned by their families but far enough away to talk about books they had read or the last goings-on in town. It was the only time he was ever interested in such subjects, when he was with her.

Now she was to be his sister, and he could not think of anything more heart-wrenching in that moment than she being Edward's wife. And now because of his foolish actions seven years ago, his brother, the man he looked up to more than anyone in the world, would bear the brunt of his ire without provocation. He despaired it would ruin them all if he could not check himself, but he was not persuaded he would be able to hold the façade of a good brother.

Evan opened the door to the rooms he was always assigned when he visited his parents' home and took off his coat. He threw it on the back of a chair, the force flinging a silver object from his pocket that spun across the room before coming to rest on the floor.

Evan stood and stared, the reminder of its existence offensive and agonizing. Deciding to ignore it, he made his way to the attached bedroom and laid down upon the bed, trying to shift his melancholy. It wasn't long before he was asleep, a small frown marring his otherwise peaceful face.

6

BALL GOWNS & GOLD BUCKLED SHOES

Fleur raised her arms and worked a pin from her hair as she sat down at her dressing room table. She gazed at herself as she pulled out each one and laid them in a neat little pile, ready to be reused.

She could see Lucy, her lady's maid, carrying her sapphire evening gown and laying it across her bed as she continued until she laid the last hairpin down.

A knock came at the door. "Come in, Julia."

Julia walked in, her dress of heavy white silk slightly trailing behind her. Lace overlaid every inch and the bodice was beaded. A soft blue ribbon wrapped around under her bust and floated behind her.

Fleur smiled, proud of the woman her little sister had become. "You look lovely. I doubt you'll want for dancing partners tonight."

Julia walked up behind her, looking herself over. "Thank goodness this is the last ball. I'm sick of wearing white, cream, ecru, and more white. It's not fair. You haven't worn white since the year before last."

Fleur laughed. "Well, I'm not exactly a new spring

debutante. It would be odd for me to wear white still. Next year is your third year and you can wear more color as well."

Julia looked over to Fleur's bed, seeing the dress she had chosen. "Why do you not wear the emerald? You know you would look stunning."

Fleur winced. "I cannot believe I let you talk me into neckline. It's much too... bold."

Julia laughed, remembering the deeper cut of the bodice, stopping just before vulgarity took over. "The dressmaker did say it was all the crack for ladies these days, especially ones who, dare I say it, are no longer new spring debutantes."

Fleur glared at her sister. "Then I will give it to you for next season."

Julia smirked. "A hit, I concede. Though it would be futile, you forget next year you'll be off busy being married, and I'll be stuck under the thumb of Aunt Lizzy even though I'm too old for a sponsor. She'll never allow me to do anything alone."

"Just because I'll be married doesn't mean I won't be there to help you though the season, in fact, I'll be able to help you even more, now that I'm not also out."

Julia squealed and bent to wrap her arms around Fleur's shoulders. "Would you? Really? Oh, please, please save me from Aunt Lizzy!"

Fleur laughed. "I thought you didn't like the idea of my being married. Suddenly you're for it now that it benefits you?"

Julia stood straight and looked down to Fleur. "I'm still furious at Papa, but Edward is a fine man," she paused, contemplating, a grin slowly forming on her lips. "And seeing as you and Edward have already kissed ..."

Fleur's jaw dropped. "Julia! That wasn't a kiss. It was a peck on the forehead. Besides he was mortified, and so was I."

"He was, wasn't he?" Julia laughed. "It was your birthday, remember?"

Fleur closed her eyes to the ghastly memory of that day, and when she opened her eyes, she looked at Julia, even if it was only in reflection of the glass. "Of course I remember," she answered.

She remembered all too well. It was one of the last memories she had of the brothers, and one of the worst. It was the day everything had changed for the two families, the day Evan left, and she had not seen him since.

"Fleur, are you well?" asked Julia.

She forced a smile, angry with herself for opening those memories. She turned to Julia, placing her hand on her arm. "I am."

Julia sighed. "You're thinking about him, aren't you? I shouldn't have brought up that day, forgive me."

Fleur removed her arm and spun back around in her chair. "Julia, not now, please."

Julia walked around Fleur's chair and knelt beside her, looking up into her eyes. "But what if..." She bit her lip, unable to finish.

"What if?" Fleur prompted, knowing she did not like the turn the conversation had taken.

"Do you think he will be there tonight?"

Fleur tittered, but her face grew pale. "Why would he come? Julia, he never does."

"Yes, I know, but tonight they are announcing his brother's betrothal. Don't you think there might be a chance? Even if slight?"

She tried to hold her hands steady as she folded them in her lap, trying to deny that Julia may be right.

"You go and finish getting ready," said Fleur, cutting off her questioning and dismissing her. "I'll meet you downstairs in just a moment, I promise." She smiled, trying to console Julia when she looked ready to argue.

Relieved that she didn't, she watched Julia nod and leave the room. Fleur sat still only for a moment before she stood and walked over to her bed and ran her hand across the blue lace of her gown. She blanched as she realized she had not seriously considered that Evan might be there. It would be perfectly natural, of course, if he made an exception and arrived that evening.

Her stomach flipped, and she felt slightly warm at the thought. What if he spoke to her? Would she be able to bear him wishing her joy in marriage to his own brother? She wrapped her arm around her bedpost and laid her head upon the cool wood, closing her eyes, fighting back her emotions.

How was it that only the *chance* of speaking to Evan made her heart ache and mind race, when a proposal from a perfectly amiable and attractive man had not? Fleur shook her head, remembering Edward made her feel guilt and shame. Her thoughts should be of him, not Evan, and if he arrived tonight she would greet him cordially, and that would be that.

Her maid walked over to her, lifted the garment, and heaved it over her head, and when Fleur emerged it was with a new frame of mind.

She owed her devotion to Edward, no-one else. He had come forward without hesitation to help her from an impossible situation. She was to be his viscountess, and one day his countess. People would be watching her, scrutinizing her every move, just waiting for her to blunder, and she had to do everything within her own power not to let them break her resolve.

She turned and looked herself in the mirror one last time and promised herself she would not give them one reason to doubt that devotion. She would forget Evan. She must.

———

EVAN HEARD a knock in the distance, but as he awoke the sound grew closer until it had his full attention. He stretched and opened one eye carefully, then the other while he raised himself up. He rubbed his eyes and then glanced at the window and saw that it was night.

"Damn," he mumbled. "Enter."

Higgins walked slowly inside, and Evan let his head fall backward. He stared at the ceiling, annoyed. "What is it, Higgins?"

"Mr. Carter has arrived, sir, he says he is here to convey you to the Brockhursts' without delay."

Evan groaned, the news of that afternoon flooded his memory, and he took a deep breath before gathering himself, trying to relieve the pressure on his chest. He imagined going to the ball and standing off to the side of the room as his father announced the betrothal, only another spectator to wish them well. He couldn't bear it.

"You can tell Mr. Carter that I'm not going."

"Sir, Mr. Carter bid me... I, of course, would never argue with your decision, but Mr. Carter ..."

Evan huffed and sat up straight, looking to Higgins. "Mr. Carter is a damned nuisance. Off with you, out of my rooms!" he shouted.

Evan leaned back, his head thumping on the headboard. "Damn," he said again. He sat for a moment, eyes closed until he again heard footsteps in his outer chamber.

"I thought I told you —"

"My, my, Evan, I know you never try very hard with your appearance, but this goes above and beyond, even for you."

"What are you doing in here?" Evan asked, startled at Nathan's sudden appearance. He scrambled out of bed and stood on the other side as if to create a barrier between him and his friend. "Get out of here at once."

"No, I don't believe I will," said Nathan, shaking his head at Evan's unbelievable appearance. "Look at you. You're a complete... are those pillow marks on your face? Evan, were you sleeping?"

Evan stared. "I'm in a bedchamber, aren't I? Daft question."

"How very unlike you," Nathan said while Evan snorted.

"To sleep?"

Nathan huffed, his patience and understanding all but gone. "To lose track of the time, Evan. You loathe when people aren't punctual, and you are never late. It's going to take you an hour to get ready."

"No, it would take you an hour. As it is, I've already told Higgins to tell you I'm not going."

Nathan smirked. "Yes, he did say as much, but I've had strict instructions to drag you there 'by any means necessary' and have been given full permission from the lady of the house to use force, if necessary."

Evan scowled, remembering his promise to his mother. Now that he was fully awake and his faculties about him he knew it wouldn't be well done of him to stay away.

"I only have to throw my coat on then we can be off."

Nathan looked scandalized. "You can't arrive like that. Comb your hair at least. It looks like all you did was run your hand through it, which I am sure is precisely what you did."

Evan ignored him and walked into the sitting room while starting to tie his cravat, only to be followed and then interrupted by Nathan clucking at him in a manner much like his own mother.

"Don't tie it like that, good Lord, you're going to a ball, not out to Tattersalls to buy a matching pair," he said as he advanced on Evan. "Here, let me do it."

"Get away, Nathan," Evan spluttered and tried to back away only to hit the wall. "I mean it! I won't be held responsible for my actions if you so much as touch —"

"Oh, be quiet. Here, it won't take a minute," Nathan said, grabbing the cravat and styling it.

Evan continued to glower at him while resigning himself to the offending hands. "Don't make it all puffy, with all those ridiculous loops yours has," said Evan. "It looks like you can't even draw breath in that monstrosity."

Nathan shook his head and finished. He stood back to admire his skill when Evan reached up, pulling at it with one finger, nearly destroying all his hard work. "Stop that," he barked while batting at Evan's hand. "You are going to ruin it."

"Too tight," Evan grumbled while reaching for his freshly pressed waist and tailcoat. Finally dressed, he ran his hand through his hair once more and declared himself ready. Nathan simply shrugged his shoulders in defeat until Evan saw him eyeing his greatly worn Hessian boots.

"Don't say it."

"Why would I waste my breath?" asked Nathan, his hands in the air, a smile on his face.

Evan actually laughed aloud and grabbed his walking stick before striding purposefully out of the room, Nathan on his heels. "You don't expect me to go around in silk stockings and gold buckled shoes, do you?"

"Well, yes, that's normally what one wears to a ball." Nathan laughed. "Though I admit you would look quite ridiculous in silk stockings and gold bucked shoes. I can't begin to imagine it."

"Well, don't try," said Evan halfway down the stairway. When they reached the entryway, Evan slipped his hand into his pocket and froze. For a split second he considered not going after it, but he couldn't. It was a part of him.

"I forgot something. Wait here; I won't be a moment."

Evan bounded back up the stairs as he heard Nathan ask him to stop dawdling. He ran into the room and slowed when he saw it, mocking him from the corner of the room. He walked over and bent down, picking up the silver piece. He stood, and gazed at it for a moment, inspecting it for any harm, before placing it back into his pocket.

He ran back down the stairs and didn't even pause to talk to Nathan before he burst out the front doors and into to the carriage that awaited them. As he sat in the box waiting for Nathan, he counted to ten and made a promise to himself that tonight he would be graciousness itself and any feelings he had on the matter would be closed. He would give his brother his love and congratulations and then be off, and anything that happened after? He would deal with as it arose.

7
DASTARDLY MEETINGS

Lady Charity Preston sat in the corner of the ballroom, fanning herself in triumph. "And Louisa was practically dying of envy when I told her I was to attend the Blackburn house party. I thought she would fall over from shock."

"Charity, you really shouldn't go around announcing to every living person that you were invited. People will think you're boasting," said Phoebe Simmons, her cousin and companion. "After all, Prudence and I were also invited."

"Yes, because you are my friends," Charity said, as though her reasoning was plain for everyone to see. "Obviously they have noted our friendship and have invited you so I will feel more comfortable. Things might finally be turning around for the better, Phoebe. Can't you be happy for me?"

Phoebe looked at her, brows furrowed, but Charity was sure she had been invited to attend the Blackburn house party because they intended to match her with their eldest son, Viscount Ravenbrook.

She told her cousin as much that morning and, once prodded, Phoebe also agreed it was odd for them to receive invitations since they really had nothing to do with the family. Phoebe thought she was setting herself up for a disappointment, but Phoebe didn't know what she knew.

The Blackburn heir fancied her, and she intended to use that to her advantage, after all, she was running out of time.

"Then how do you explain Prudence?" Phoebe tried to reason, again. "They wouldn't invite her because she's your friend. You hardly even speak to her unless I'm with you."

"Whoever cares, Phoebe, but I know I'm right. I've seen the way he looks at me from across the room. Look! He's doing so right now." She turned and gave an easy but calculated smile to the viscount, who looked back unabashedly, not even shocked at being caught staring at her so openly.

Phoebe turned her gaze and started, quickly looking back to Charity. "Has he been staring at you like that all evening?"

Charity smiled. "More like all season."

Phoebe gasped. "Has he spoken to you? Surely not."

"How could he? We've never been introduced," said Charity.

He had always watched her from afar, and why wouldn't he stare? She knew she was considered beautiful. With her golden hair and light blue eyes, her cornflower blue dress cut just so to accentuate her figure. Phoebe's own blonde hair was not quite so golden, and her blue eyes, not quite so blue.

Even so, she knew Phoebe had something she didn't that inspired people to like her, even love her. It wasn't that she didn't have love of her own. She did. Her father loved her, she knew, but everyone had always gravitated towards Phoebe. Her life had been free of strife and loss, and it showed on her glowing face and kind eyes. Charity loved her cousin for her interference in her own life but knew she must take every opportunity presented to her, especially one such as this.

"Perhaps you're right about the house party. Still, I don't want you to get your hopes up only to be hurt," said Phoebe. "There could be many other reasons for the invitation."

Charity opened her mouth to answer, only to be interrupted by Prudence Wilson sitting herself down beside the pair, her caramel colored curls bouncing as she tried to catch her breath. "You will never guess what I saw a moment ago."

Phoebe turned to Prudence and smiled, while Charity tried to appear uninterested but leaned towards her to hear just the same. "What is it? Go on, tell us. I can see you'll absolutely burst if you don't."

"Well, I was waiting to greet the hostess — oh, was the line ever long — and I saw Julia standing with her sister and Lady Blackburn. They were right behind me, you see, and do you know what Julia told me?" Prudence asked excitedly, her brown eyes sparkling and her cheeks flushed from the crush of the room.

"Get on with it already," Charity said testily.

Prudence gave her a look before continuing. "She said that she and her sister arrived here in Lady Blackburn's carriage, that they all came together!"

Phoebe patted Prudence on the arm as Charity deflated at such dull news. "That's not very extraordinary," Phoebe said kindly.

Prudence shook her head. "Yes, but that's not all. I

heard Lady Blackburn tell Fleur that the announcement would be made before supper. The *announcement*. Don't you see, I've figured out the puzzle. That must be why we were all invited, because of the Osborne girls. Julia is a particular friend of mine, and you two have known Fleur for ages. It all makes sense now that there will be an *announcement*." She giggled, happy at the idea of one of them finally marrying.

"Hush, Prudence, now you're just speculating," Phoebe said, trying to un-ruffle some of Charity's feathers. "The Duke of Norfield is old friends with the Earl of Blackburn, but it doesn't have to mean marriage between the families."

"Oh, Phoebe, what else does one announce at a ball?" she asked, exasperated at their lack of enthusiasm. "It's obvious to everyone that they would be perfect for one another." Prudence lowered her voice and leaned towards them. "It must be that there is an understanding between them."

Charity leaned back in her chair with an indignant huff. "How absurd."

"That will be enough, both of you," said Phoebe. "We don't know anything right now, and I do not like gossiping about Fleur like this when she's not here to speak on her own behalf."

"Very well," said Prudence, while Charity looked about the room, continuing to fan herself. To the world, Charity looked cool and confident, but she was quickly becoming worried. What if Prudence was right? If he were indeed to marry Fleur, she would have no prospects at all until next season, and that would not do at all.

She stole a glance at the viscount, and sure enough, he was still looking at her with unabashed curiosity. She really couldn't figure out what the man was about, but she hoped for her own sake that Prudence was wrong, though if she wasn't, she was prepared to wish Fleur well. Securing her own future was important, but not at the cost of her own dear friend's happiness.

———

EVAN MADE his way into the ballroom with Nathan looking for his cousins and brother. He'd never attended a *ton* ball, only country assemblies back home, and the opulence both amazed and petrified him. He gazed around the room and saw much to scorn, but he also admitted — even reluctantly — that there was also much to praise.

Couples young and old danced in the center of the room, talking and laughing. Matrons guarded their charges like the fierce lionesses they were and men both respected and feared them as they circled, gathering courage to speak.

It was a choreographed dance, this mating ritual, and it fascinated him.

He walked further into the room and spied Edward in his usual pose, leaning against a wall, nonchalantly looking across the ballroom floor. His cousins, Felix and Dominic, were on either side of him, and Evan's tense shoulders relaxed with relief at seeing familiar faces.

Nathan and Evan made their way towards them into the thick of it, and the whispers and words of his arrival did not go unnoticed by him.

"Everyone is staring at me," he whispered to Nathan.

Nathan laughed. "Of course they are. Had you done your duty like a good little gentleman and attended these things before, then you would have been as unremarkable as the rest of us. As it is, you're like the new act at a traveling circus. Everyone wants to get a good look at you."

Evan looked around and saw no fewer than four ladies in white staring at him from behind fans beside the refreshment table. He quickened his pace.

Arriving, Felix clapped him on the shoulder, laughing at his practical gallop to their side. "Ah, Evan, fancy seeing you here. Stay by us, young cousin, and we shall protect you."

Dom laughed. "He looks ready to bolt, Carter. Didn't you warn him at all?"

Nathan smiled and shrugged.

"Leave him be," said Edward, his amusement obvious only to those who knew him.

Evan pulled at his cravat with a glare from Nathan. "It's so hot in here. I don't know how any of you stand it for long."

Felix smiled and shook Evan's shoulder once more. "That's why God invented the card room, Evan, so men would have a place to drink and tarry and loosen their collars with stories that weren't made for ladies, young or old."

Evan looked at his cousin, completely diverted. "Your turn of phrase is as quick as ever, Felix. Damn if I didn't miss you."

They laughed, and Evan couldn't help the small tinge of regret that told him had he just swallowed his pride, he could have been here with them always, enjoying their company, and not just during the few times a year he allowed himself to return home.

He had discovered many regrets that day, though not all were so easily remedied, and some he knew he would never have the chance too, not as he wished.

Feeling rather gloomy now and at odds with the frenzy of the room, he jerked his head at Nathan. "Want to show me this card room?"

Nathan nodded and asked the others to join them. Felix and Dom declined, having dance partners of their own, and Edward just shook his head with a smile and looked off into the distance.

Evan followed Nathan to the card room, and this time searched the room meticulously for a certain young woman with raven hair and fine blue eyes. He did not know if he would find her, or what he would do if he did, though the thought made him breathless and nervous with anticipation.

He only knew he wanted to see her again, even if it were only to glimpse her from afar. It was in that moment that Evan knew he should have had the foresight, the knowledge of his own character to know when he did find her, something dastardly would happen.

———

FLEUR STOOD in the large entryway to the ballroom with Julia, both looking for the other girls. Had she not been so preoccupied, Fleur would have been in awe of the splendor before her. Marble floors that gleamed in the lowered candlelight of the many chandeliers, the whole of the room a soft white with cool tones of blue.

She finally saw them, sitting off to the side as always, conversing among themselves. She followed Julia as she weaved between the guests, pausing to say hello to a few acquaintances here and there until finally, she stepped around Julia to take the seat next to Charity.

She looked to her friend, and the tension of the day eased just a little bit. She was always more comfortable at these things when her friend was around. Charity leaned forward and kissed her cheek. "Fleur, you've only arrived and already you look done for. Your cheek felt warm, are you feeling well?"

"Yes, I'm quite well, though I suppose I am a bit warm. Why do these things always have to be such a squeeze?"

Charity smiled and took Fleur's hand in her own. "Because it's everyone's last chance to be seen before they retire to the country. They couldn't miss that, now could they?"

Fleur followed Charity's eyes to a dancing couple and winced when Mr. Trentham trod all over Charlotte Smith's toes, something they had all experienced, poor man. "No indeed, what would one have to talk about all winter if one missed the last social event of the season? So much excitement."

Charity cleared her throat and looked back to Fleur, trying not to laugh when she heard Mr. Trentham apologizing to Miss Smith once more. They looked at each other in all seriousness, trying to keep control lest they burst out laughing. "I'm sure they would think of something, would they not?"

Fleur laughed behind her fan and eyed her friend. It was good to see Charity in such happy spirits, at last, the pain of losing her elder brother lessening with time.

"What are you two laughing about?" asked Julia, now seated between Prudence and Phoebe.

Charity lowered her fan. "Poor Charlotte Smith is dancing with Mr. Trentham."

"Oh, poor Charlotte," said Julia before turning back to Prudence.

Fleur sighed. "My father wished me to express his regret of not seeing your own father in town. Though he understands he's been much occupied with everything at home, Papa had hoped he would come."

Charity's smile faltered, and Fleur regretted reminding her friend of how her father remained at home mourning her brother, though he'd been dead more than a year.

Charity smiled again though Fleur saw through it. "Yes, I'm sure he'd love to be here, and he's promised to bring me up next year himself along with my aunt. You know how my father loves a ball."

"Of course, I remember. He always is such a delight at the assemblies at home, making sure everyone has a partner and not one young lady is left standing in a corner. What would he say if he could see us now?" asked Fleur, grateful for the turn in conversation.

"He'd have all of us paired off before we knew it, one of us to Mr. Trentham, no doubt."

Fleur laughed and then looked out into the room. "I do miss home."

"Don't worry, in a few short weeks you will you be on your way back to Norfield."

Fleur tried to smile but couldn't find it within herself. She wouldn't be on her way to Norfield anytime soon, not any longer.

She thought of home and of Mrs. Davis, who always sent up warm milk on fall and winter nights to warm her before bed, and of Mrs. Finch, the housekeeper, who always bickered with Mr. Baines about leaving her father's shirts too long before pressing them.

Suddenly she felt like weeping. When she left, she had no way of knowing that would be her last day at Norfield. She knew she would return for holidays and family visits, but it wasn't the same, not at all.

Fleur jumped when she felt Charity's gloved hand touch her shoulder. "Whatever is the matter?"

She looked over at her concerned friend and scolded herself. How could she be wallowing in self-pity in front of Charity, who had only been out of mourning a few months? She should be helping her forget her troubles, not adding to them.

"It's nothing. You know how I feel about these things."

"Yes, but it's more than that. I've known you too long, Fleur, so tell me what is wrong."

"It's only the heat of the rooms. Perhaps we can walk? The gardens?"

Charity nodded, and they stood to leave, mindful to tell the others where they were going.

"Should we all go?" Julia asked.

Phoebe sighed. "I've promised the next set to Mr. Brandall." Her eyes became wider, and she looked at them quickly. "Please don't leave me here alone. I shall die if I'm on my own when he comes to fetch me."

Prudence laughed. "Sorry, but I've promised Mr. Henderson the next."

Charity sat back down, shaking her head. "For goodness sake, I'll stay. Julia, you and Fleur go. Honestly, you two. Fleur, I'll find you later?"

Fleur nodded and joined arms with Julia as they made their way towards the door. She heard Charity call Phoebe silly for getting worked up over Mr. Brandall, the biggest flirt to ever step foot inside of a ballroom.

Julia laughed and Fleur gave her a look. "Well, it's true," she said as she shrugged her shoulders.

"She shouldn't say such things, especially where she can be overheard, and neither should you."

"It's Charity," she said as if that explained everything, and it did.

Fleur lost herself in her own thoughts while following Julia, and she was halfway across the ballroom when none other than Nathan Carter came bounding up to her.

"Lady Fleur, this is a pleasure," Nathan said, rocking back and forth from his heels to his toes. "And Lady Julia, nice to see you again. You look quite fetching, even with that frightening scowl on your face."

Julia crossed her arms and looked upwards toward Nathan as he stood a good head over her. "Must you always be so loud and... oh, I don't know... full of *bounce*?" asked Julia.

Fleur stared at her sister in astonishment. Her gaze was broken by a deep rumbling laugh coming from behind Nathan, causing her to stiffen. She knew that laugh, a laugh that never failed to shake her to her very core.

"Nathan is never in any other humor but joy and merriment," said Evan. "He practically wrote the book on how to be pleasant in every scenario known to man. I don't think he knows any other way to be."

"Yes, I noticed," said Julia. "He is very pleasant indeed, though what he could be so happy about all hours of the day I do not know. Are you ever serious, Mr. Carter?"

Fleur was mortified. "Julia, really —"

"Don't worry about Nathan, he can hold his own," said Evan, looking directly into Fleur's eyes. "See, look at them, matching each other word for word like they have been doing so for years."

Fleur ignored the bickering two beside her and stared into eyes she had thought she'd never see again. *So dark,* she thought, just as she remembered. Evander Woolf was standing in front of her, his hair darker and shorter than it had been as a young man.

She couldn't breathe — oh, why couldn't she just breathe?

He wasn't overly tall, not as tall as his brother, but he still stood above her, the top of her head reaching his nose. His attire, however inappropriate, showed off his well-defined chest and shoulders. He was, she thought, perhaps not as elegant as some men in the room, but he was Evan. She again reminded herself to breathe.

"I hear congratulations are in order, Lady Fleur, as it seems you are soon to become family," he practically sneered, taking a step towards her as she fought not to take her own step backward. "We shall have to try our very hardest to make you feel welcome, now won't we?"

The words could have been the sweet words of a caring brother if not for the obvious ridicule in Evan's voice, and the hard look in his eyes, a look she had hoped she'd never see again.

Nathan and Julia stopped talking when they heard Evan's words and stared at him.

"Yes, Mr. Woolf, I thank you for your *kind* words of welcome to your family," Fleur said, trying in her own defense to match him, her anger coming forth.

Evan's laughter at her words held no joy, while Fleur's eyes darted around them. She was relieved and amazed to see no one had taken any notice of them.

"Evan, what is this?" Nathan asked quietly, grasping his upper arm while Julia stepped in front of Fleur, prepared to give him what-for.

Evan ignored them both. "You haven't changed at all, still silly, frightened Fleur, protected by her brave little sister, who at the age of six had more backbone than you carry now," Evan said. His lip curled, and his eyes narrowed while he looked her up and down as if to assess her. "If you will excuse me, I think I've seen enough."

Fleur couldn't move. Frozen, she couldn't turn her head to watch him walk away. Not again, she wouldn't.

"Lady Fleur," said Nathan. "Apologies are not enough, but let me try in Evan's stead, he does not do well with... well —"

"People?" Julia asked, her anger ready to boil over. "What a horrible man he has become. Though I don't know why I'm surprised, he's always been high and mighty, but how dare he —"

"Julia, please," Fleur begged her sister. "Really, Mr. Carter, it's nothing I haven't seen before. I've known Mr. Woolf all my life, and I'm well used to his character. If you both will excuse me, I will step outside for a moment."

"Fleur, wait, I will accompany you, it won't do for you to be —"

Fleur stopped Julia with a hand on her arm. "No, Julia, please. I think I'd like to be alone, for just a moment. I'll go out into the garden — there are people there strolling and it is well lit. You go and find Prudence then join me. Thank you, Mr. Carter, it was a pleasure to see you again." Fleur turned on her heel and hurried her way to the garden, but not before both Nathan and Julia saw tears in her eyes.

"Has Evan lost his bloody mind? Oh, do excuse me, Lady Julia. "

"He lost his 'bloody' mind a long time ago. This is not the first time he has hurt my sister." Julia said in agreement, making Nathan want to stare at her in shock, or laugh at her boldness, he couldn't decide which. "Keep him away from her, do you understand? I will not have him upsetting her any more than he already has."

"I assure you, Lady Julia, I will make sure Evan has no opportunity to do more harm this evening. Now, if you will excuse me, there is someone I must find."

Julia stood in the hall. In the room next to her were dozens of people, but the only thing she could see was the angry look on Nathan's face before he walked away, his jaw set, his stride purposeful. She could not help but stare at him as he departed, catching her breath from her anger as one thought ran through her mind. Apparently, Mr. Carter could be serious after all.

8

MURDEROUS FLOWER POTS

Fleur stepped quickly into the gardens just beyond and to the side of the ballroom doors. Not wanting to wander too far in case Julia couldn't find her, she stayed close, but she needed to escape from the crowds, to disappear if only for a moment.

She had been taken aback by him, even though she knew there was a slight chance he would appear. He was not supposed to be there, he never was, and she had counted on that constant. Evan knew about the betrothal, that much was certain, and everything he had predicted to her the night he left had come true. His parents, her father, everyone had gotten what they wanted.

Everyone but herself and Evan, even Edward hadn't wanted this.

It was always the same. Every year she and Julia would wave to them as they went off to school, Evan to Eton, and Edward to university, while they went home to Norfield. When she was little her father told her it was a game. She would count the days till they returned to Blackburn Hall to see them all again. Every Sunday her father would ask her the days on their walk home from church, and she would excitedly ramble off her answers.

But as she grew the game became childish, though her feelings became just the opposite. She missed both brothers terribly, but Evan even more so, and when he finally returned for Christmas from his first stint at university, with Edward for an escort, she and Julia had both rushed to their sides, greeting them at the stables.

He had greeted her, not coldly, but not with the same warmth as before, and as they walked to the main house together, Edward and Julia before them, he barely spoke a word to her, all politeness about the weather and her family's health.

All her prior fears that he would not want to remain there with her and return to his life outside of Blackburn Hall came rushing back to her. That was until he had finally laughed and teased her about her red nose and cheeks from the December snow.

He had smiled at her then, and it took her breath away.

It was then he had stopped her mid-stride, and looked at her with all seriousness as he asked her to meet him in secret that night at the stables, telling her that he had something important to show her for her birthday. She knew she shouldn't, that they would both be in trouble if she agreed, but agree she did and promised him she'd get away as soon as she was able.

Later that night, she buzzed with anticipation, especially once Evan had stolen away. Several times she tried to get away but was thwarted at every attempt. First Madeleine had requested she play the pianoforte, and then Julia insisted they all play charades. When she had finally made her excuses and walked towards the doorway, she made the mistake of stopping to say goodnight to

Edward, who had been leaning against the doorframe reading.

Her father had laughed and asked Edward if he had been standing in the doorway all night to catch her. Fleur was confused until a smiling Lord Blackburn pointed at the small bundle of mistletoe in the doorway. She immediately wanted to flee.

Edward, being the gentleman he was, relented, his own embarrassment gracing his face. He had closed his book and leaned down to kiss her cheek only to veer off last-second to her forehead. He'd smiled at her afterward, and she was so thankful for his thoughtfulness, she had beamed at him before running off upstairs.

After delaying to her room to find her heavy woolen winter cloak, she had walked quietly down the hall, wondering what it could possibly be that Evan wanted to show her. But before she reached the back stairs, she heard her name. It came to her barely above a whisper.

She stopped and turned, finding him in a small parlor room, his dark silhouette contrasting against the unusual brightness of the room, the moon shining off the snow outside and reflecting on the walls.

He said her name again as one of his hands raked through his hair. Something about his voice and manner disturbed her. His eyes were hard and his jaw firm, his face ruddy, not only from anger but from the cold of the outdoors, from waiting for her. Her heart sank at the thought. She tried to explain, but he wouldn't listen. He never did when he was upset.

He had rambled then, telling her he knew his efforts were all for nothing, the years he spent at school to make something of himself so he could have a chance to win her affections. The constant arguments he'd had with his father to not be send off into the military so they could be together, all of it, spent in vain. Her heart had soared at his declaration but then came crashing down the next moment.

His voice was full of accusation, and he cut her down as he relayed what he'd witnessed — she and Edward under the mistletoe. Evan had never known her to be so shallow, he never pegged her to be one to prefer the heir, he'd said, that she was the same as all the other feather-brained debutantes out to seek a fortune or a title, and that he regretted thinking her different.

And so she had shot back, her own pain overwhelmed by the shock of his words, and in her anger she compared the brothers. She asked him why she wouldn't prefer someone who could check his temper, who would never treat her the way he was treating her now, calling her names and assuming things about her character he knew not to be true. That Edward had always treated her with patience and care, and had never spoken thus to her.

Evan had walked away from her then, and she, regret-ting her words, called after him, but he ignored her and shut himself in his rooms. She had stood in front of his door, poised to knock but never finding the courage when her father found her there.

She ran into her father's arms, and he consoled her, and she promised herself the next morning she'd find Evan and explain. That she didn't mean it, that she never wanted him to be anyone other than himself, but that he needed to think of others too. All of her hopes were pinned on speaking to him but when she woke, Evan had left, leaving only a note saying he was returning to school.

The next season her father and her finishing governess had deemed her an age where it was inappropriate for her to frolic with the boys at Blackburn Hall, and they stopped visiting, only seeing one another at social functions during the season.

It was two years before she saw Edward again across a crowded ballroom. His mother, her sponsor, had reacquainted them, but by that time he had become Lord Ravenbrook, and she, Lady Fleur.

As for Evan, she hadn't seen him since the night of her sixteenth birthday. Later as she grew into a young woman, she finally understood everything she couldn't understand then, that neither one of them in their immaturity knew how to handle their feelings or their families' expectations. That Evan was afraid that if she married into the earl's family someday, it would likely be as the Viscountess of Ravenbrook, and not as his wife. His worst fear had come true after all, though not in a way anyone expected.

She leaned against the stucco wall, letting it hold her as her breath heaved. "What am I going to do?" she asked no-one, the night hiding her from everyone's gaze.

She felt like her whole world had stopped and centered on him when she saw him again. When she heard him laugh, her heart had raced, and when he spoke to her at first, she was so relieved, she thought for one blissful moment that they would talk again as old friends. Then in one tiny moment, everything shattered.

He had been so hateful, so cruel. His was the same voice that once laughed with her, had sat beside her while they abused the piano singing silly songs to make Julia laugh when they were stuck indoors from the rain, the same voice that used to greet her daily.

Evan hated her. She knew it, she felt it deep into her very soul.

A sob rolled through her, and she held her breath to

stop it. Once she had control, she let it out in one shuddering breath. "What's the matter with you? He left you ages ago, remember? You do not need his approval nor his company," she whispered to herself. Her anger flared and then quickly subsided when she realized Julia would come for her any moment.

As she walked below the upper veranda, not far from the ballroom doors, she could hear the boisterous voices and laughter of the young men above. They were talking animatedly and smoking cigars, and she wondered if it was the card room as it seemed to be rowdy enough and there were no ladies present.

She was just about to make her way back to the main door stairway when she felt something slam into her from behind, knocking her down to the ground and her breath away from her. Dazed, she looked up into dark eyes just before all hell and the devil broke loose.

———

EVAN STORMED through the halls of the Brockhurst home before finding an exit to the side yard, needing a brisk walk and the cool night air to clear his anger. What had he bloody said back there? Silly, *frightened Fleur?* Good Lord!

He had been a complete beast — no, he was worse than that, he was the one who was frightened. If any other man had dared to be cruel to Fleur in the manner he had just been, he would have drawn his cork right then and there.

Shamed, he stopped and threw his back against the wall as he leaned and looked up into the night sky, trying to understand himself. He saw her standing there with her sister, his wish of finding her coming true, and before he knew it, Nathan had walked up to the girls before he could stop him.

In that moment he felt uncontrolled and unrelenting jealousy. It had overwhelmed him, and thinking back on it; he couldn't say whether it was the thought of her marrying Edward or the scene of her speaking so easily to Nathan that did him in. Any and all good sense he had gained over the years left him, and all he knew was he wanted to lash out at her. Blame her for agreeing to a match she swore she never wanted.

He had repeated past mistakes without even a pause or a second thought, and the knowledge of it made him cringe. Like so many times before, he had let his emotions run away from him, and he exploded before running from her, leaving her to pick up the pieces he left behind. Would he never learn from his past mistakes?

He was distracted from his sulking when he heard laughter come from above. He lifted his gaze and saw Lord Brockhurst's youngest son teetering on the edge of the veranda in his drunkenness, only the railing keeping him upright. He snorted when he saw the man barrel into a few of the potted plants situated on the railing, sending them into a spin. His eyes couldn't help but travel to see where the plants would fall and what he saw made his blood run cold.

Evan looked back up just in time to see two of the pots sway dangerously. Without even stopping to think, he ran. He ran faster than he thought possible and blindly jumped a hedge. Just before he heard two loud crashes, he flung himself at Fleur, knocking them both spectacularly to the ground in a tangle of skirts and limbs.

When Evan lifted his aching head, completely disoriented from the hard landing, he couldn't tell what happened first, the ladies screaming around them or the loud promises to kill him that came from above. Overwhelmed by the shocked murmurs that he could hear from just inside the ballroom as people gathered at the door, he started to come around and shook his head trying to clear the fog when he heard someone cry out Fleur's name.

He looked over and saw Lady Julia with no fewer than three other ladies, as a small crowd started to form around them. To his right, he saw his father's pale face and the Duke of Norfield barreling toward him with a face so red he thought the man might be choking. He followed everyone's eyes down in confusion only to meet a wide blue gaze.

It was then that Evan finally noticed he was lying right on top of the lady with her legs tangled about him and his hand so far up her skirts, he was touching her stockinged thigh above her knee.

Evan whipped his hand out of her skirts and jolted backward, falling onto his backside in the grass. He saw Fleur's face, burning with deep embarrassment, not unlike his own as he stood and backed further away.

Once he moved, Lady Charity Preston and Julia ran towards her to set her skirts to rights. He didn't see much more, however, as a fist came sailing through the air, hitting him squarely in the jaw.

"Norfield, stop this. Julian, no!" Evan heard his father say. He touched his hand to his lip, blood seeping through his fingers and looked up to see his father and brother holding steadily onto a very angry duke.

"Papa, please stop. It's not what it seems," he heard Fleur say, trying to cut through her father's angry fog.

The duke looked her over and satisfied she wasn't hurt, began his tirade. "Not what it seems? Then what the devil was it that gave him cause to have you on the ground screaming?" he asked before turning to his own father. "I'll have your whelp's answer by God, Blackburn, or I swear I'll slap my glove in his face right now and meet him at dawn!"

"I say, Norfield," a blustering Lord Brockhurst interrupted. "Let's get the lady inside and then we can all discuss this rationally."

"Yes, Julian, let's all go inside," Evan heard his mother rush to whisper, "Fleur has had a shock and it will not do for her to stay out here."

Lord Brockhurst broke up the small whispering crowd, sending them all back into the ballroom while Lady Brockhurst escorted them into the library, away from the onlookers and the gossip that was surely already brewing.

They were all there — his parents and brother, and of course her father and sister. Even his cousins Felix and Dom were standing off to the side with a clearly upset and confused Nathan. Evan looked over to the door when he heard it open, and Lord Brockhurst came in, breathing heavily from walking briskly, the excitement likely the most exercise he had in decades.

"Now, let's all stay calm and see what's happened, shall we?" Brockhurst asked as the duke continued to glare at Evan.

Evan knew what it *looked* like he was doing, he knew he should be careful with his next words, but that had never stopped him before, not when he temper was so far gone.

"Your brat is what happened, Brockhurst," he said angrily. "He was doing a drunken dance on the veranda and whilst doing so he knocked over two pots from the railing. I only reached Lady Fleur in time. One more second and they could have struck her on the head and killed her."

"Oh, I say," Brockhurst said, his mustachioed face puffing up as his wife ran over to comfort a shaken Fleur.

"Oh, you poor dear!" Lady Brockhurst exclaimed. "I shall make sure the gardener removes every pot from the railings, to think you could have been killed!"

Evan threw his hands in the air at the complete absurdity of the situation before clasping them behind his back to pace the room.

"Why the devil did you not say as much outside?" the duke asked. "And did you have to knock her clear down to the ground, her skirts above her ears for all and sundry to see?"

Evan stopped and glared at the duke while the ladies gasped at his words. "Why yes, you are absolutely right, your grace," said Evan, "Next time I'll just let the pretty little pot fall on her pretty little head while I decide how best to save her with *dignity*, shall I? Would that have suited you better, Lord Norfield?"

Fleur burst into tears then and buried her head in her sister's shoulder. He wanted to go to her, but the duke was already in front of her offering his handkerchief.

"Evan, that's enough," his father commanded. "Julian, it's clear that Evan was saving your daughter, not debauching her, and as you can see she is fine, though understandably shaken. I suggest you take her home, and tomorrow we can discuss what is to be done. In the meantime, Felix and Dom, along with the Brockhursts, will spread around the story, making sure to bury any suspicions of impropriety."

Edward moved from the side of the room towards him, speaking for the first time. "Evan, I think you should go home. I'll fetch you when it's time to meet tomorrow. Nathan, you will escort him, won't you?"

"Yes, of course —"

"I don't need a damned guard. I can take myself off!"

Evan yelled at Edward, storming past him and yanking the door open. Nathan apologized to the ladies for his friend for what seemed like the hundredth time that day and quickly followed after him.

"Come, Fleur, Julia, we are leaving. I'll see you in the morning, Blackburn." Julian escorted his daughters out of the room, followed by the Brockhursts.

Lady Blackburn paced the room, much as her son had earlier. "Charles, what a ghastly nightmare. How could things have possibly worsened since this morning? I must go and find Lady Brockhurst. I love the dear, but I need to know she is saying the right things. The woman could talk the ears off an elephant," she said before walking towards the doorway.

Felix stepped towards her, grasping her hand in his own. "No, Aunt, let Dom and I handle this. If you walk out there now you'll be... just let Dom and I," he said, trying to calm her nerves and spare her the hurt she was surely to feel if she went out into the fray. "We will go and try to control some of the damage in the ballroom, and later we will even go around the clubs to make sure all is well and nothing untoward is spreading. I'm sure you will be announcing their betrothal on the first night of your house party, so why don't you let Uncle and Edward escort you home."

"But I really must —"

"Madeleine," said Charles, the use of her full name breaking through and drawing her attention. "Felix is right. We must let them handle it the best they can. If you were to arrive now, they would pounce on you, demanding to know what your announcement would be and as we don't know... that is to say... we can't be certain of anything now. We need to discuss the situation with Julian first."

"But, Charles, what if we can't protect her from this?" she asked, gripping his arm, her small hands shaking from the force.

Edward stepped forward. "Mother, nothing has been done that we can't remedy later. Let us take you home, and we can discuss it."

Madeleine nodded and took a deep breath. "Felix," she said, looking over to him and Dom. "You always were a good boy, you and Dom both. I know I can trust you not to get carried away. Don't confirm anything, just remind them that the duke and his daughters are close friends of ours, it's not so strange she would be in the gardens alone with Evan..."

She trailed off, her own bravado failing. "Just do what you can."

She took Charles' arm, and he escorted her out of the room. The three younger men somberly followed, expecting everything to go as planned as it was too much to hope that even the *ton* could find a new scandal to gossip about by morning.

———

FELIX MEANDERED through the clustered crowd, silent but observing. As he looked across the broad room, not one person was dancing, though music played, barely heard over the multitude of voices. All were gathered around the ballroom, all speaking rapidly in false hushed tones, as they all wanted to be heard. All about Lady Fleur.

"Lady Blackburn did say there would be an announcement this very evening. It's a shame the Osborne girl had to ruin her moment of triumph. She was surely announcing an engagement, oh how disappointed she must be," He heard Mrs. Tildon say.

"Apparently she was alone with him before it happened, she was seen sneaking off to the side of the house... alone," Lady Ashton replied.

"I don't believe it," said Lord Crowley. "The younger girl, yes, I would believe it of, but not Lady Fleur. Never was there such an affable and steady girl, I just don't believe it," he said once more, shaking his head.

Felix looked back towards his brother when he heard his name being called.

"Felix," said Dom, jerking his head to the side towards an empty room. The both rushed inside and once over the threshold; Dom shut the door with a heavy sigh. "This is much worse than we feared, the gossip ranges from an innocent stroll to, and you won't believe this, Lady Fleur planning to run away and *elope* with Evan. Apparently, her father found out and chased them down, attacking Evan to stop them. They aren't even trying to remember the particulars of what actually happened out there."

Felix closed his eyes and gritted his teeth. Of course they weren't. The truth isn't near as interesting as an imagined anvil wedding. "An elopement, you say? Of all the nonsense to invent."

"What do you want to do?" asked Dom.

"Damn Norfield and his temper, if he hadn't attacked Evan... but no matter, what is done is done. You go on home for the night. I want to stay here for a time longer."

"What about the clubs?"

"Do you think it will be any better than this?" asked Felix, sighing. "Go home. There is nothing that can be done here.

Dom nodded and walked towards the door before he stopped and turned to look at his brother. "Felix, don't do anything stupid," he said, giving him a look before leaving.

Felix smiled and followed at a more sedate pace thinking about what Dom had said earlier. An elopement between Fleur and Evan. The thought made him smile as he walked amongst the crowd, people were dancing again, but there were a few still going on about the incident.

He walked over to the refreshment table, pretending to peruse the items as he listened. He could see Lady Brockhurst with a group of young ladies accompanied by their chaperones. She was floundering.

"An elopement? No, no, my dears, you have it all wrong, Lady Fleur was simply walking in the gardens when a great pot nearly fell on her head! Mr. Woolf saved her! I think it was quite heroic of him."

"Oh, come now, Wilhemina, that is too absurd," said Lady Dudley, fanning herself while laughing. "Murderous plants?"

"We know Lord and Lady Blackburn planned an announcement tonight, is that true, Lady Brockhurst?" asked a young indistinguishable girl in white.

"Well, I don't know —"

"Of course you know," Lady Dudley prodded again. "It is *your* ball so you must know."

Felix saw Lady Brockhurst's face pinch and decided it was best to intervene.

"My goodness, ladies," said Felix, walking into the group, his signature smirk slanted across his face. "You have it all wrong."

Lady Brockhurst looked relieved as the rest tittered. "Really, Mr. Woolf? Then pray, tell us, what is your take on the situation?" asked another girl, in another shade of white.

Felix thought quickly. Really, there was only one thing to be done, and considering what Edward had told him earlier about his upset with Evan, maybe this would be the best solution.

"Lady Fleur was simply walking in the garden, as Lady Brockhurst said, but you are correct, she wasn't alone. Her fiancé escorted her."

Gasps made their way around, and Felix waited for everything to fall into place.

"Fiancé? You mean to say that Lady Fleur is to marry Mr. Evander Woolf?" asked Lady Dudley, her brow arched as the puzzle pieces came together for her. "And the announcement was to be made this evening, how awful that this ruined their special night."

Lady Brockhurst quickly looked between Lady Dudley and Felix, no doubt wondering what he was doing.

"Indeed, a tragic loss, what girl doesn't look forward to her engagement announcement?" he asked, smiling at the young girls as they nodded. "And you know, Mr. Woolf is quite the hero, as Lady Brookhurst mentioned. Why she might have been killed, or worse," Felix looked around the room and then leaned in to whisper, his audience intrigued and ready, "She could have been maimed."

The ladies all gasped predictably in time. They then took up with the story and ran away with it. Words of congratulations, romance and heroics abounded as a wedding between two prominent families would take place, and in the excitement of being the first to tell others all had forgotten that just a few short hours before, the head of one family had punched the supposed groom of the other.

Felix watched and knew his job was done. By morning everyone would know, now he just had to figure out how to tell his own family without receiving a punch of his own.

9
WOOLFS IN LONDON

Julia sat in her own room the next morning giving instructions to the maid about her packing. They were to leave for Blackburn Hall the next day and Fleur had shuttered herself in her room, refusing to come out since the night before and leaving her to deal with the house.

Pointing to another round of bonnets to be packed, she told her maid she would return and walked to Fleur's room to make her come out. Slamming open the door, she stopped just inside and eyed Fleur. Her hair was a mass of dark disarray around her head, with her nightgown twisted around her legs. She gripped a pillow in her hands, raising it before slamming it down.

"Uh, Fleur? Dear? You look a little unhinged. It's quite frightening as a matter of fact."

Fleur turned to her sister with the most pitiful look she had ever given, and Julia could not help but laugh, then wince. "Forgive me, I did not mean to laugh."

"Oh, Julia, it's not funny. Honestly, I never want to be seen in town again."

Julia straightened up and cleared her throat as she walked towards Fleur. "It's not that bad, really," she said, petting Fleur's head and trying to tame some of the curls.

"Not that bad?" she asked disbelievingly. "Half of England saw my garters, and it's not *that* bad?"

"Well... it could have been worse... perhaps?"

Fleur took her pillow and raised it suddenly, pressing it to her face.

"Stop that, for heaven's sake, Fleur," said Julia, taking the pillow from her.

Fleur leaned back onto her headboard and sighed. "How can I ever show my face in society again? I'm a disgrace! And all because of a poorly placed flower pot," she wailed.

Julia clucked her tongue. "You could never be a disgrace, not as long as I'm around. Give me until next season, then I'll be sure to outdo your scandal, and then no one will remember this day."

Fleur giggled and then became dreadfully serious. "You had better not."

Julia smiled. "Come now, you must rally, and you certainly must get out of this bed and do something with that hair."

Fleur huffed and shook her head.

"Papa will be home soon, and don't you want to know what has happened at the Blackburns?"

Fleur didn't answer and just looked to the side of her room, pushing her hand through her hair before sighing.

Julia watched her, and her suspicions grew. "Are you thinking about *him*?"

"No," said Fleur, whipping her head around to meet her sister's disapproving look.

"You are, and why I have no idea, since he's the very *reason* you're in this predicament in the first place."

"I said I'm not," argued Fleur.

"You are," Julia countered. "Listen, it's not that I don't understand, I do. The love of your life since childhood suddenly arrives after spurning you for seven years, only to find out that you're betrothed to his brother? If the flower pot had stuck you on the head you'd have been a Greek tragedy!"

Fleur looked at Julia, stricken. "Is this really my life?"

"Yes, I'm afraid it is," she said, patting her sister's knee.

Fleur closed her eyes, her mouth a thin line.

"Is it really so bad? Edward is a very agreeable man and he cares for you, and Lord knows he is handsome. He would never intentionally upset you or make you cry, he certainly wouldn't snip at you like *others* we know."

"Yes, but Edward never held the power to upset me in that way, Julia, he's... Edward. I don't think you will understand until one day you fall in love yourself."

Julia wrinkled her nose. "So unless he can make you cry and anger you to the point of madness, it isn't love?"

"Yes," said Fleur, before rolling her eyes at her own answer. "You know what I mean, don't you?"

"No, I'm not sure that I do. If that's love you can keep it."

Fleur smiled at her as if she knew some secret she had yet to discover, and she placed her hand on her hips. "Get up and dressed, we have work to finish, the house is nearly packed but there is still more to do. Come and find me when you're done here?"

Fleur nodded, and Julia walked towards the door. "See you in a moment?" she asked once more. When Fleur again agreed she walked out of the room and frowned. Her sister most definitely was still in love with Evan Woolf.

She could not understand why someone would cling to a love that was so obviously painful. She hoped Fleur was wrong when she said one day Julia would understand — not if it made nitwits out of otherwise perfectly reasonable people.

She would grow old, and live with her father, taking care of his home and doing the things she wanted to do, happily playing spinster aunt to the brood of children Fleur was sure to have. She would never marry, as no man would ever hold that power over her, she was certain. And if she ever fancied herself in love, she would think back to this day and remind herself to hold onto good sense, and never lose reason.

———

EVAN WOKE to a loud knocking on his bed chamber door and his brother calling his name. He instantly regretted his instructions to Eliza the night before to let his brother up when he arrived. He was about to get out of bed to answer when the door burst open and in came Edward, Felix, and Dom.

"Morning, my love," Felix shouted, jumping on the bed and shaking Evan relentlessly before he was shoved to the floor.

"Can't you go two seconds without acting like a fool, Felix?" Dom asked while helping him off the floor.

"It's because I'm in such good spirits. A very good deed was done last night, and by none other than yours truly —"

"Let's not veer off course," Edward stated. "Evan, get up

and get dressed, we will be downstairs waiting. Do not go back to sleep."

Evan growled as they walked out of his bedchamber. It wasn't as if he could go back to sleep knowing what lay ahead. He was amazed he was able to sleep at all.

Throwing the covers aside and rising from the bed, Evan wondered what was likely to happen once they reached his parents' home. His brother would have to marry her despite the scandal, there was no doubt about that, and for the first time since he learned of the engagement he let himself think about how all this had affected his brother and Fleur.

He had not even congratulated Edward when he told him the news, and he had acted like a spoiled child, something Edward was well accustomed to, and the knowledge of it shamed him. Lady Fleur was no longer his childhood playmate, but Edward's betrothed, and a grown woman.

His brother's soon-to-be wife.

God, he was a fool. He was going to have to live with the knowledge of it and find a way to be happy for both Edward and Fleur. He must.

As he finished dressing and made his way downstairs, Evan resolved himself to do better. This was a delicate situation and they didn't need his temper making things worse. As it was, he was lucky he hadn't been called out by her father, or worse, her cousin. Her very short tempered and military-trained cousin, that is. Evan shuddered and willed the frightening thought away and thanked his luck that the Captain was away.

"Ah, there you are, Evan," Dom said, breaking off his quiet conversation with Felix and Edward as they waited in the entryway. "Let's get this over with, shall we? We've only a quarter of an hour to arrive."

Evan nodded and walked out the door, telling his cook he would return later, and would she please start packing for the trip to his new estate.

Protest from the other three rang in his ears as they made their way to the sidewalk, arguing that he should come to the house party.

"We're trying to dissolve a public scandal," Evan explained. "I think it's best if I stay away for a while. Besides I'm sure it would make the lady uncomfortable if I were to come."

"While your thoughts to her comfort do you credit," Dom said, giving a pointed look to Edward and Felix. "After last evening I do believe staying away would be worse. People will speculate why you're not there and draw all kinds of nefarious conclusions, much more so if you were to just go and behave normally, don't you agree, Edward?"

"Yes, I do," Edward said, stopping on the sidewalk to look at Evan. "Don't let this become a barrier between us. If you feel uncomfortable now think how it will be in a month, or six months from now. I'm not going to let this be the reason you shut us all out for good, Evan."

Evan stared at his older brother and once again felt his protective calm wash over him, as it had so many times before. "I... I have behaved badly towards you, Edward, I don't know why I can't control my temper when it comes to... well, I took it out on your head and I'm sorry for it."

Edward smiled and began to walk again when he heard a loud voice calling to them from behind to stop.

"Ah! This is a rare sighting, a pack of Woolfs roaming the middle of London," Christopher Powell said while shaking their hands in greeting. "I hear congratulations are in order, that you are to marry the Duke of Norfield's daughter."

Evan stood frozen as Powell addressed him with words of congratulations. Was the man daft? Why was he not speaking to Edward?

"Thank you, Powell," Edward replied. "We are all looking forward to welcoming her to the family."

They said their goodbyes and continued on, but it wasn't long before they were again accosted with strange words of congratulations as they walked.

"I hear the little flower is to become a Woolf. Congratulations!"

"It's being said all over town that you're to marry, Woolf! Never thought it would be you before your brother!"

"How does it feel for your brother to get the jump on you in the marriage arena? Probably glad you dodged a shackle, eh?"

Evan stopped in front of his parents' stairway and looked to the other three. "Is it just me or does it seem like..." Evan quieted, not knowing how to explain.

"Like they are congratulating you and not me?" Edward finished with the same air of confusion.

"It is most odd," Dom added.

When silence greeted them, they all looked to Felix, who was sheepishly looking at his feet. "You know that good deed I was going on about earlier? Well... I may have led everyone to believe that Lady Fleur is to marry Evan... instead of Edward."

Edward and Evan gaped while Dom whispered angrily. "May have what? What did you do, Felix? Just what in God's name did you *do*?"

"I will kill you," Evan growled, having finally found his voice and his fists as he sprung forward.

Edward reacted first, grabbing Evan around the chest

while Dom stood in front of Felix, though he didn't know why his brother deserved his protection.

"Evan," Dom whispered frantically, "You cannot kill Felix."

"Why not?" Evan shouted.

"We're in the middle of *Mayfair*." Dom said, still trying to keep his voice down, as they were already drawing attention from the road. "I don't think Aunt Madeleine would appreciate us brawling in front of her home for all to see, and especially not after last night, do you?"

Evan quieted at the thought of his mother, raked his hand through his hair, and glared at Felix. "How could you do this?" He asked before turning away and walking inside his parents' home with a slam of the door.

"God in heaven, Felix, please tell me you have some... some semblance of a good reason for doing this, because I can't imagine why you would take an impossible situation and make it worse," said Edward, his brow furrowed and his heart still beating fast from his struggle with Evan. "And when exactly were you going to let us know about this?"

"I tried to tell you earlier, then there were the constant interruptions on the road so I planned to tell you just before we went inside. Listen, yesterday you said not to bring up your engagement in front of Evan, that you thought he was upset and possibly still infatuated with the lady, did you not? You're not in love with her, too, are you?" Felix asked.

"What? No!" Edward spluttered. "But what are we to say to everyone? And what about Lady Fleur? She's not a deck of cards we can just pass around for our own amusement; this is not a game."

Felix sobered. "No, it's not a game. Do you really want to marry the love of your little brother's life? Do you think you can just move forward normally as a family after that happens? That you'll all meet for Christmas and it won't be soul crushing to know Evan is miserable? And he will be, Edward, and so will you."

Edward swallowed. "Of course not, but—"

"The gossip was vicious, Edward," Felix continued, "and by the time Dom and I made a few rounds last night she was common fodder for the masses. What do you think would happen if she were to marry the titled brother after being found in a compromising position with the spare? Don't you see, Edward, this is the only way, and Evan could be happy again."

"I can't believe I'm saying this,' Dom interrupted, "but Felix is right, Edward. It not only solves the problem of them in the garden, but also the issue of your brother being in love with your soon-to-be wife," Dom said, letting the gravity of those words sink in. "I regret that this has happened to the lady, but if she were to marry you now, you know there would be a break in the family. Do you really want that?"

Edward shook his head in defeat. "But what if we are wrong? What if she doesn't love him anymore, after everything that has happened?" he asked.

"She doesn't love you, and that wasn't a concern," said Felix.

"Yes, but I'm also not in love with her," Edward replied, hoping that they could understand the difference. "That changes everything."

Edward looked up to the sky, a hand on his hip and the other rubbing his nose under his spectacles. He knew they were right, it was just that everything about the situation was so absolutely wrong.

10

OVERDUE CONVERSATION

Julian sat in the drawing room of his friend's home. A home he knew as well as his own, so long had he visited its halls, but today he felt like an intruder. His fists clenched when Charles cleared his throat for what seemed like the hundredth time, and Madeleine fiddled with the tea tray, ignoring them both. The silence was maddening.

Damn, Julian thought. He had overreacted the night before... perhaps, but what father wouldn't have? He'd heard the commotion from the card room, and, like the others, he stood to look out the windows, and a man, Evander Woolf of all people was attacking his... no, *saving* his daughter. Flying into a rage, he had punched the little bastard without thinking, and in front of a few dozen people at least.

He had struck his best friend's son!

He knew he should apologize, but looking at Charles sitting across from him in his damned stubborn silence, he didn't want to. He knew it was petty, but he couldn't bring himself to care. His daughter was all but ruined, and just after they thought they had put a stop to one scandal, another erupted.

"Are you two going to sit and sulk all morning, or are we going to actually discuss the matter?" Madeleine set her tea cup on her saucer, looking from one stubborn man to another. "The boys will be here any minute and you're both acting like children."

"He started it," the earl mumbled, then withered under his wife's glare. Julian smirked.

"I think under the circumstances a traditional wedding is out of the question. Just imagine sitting through the banns week after week. I will not put Fleur through that nor make her the topic of conversation for more people to tarnish her character. What do you think, Julian?" She set her tea down on the side table and folded her hands in her lap, waiting patiently.

When nothing was forthcoming, she huffed. "They must marry, and straightaway. The only thing to do is have Edward obtain a special marriage license. We can hold the ceremony in your home, Julian. Fleur will feel more comfortable there, and then we will all leave for Blackburn Hall tomorrow morning after they are wed. We can have a small celebration when the other guests arrive for the house party." The first hint of a smile crossed her face. "Don't you *both* agree?"

Charles nodded vigorously while Julian, usually the more sensible of the two, grunted.

She pursed her lips and Charles could see she was about to let Julian have it when he heard the door slam from just outside the room. Twisting in his chair, he saw Evan standing in the doorway.

The boy looked positively livid. *How wonderful,* Julian thought, crossing his legs with a smirk on his face. It was only fair that they both were miserable.

———

EVAN SLAMMED THE FRONT DOOR, a tinge of satisfaction sweeping through him as Higgins retreated without a word.

How could his cousin do this to him? To Edward? The whole thing was preposterous! He flung his hat and gloves onto the entryway table, carefully laid-out letters scattering to the floor. Not bothering to pick them up, he stomped to the side drawing room where he knew his mother and father would be with Lord Norfield.

He tried to calm himself before he reached the door but must have failed miserably since his mother was now staring at him, her brow furrowed.

"Darling, are you all right?" She rose to meet him at the door then ushered him inside, giving the duke a wide berth.

"Good morning, Mother." He kissed her cheek and moved over to the window where he could see Edward, Dom, and Felix still standing outside. They were arguing, that much was certain, and then he saw Edward's shoulders slump in defeat. Never before had Evan seen such a weary expression on his brother, and upon seeing it, something inside him crumbled. He felt absolutely wretched.

He turned to his mother when she spoke. "Where is Edward? We were just discussing the arrangements. We think a marriage by special license first thing tomorrow morning is best."

Evan inhaled sharply. "There may be a difficulty —"

He was interrupted by the commotion in the front

entryway that was his brother and cousins. *This is it*, he thought, *there's no turning back now.*

"There you three are, what kept you?" she asked, moving to greet them.

"We were just outside, Mother, we came with Evan." Edward glanced at him, a meaningful look full of concern, and he almost laughed. The man was about to be jilted, the reason being his very own brother, and yet he was still playing the part of protector.

"Mother was just telling me, Edward, how she thinks you should be married by special license. In the *morning*," said Evan, giving Felix a pointed look.

Edward froze, his eyes widening while the duke bristled. Good God, but was this a disaster.

There was no skillful way to break the news gently, so he pressed on, hoping Lord Norfield would accept the situation gracefully. He wasn't keen on being hit by a man who had at least two stone on him... again. "There have been some developments in the matter. You should all know that last night —"

"No, Evan, I'll tell them." Felix stepped forward, his words brave, but Evan was sure he was scared as a newborn colt. "After all, it was my doing."

"And mine," Dom joined in, siding himself with Felix.

The duke stood from his chair. "What's going on?"

His father walked towards Lord Norfield and set a hand on his arm. "Come now, let them explain. We need to be rational at times like this." He stepped forward in front of his nephews.

"Felix, Dom, what have you done?" he hissed. "If you've caused trouble, I'll have both your hides. It will make the time you stole chickens from —"

"Charles, my dear, why don't we let the boys handle the

situation?" His mother slipped her hand through his father's arm and gently led him away. Felix and Dom both looked terrified.

Rational indeed, Evan thought.

Edward cleared his throat. "It seems that word has spread far more quickly, and maliciously, than we expected. The only way to extinguish the gossip was to... we..."

"You what?" The duke thundered, all patience lost. Evan had enough when he saw his brother flinch in the face of Lord Norfield's anger and stepped forward.

"They told everyone that Lady Fleur is to marry me. That we were walking in the gardens last night as a betrothed couple before the accident."

His mother gasped and his father put his head in his hands in groaned.

"You what?" the duke asked, his voice soft and wavering.

"Why the devil would you say such a thing?" his father blustered.

"There wasn't time, Uncle," said Felix. "Word had already spread that the lady... well, it was *less* than flattering, I'll venture to say. Now the story is full of romance and saving damsels in distress. The *ton* will be speaking of Evan's heroism till at least Christmas!"

Evan glared. *Flower pots. Blasted, unnecessary, trifling, frivolous flower pots!*

"So you saved her from ruin?" His mother sat in her favorite chair, smiling of all things. "I suppose it was foolish to hope she wouldn't be compromised. Oh, of course it was foolish, but you've done a wonderful thing, Felix!"

Felix flushed, and Evan wondered if it was, in part, from guilt. The answer was a resounding no when Felix put on his most dashing smile and preened. "Well, I was only doing what any gentleman —"

Dom elbowed Felix hard in the ribs and he coughed. "I'm sorry, Lord Norfield, but under the circumstances it was the only thing we could do to put the situation in a positive light."

"Hmmm... and you, Ravenbrook, how do you feel about all this?" Lord Norfield asked.

"I wish Lady Fleur every happiness and will be honored to call her sister. I think Evan is as capable as I to make her happy. I think the real question is how does Evan feel?" Edward turned towards his brother.

Evan snorted. "How do I feel? How do you expect me to feel? An arranged marriage, all due to a blasted flower pot," Evan mumbled, shaking his head at the absurdity of it all. He started to regret his words when the Duke of Norfield walked towards him.

"How dare you? You'd be lucky if she lowered herself to marry such a —"

"Now, wait just a minute, Julian, you can't speak to my son that way."

"I will speak to him however I please, and alone. Out, everyone out now!" Norfield waved his hand towards the door.

Evan watched as everyone in the room froze. The first to react was Edward, ushering out Felix and Dom, whispering something to his father, who then looked at him as if to ask if he would be fine. Evan nodded and his mother took his father's arm. As they walked out the door he could hear his father whisper. "I wonder if it ever occurred to Julian that he hasn't the right to order anyone out of *my* drawing room."

Evan almost laughed when he heard his mother shush

his father, but then the duke stepped directly in front of him. *This was sure to be fun*, he thought as he looked the Duke of Norfield straight in the eyes. All of a sudden, Evan felt angry. Angry at Edward for asking for her hand. Angry at Fleur for accepting, and angry at his whole family for picking Edward for her all those years ago, and even now, instead of him.

"What is the matter, your grace? Bee in your bonnet? You need not worry as I have no intention of leaving your daughter to disgrace and ruin."

"What is the matter with you?" Norfield flung his hand in the air, exasperated with Evan's flippant tone. "Do you ever stop to think before your mouth runs away with you? Do you think that you could do better than my daughter?"

"No. No, indeed I could not do better," Evan stated matter of factly.

Norfield cleared his throat. "You do intend to marry her then? Please, tell me straight, I must know. Will you marry Fleur?"

Evan sighed and ran his hand through his hair, the anger suddenly flowing out of him leaving him tired. "Of course I will, if she'll have me. It's the only thing to be done in this situation. I know this isn't what you wanted for her —"

"That, my boy, is the understatement of the –"

"However." Evan glared and tried to bring the conversation back to firm ground. "I will do my duty by her and make sure the jackals have no reason to snip at her."

Julian shook his head at Evan's answer. "You must know I don't like you, Woolf."

"And what did I do that was so awful to you?" asked Evan.

"What did you do?" The duke stepped closer to Evan.

"After you left, I had to watch her as she locked herself away in her bedchamber for days after we arrived back to Norfield. She doesn't know that I know, but she wept for months after you left. All of this, because of you, because of that night. I saw everything, you know, in the corridor on her birthday. I went up to check on her and saw everything."

Evan stood still, eyes wide, his defenses rising.

His voice shook, control all but gone. "You were as much to blame as I, you know, you, who was like another father to me, you knew that I loved her, but all of you kept pushing her towards Edward all because I wouldn't fall in line and go into the military?" Evan took a deep breath, calming himself. "I do not know why I've never been enough for you —"

"It was never that, my boy. Don't make the mistake of thinking I never cared for you, but until that night I was not aware of just how deep your feelings ran. I apologize for that, I should not have let your refusal to accept a commission sway my thoughts on you, but you refused the one thing that would ensure you could take care of my daughter, despite the fact you have done well for yourself, I will always maintain speculation is a risky business."

"So do we continue to blame one another?" asked Evan. "I should have come to you as well, but I was young and stupid, and then I didn't know how to take it back."

The duke nodded, understanding. "What I need from you now is to know that you can take care of her, I still have the same doubts I had then. Can you provide for her needs? All of them? Where will you live?"

Evan huffed. "What is this? An interview? I have already agreed to marry the lady, so I don't see the point in all of this."

"You will see the point when you have daughters of your own one day."

"Daughters? Me? Absurd." Evan nearly laughed at the thought. He had long come to terms with the fact that he would never marry or sire children and the events of that morning were not enough to erase that vision of himself, not yet.

"You do realize my daughter will want children of her own? She is just the sort of woman who looks forward to being a mother."

"I... children?" Evan faltered.

"Yes, and several. I have often heard her speak to her sister about her ambitions of having at least, oh, seven or eight children, I think it was."

Evan paled. "Eight... eight?" he asked, searching the duke's eyes for truth.

The duke smiled at his discomfort and fell into a chair beside him. Evan followed suit, though more from not being able to remain standing. Eight children!

"Come now. I was only teasing, but it's true Fleur will want children of her own. How will you be able to provide for them? For her?"

If Evan weren't so relieved, he would have had the mind to be angry. Eight children indeed. "I have never speculated wildly. All of my investments are carefully considered and most in traditional avenues that have a long history of returns. I have a townhouse here in London and have recently purchased an estate not far from my father's in Kent. I plan to settle the land with renters, though my investments alone would keep your daughter well off for her lifetime. She will want for nothing, your grace."

"Now, was that so difficult? About her dowry—"

"There is no need, sir, settle it on Lady Julia. Lord knows

you will need all the bribes you can muster to marry her off."

The duke smiled. "This is true. However, Fleur will have a dowry. Save it for those eight children, surely you will have many daughters."

"They will probably *all* be daughters if I know Lady Fleur. It would be just my luck."

"Your privilege," the duke insisted. "Having daughters is like nothing else in the world; there is nothing better."

"Well you needn't worry, I will care for the lady and any offspring in every way that matters."

"Not in *every* way, I fear," said the duke as he wistfully looked out the window. "Evan, do you still love my daughter?"

Surprised at the question, Evan hesitated, not wanting to pour out his soul. He gave a cautious answer. "Apart from last night, I haven't seen Lady Fleur in more than seven years."

"I understand," said Julian. "It will take some time for you to reacquaint yourself with my daughter, of course."

Evan wondered at the duke's sudden melancholy and decided to move on to important business.

"I will procure the license this afternoon. I'm afraid there isn't much time, so I won't be able to formally speak my addresses to Lady Fleur. Please relay my apologies."

"Running away again?" the duke asked in a joking manner, but Evan doubted it did not bear weight or truth.

"No, but I feel the lady should have time to adjust to this sudden turn of events. I had my family with me when I found out. I would wish her the same before tomorrow."

Julian nodded. "I will inform her. Be at my home with your family at half past ten. We can all away to Kent together." The duke started to rise but then stopped himself.

"Evan, I hope you understand that I didn't mean to be so harsh yesterday. I was... well, I was shocked. Forgive me if I hurt you in my haste to protect her."

Evan rubbed his jaw. "Any father would have done the same, so let us say no more. We shall be family from tomorrow onward, and we will be together at the house party in the next few weeks. My mother will be overjoyed that we have come to an agreement, or at least some semblance of civility."

"Yes, you are right, besides I must own that if it wasn't for myself and your father, if we had not been so very drunk the other night, then none of this would have even begun."

Evan looked into the duke's eyes, trying to read him. "What do you mean?"

"You don't know?" Julian asked.

When Evan shook his head the duke sighed. "Your brother was only set to marry Fleur because your father and I made an enormous mistake at Whites the other night. We were talking loudly about our dream of joining our households. They story flew through London faster than a pair of matched greys. Edward was our solution."

Evan remembered something that had been nagging him. When asked, his brother said that his marriage to Lady Fleur was a delicate situation. "You mean *that* is the reason they were betrothed? Why didn't anyone tell me?"

"I doubt anyone had time, it all happened so quickly, not that it matters now. You run along with the boys to procure the license, and I shall inform your parents and then go home to Fleur. I shall see you in the morning."

"Good day, your grace," Evan said absently as the duke took his leave.

He sat rigid as his mind raced at the news he had only

just learned. So it was not planned by the elders at all, but a solution to some mishap.

Evan laughed. It was almost too much to believe.

A woman compromised once was deliciously shocking, but a woman compromised twice in less than a day and betrothed to two brothers in the same amount of time? He doubted even France could provide such a scandal.

11

WILL YOU HAVE HIM?

Fleur bounded down the stairs in search of her sister. After finally getting out of bed, she quickly dressed and made her way down to see to the rest of the house closing. She reached the front entryway and stood before a table picking through letters when Craigs came in.

"Mr. Craigs, have you seen my sister? She wasn't in her chambers or the breakfast room."

"I believe Lady Julia is in the music room, milady."

"The music room? What on earth is she doing in there?"

"She seems to be practicing," Craigs sniffed then bowed before he took his leave.

Fleur made her way to the music room. There really was so much to be done before they left in the morning. *What could Julia be doing*, she wondered. She rounded the corner into the drawing room that opened into the music room and looked around.

"Julia? Are you in here?"

"I am here!" Fleur heard her shout.

"Here? Where is here?" Fleur smiled when Julia stood up from behind the large pianoforte.

"What on earth are you doing?"

"Practicing."

Fleur raised a skeptical brow and Julia laughed.

"Yes, practicing. Is that so hard to believe?"

"Frankly, yes. Papa has been urging you to practice for years. Why the sudden interest?"

"Because now *I* wanted too," Julia said as if it were obvious.

"Right. Of course, you would choose this very moment," Fleur said, giving Julia an exasperated look. "Are you ready to depart tomorrow? Lucy finished with my packing, and we are set to close the house. Do you need any more help?"

"No, I am also ready, though I'm already tired just thinking about the next few weeks. Two weeks in the same house as Charity." Julia shuddered.

"Don't be unkind. If it weren't for her, I would still be lying on the ground with my skirts around my head while you just stood there with everyone else staring."

"I was in shock," Julia protested.

Fleur laughed. "Yes, I suppose it was very shocking."

"You're being awful lighthearted about it now." Julia moved her music sheets back into a neat pile.

"Oh, Julia, what else am I supposed to do? I have to laugh or I would just... but what is done is done, and I'm determined to put it behind me and enjoy our time with our friends."

"It really is laughable, you embroiling the family in scandal when you know everyone thought it would be me."

"Yes, I am laughable," Fleur said while pushing Julia over so she could sit down on the bench beside her. "I'm positively wretched."

"No, you're wonderful. And you will be happy with Edward, you'll see. Evan is the wretched one."

"He saved my life, Julia," Fleur said disbelievingly. "No matter what has happened in our past, I think we owe him our gratitude."

"Fine, I'm grateful, but that's all. Honestly, he's such a —"

"Julia."

"Well, he is. Even Papa thinks so."

"I think what?" Fleur and Julia both looked to the door when their father walked in.

"Papa!" Julia ran to her father and greeted him with a hug and a quick kiss to the cheek. "We were just discussing the fact that Evan Woolf is an —"

"Julia!" Fleur and Julian both snapped at her.

"I was going to say he's an abominable man," she said, hand on her hips, nose raised.

"Of course you were, dear." Julian shared a long look with Fleur.

"Fleur, I'd like you to speak to you alone in my library, now, if you please. Julia, will you see to it that everything is ready for tomorrow?"

"We handled everything this morning, and you are just trying to shoo me away so you can talk about what happened at Lord and Lady Blackburn's this morning."

"Julia —"

"No. Fleur is my sister, and I have a right to know what's going on. She will just come tell me everything when you leave anyway."

Julian sighed, knowing her words to be true.

"Fine, you may stay, but I want your word you will keep quiet until I have said everything there is to say on the matter. I won't hear any arguments, understood?"

"Yes, Papa."

"Did something happen?" Fleur stood and walked

across the room to her father and laid a hand upon his arm. "You seem out of sorts."

"There has been another difficulty..."

Fleur urged him on. "What is it? I know you are worried for me, Papa, but after last night really what else could possibly go wrong?"

Julian wished she had chosen her words differently. "The gossip, my dear, it was more than we expected. You know how people love to go on about the latest scandal. It was unflattering to say the least."

Fleur reeled back as if slapped. "What is being said?"

"That doesn't matter. The important thing is the situation has been handled, and there will be no more unsavory gossip about our house."

"I don't understand," Fleur said. "You said there was a difficulty. Was Lord Ravenbrook... was he reluctant to honor the betrothal?"

"No, my dear, no, nothing as bad as all that. He would have married you gladly."

"Would have?" Julia asked as she crossed her arms with indignation.

Feeling as if he was being ganged up on, Julian cut to the heart of it. "It's been decided that tomorrow morning you will be married by special license, but not to Edward. You are set to marry Evan... if you feel so inclined..." he trailed off lamely.

"What?" Julia gripped her father's arm, hard. "You cannot be serious, Papa, you cannot. He's a tyrant. Fleur, say something."

Julian looked to Julia. "I have to think of your wellbeing, along with Fleur's."

"I don't care. I don't care if I never marry. I won't be made the reason, no, the sacrifice upon which Fleur throws her life away on that man. Fleur, say something, please."

Fleur moved backward, and laughter bubbled up within her until it exploded into great guffaws.

Julian stepped forward, gripping her by the shoulders, worried she may have an episode. "Fleur, are you well?"

"I am to be Evan's wife? After everything?" She continued to laugh until she broke free of her father's grasp and walked halfway around the room before leaning upon the harp to help control her laughter. "When people announce me, I shall be The Lady Fleur Woolf! It's hilarious, isn't it, Julia? Absolutely absurd!"

Julia stepped towards her sister. "Fleur, please, what on earth is the matter with you? This is serious."

"Serious? Coming from you? Do you know the meaning of the word?" Fleur sobered when she saw the flash of hurt in Julia's eyes. "Oh, I'm sorry. I don't know what's come over me, Julia."

"I do, you have gone positively mad. The news has unhinged you. Papa, don't you see how foolish this is? She cannot marry him."

Julian placed his hand upon Julia's cheek trying to soothe her before turning to his eldest. "Fleur, you know the consequences of refusing Evan's hand. However, you know I will stand beside you no matter what course you take. After all, I am the Duke of Norfield and therefore impervious to scandal or gossip." He winked at Fleur, and she laughed once more. "But I would advise you to agree to the match. What say you? Will you have him?"

"Yes!" Fleur ran to her father, smiling, and threw her arms around him. "Yes, Papa, I will marry him. There is so much to do before tomorrow. I'll need to unpack my... " Fleur babbled as she walked out of the room while Julia and

Julian stared at one another, surprised at the vehemence with which Fleur agreed to the plan.

"I must say I'm a little relieved that it all turned out this way," Julian said.

"Relieved? I am completely astonished, what has gotten into her? It's like she *wants* to marry him."

Julian smiled at his younger daughter. "I think we both know whom she would prefer to marry, don't we, Julia?"

Her lips thinned. "I can't imagine why."

"You will, one day," he said, and when she gave him a look, he laughed.

"I wish everyone would stop saying that, good Lord!" Julia shook her head then reached up to kiss his cheek. "I'll go check on her. She walked out of here as if on a cloud, and by now she probably has undone all of Lucy's packing looking for a suitable dress for tomorrow. Will we see you at dinner, Papa?"

"No, I have business at the House of Lords, so I will return late. I'll see you bright and early. Tell Fleur the wedding will be here, and then after, we will be off to Kent."

Julian watched Julia nod and practically run out of the music room to find her sister. He really would never understand his daughters, but he loved them fiercely, and he felt as if past wrongs had finally been set right. Maybe they had not come around it in the best of ways, but they had come full circle, and that was the most important thing of all.

———

Fleur rushed to her room, flung open the door, and barely reached back to close it before she ran and threw herself down onto her bed, head buried in her pillow.

She lay on the bed and felt relief, unabashed and unrestrained relief. Until the moment her father told her the best option was to marry Evan, she didn't know how scared and nervous she had been about marrying Edward. He was a fine man, yes, but he was Edward.

Evan, she thought and smiled.

Her euphoria came crashing down when she remembered how angry he was the evening before. She sat up slightly, propped on her hands, and she frowned. Evan hated her, did he not? Last night he was so horrid to her, and then in the anteroom with the families and the Brockhursts there, he didn't look at her, not once.

She laid her head down on her pillow once more and closed her eyes. If he hated her so, why would he agree to the marriage?

She knew Evan. She knew he would attack and bite if he felt threatened, but she also knew he regretted the action almost instantly. They were the best of friends once, and she was sure that they could come to some sort of understanding if only he would talk to her.

She didn't know if he would ever forgive her for that night at his parents' home, and she didn't know if they could have romantic love, but she knew they could be friends and care for one another, and she vowed to start there.

———

EVAN SAT in his carriage the next morning wondering how he would explain the latest developments to Nathan. It was early still, much too early for a social call, but he needed his best man and witness. It was his wedding day after all.

The night before, he decided he would ask Nathan to stand up with him as asking his brother under these circumstances would be awkward at best. After he had spoken to Fleur's father, he went with Edward, Felix, and Dom to procure a special license, not an easy feat, but he was able to do so using Edward's name and influence. Just one more thing that indebted him towards his brother.

He had left on better terms than he could have hoped for with the duke. He knew he was brash and quick to anger, but so was her father. It was a wonder they didn't come to blows, and it was not lost on him that perhaps they were more alike than he had ever realized.

From tomorrow onward they were to be family, and he didn't want to hurt Fleur through spurning her father. After the way he treated her at the ball, he had wanted to make a real effort, and that was just when he thought she was to be his sister-in-law. Now she was to be his wife.

His wife.

If he wasn't already sitting down, he might have swooned from the shock of it. The would live together, breakfast together, spend their nights together. Beget children together.

Evan rubbed his chin as he felt his face heat and he shook his head at his own foolishness. There was no reason to get ahead of himself, but he couldn't help but think that maybe, just maybe they could be happy together. Maybe he could keep his temper in check and offer her a real home of her own. Someplace she could be truly comfortable, the life she wished for and talked about when they were children.

Their families were close, which was ideal, and they would be able to holiday together. When they removed to his country estate, she wouldn't be far from his mother. That would make settling in easy for her.

She would not hold a title, though as a duke's daughter she would always be a lady by name, she would be plain

Lady Fleur Woolf now. Evan schooled his features and coughed when he found himself smiling like an idiot. How absurd he was behaving, almost if he was — dare he think it — happy?

By God, but he was. He was a simpering, bubbling lovesick fool, and he was happy. He sat up straighter in the carriage and cleared his throat when a thought crossed his mind.

What if Fleur didn't truly want this?

He pushed the thought away. He could not know, not until he spoke to her.

Evan covered his mouth, rubbing his face as the carriage stopped at Nathan's townhouse. He gathered his wits about him and opened the door before jumping down and nearly knocking the waiting footmen over.

"I beg your pardon, sir," the footman said as he bowed and made way.

Evan nodded at the young man and ascended the steps with quick jaunty leaps before landing three bellowing knocks on the front door. As he waited, Evan wondered what Nathan would say. He would probably call him mad. Indeed, the whole thing was mad.

As the door opened to reveal Nathan's butler, Evan started to feel nervous.

"Ah, Mr. Woolf. I'm sorry, but Mr. Carter is — "

"I know it's shamefully early, Hobbs, but I really must speak to Mr. Carter, it's of great importance."

Hobbs looked him over and nodded before leaving. Evan couldn't remember a time he'd met such an unfussy but reliable servant. Always to the point, was Hobbs. If only he could find help of his own like that, maybe he wouldn't mind the invasion of his privacy.

Evan was broken from his thoughts when Hobbs

returned and led him into the library where he knew Nathan preferred to take his meals since he lived alone. When he arrived, he saw his friend sitting at a small table devouring a sausage.

Evan sat down across from him and spoke. "We've to be somewhere within the hour so finish your breakfast."

Nathan swallowed a mouthful of hot coffee to quickly and tried his best not to choke. "Be somewhere? We're to away to Kent within the hour, where could we possibly need to be?"

"Slight change in plans," Evan said as he swiped a sausage from Nathan's plate, wondering why his friend was not asking him about Fleur.

Nathan didn't even bat an eye, so used was he to his friend's bad manners. "What's going on? Are we to delay? Did something else happen with your brother and Lady Fleur?"

Evan sat back in his chair. Could it be that Nathan didn't know? "So you've not heard? Where have you been since yesterday, in a cave? It's the talk of the whole town."

"Heard what? You were able to settle the gossip, weren't you?" Nathan lowered his fork and stared at Evan in worry. "I didn't go out yesterday. I spent all day writing letters to my solicitor and giving instructions to the staff. What's happened?"

"A lot has happened. Lady Fleur will no longer be marrying Edward."

This time Nathan actually choked on his coffee, and Evan took pity on him when tears started to appear in his friend's eyes. He leaned forward to give him a firm slap on the back.

"T-thank you," said Nathan, clearing his throat. "But

what do you mean? They know the consequences if they do not."

"Precisely. I never said she wouldn't marry. I only said she wouldn't be marrying Edward."

"But that makes absolutely no sense. She was certainly compromised from the situation, the only other person for her to marry would, well, it would be you." Nathan snorted with laughter then took another bite of sausage. He chewed greedily, his eyes locked with Evan's serious ones. His jaw stopped working and then dropped as bits of food fell from his mouth onto his plate.

Nathan swore. "How on earth did this happen?" he asked as he stood, wiping food from his mouth, and Evan, feeling at a disadvantage, stood as well.

"Felix happened. He led everyone to believe that Lady Fleur and I were betrothed when it became apparent that gossip was more vicious than we first realized. If Edward's name had been brought into it, things would have just deteriorated. So it was decided I will marry the lady this morning, and then we shall leave for Kent."

Nathan stood staring at Evan like he'd lost his head. "Come again?"

"I'm not repeating all that again, Nathan, it's becoming monotonous."

"It's just... how do you expect me to react? I'm stunned!"

"Yes, I can sympathize," Evan said dryly. "But the fact remains that we must be at the Duke of Norfield's home in half an hour, so we best make haste. I'd rather arrive too early than be late seeing as how I've just struck a civil temper with her father. Imagine if he thought I was going to leave her at the altar?"

Nathan grimaced. "I don't envy you there. He can be quite frightening, but Evan, does her cousin know?"

Evan's eye twitched, and he would never admit to it, but he may have paled just slightly. "How would he know? He's on his ship only God knows where."

"Well, don't worry, if he calls you out I am sure we can find someone to be your second," Nathan said while laughing.

"Why would he call me out? I'm marrying her, not crying off."

"Hmm, I don't think that will matter to Osborne, as he's always been fiendishly protective of Lady Fleur and Lady Julia. I'd wager they are the only people he cares for in all of England. It is well known he even hates the duke, which is odd, seeing how he is the heir to the dukedom."

"He has no reason to have it out with me. I'm doing my duty. Besides, I'm counting on him being away for quite some time. By the time he returns we will have been married several months."

"Aha! So you are afraid of him."

Evan stomped towards the door. "I'm not afraid."

"You... areeeee...," Nathan singsonged as he threw his napkins on the table and followed Evan out.

"Nathan, I will not have this childish discussion with you. Now, are you coming to stand up with me or not?"

"Yes, yes, good grief. Let us go. We would not want to keep the lucky lady waiting, would we? Give me a moment to instruct my driver to meet me at your home, and I can travel straight from there."

Evan rolled his eyes upwards but followed his friend with a smirk. Even the mention of Fleur's devil cousin hadn't soured his good mood.

12

DEARLY BELOVED

Fleur sat in the music room, her back ramrod straight, slight pain blooming behind her eyes as her attention swayed back and forth between a frantic maid and her sister.

"And the flowers, milady, are they to your liking?" asked the maid.

"Yes, Mary, they are beautiful, thank you —"

"I can't believe you're going to go through with this... this farce of a marriage to that... that...," muttered Julia, quickly walking across the room.

"Are you certain, milady? I had to take the flowers from the morning room so they are a bit sad and wilted, 'tis all I could do on such short notice."

Fleur tried to smile. "You have done a miracle with this room with the little time offered to you, Mary. Everything is perfect —"

"He is deceitful. That is what he is. He planned this entire thing. I just know he did. I will strangle him..." said Julia, quickly making her way back across the room.

"And the chairs, should we move them back a bit more, or closer, should they be closer —"

"I'm sure the chairs are fine, Mary –"

"I cannot stand the thought that you will be living all alone with him only God knows where and we won't ever see you again. He is sure to keep us from you."

Fleur rubbed her temples and closed her eyes. "Mary, on second thought, I think the mantle could use a few more flowers after all. There are several in the upstairs bedrooms, would you fetch them?"

"Yes, milady, I'll try to find blue ones to match your dress. Oh, you look so beautiful, if you do not mind me saying so. Your betrothed will faint dead away when he sees you."

"We can only hope..." Julia muttered.

Fleur looked long at her sister as Mary left until Julia cringed and folded her arms. Fleur knew the silence would not last long.

"Really, Julia, will you stop being so dramatic and sit down? My nerves are simply shattered between the pair of you."

Julia sat down beside Fleur, looking her straight in the eye. "Because you know this is madness. Fleur, please, for the last time, do not do this."

Fleur sighed, gripping Julia's hands. "You are the best sister, did you know? You are absolutely lovely, and I love you, Julia, but you are going to have to let me go. I *want* to be married and have children. I *want* the country estate with the dogs and barn cats. Everything, I want it all. I want *thi*s. What are you so frightened of? You knew one day I would marry."

"Yes, but this is all so sudden, and he is so disagreeable. I cannot like him after his behavior towards you."

"Cannot or will not?" Fleur asked, reaching to push a stray piece of hair behind Julia's ear.

"Both. He is a —"

"He is a perfectly respectable man, even with his... shall we say... quirks?" Fleur smiled.

"Quirks? He's a menace. I wish it were Edward. Your life with him would have been so much easier."

"Yes, it would have been," said Fleur, thinking how life with Edward would have been perfectly polite and ordered, though never passionate and never challenging. "I know this is going to sound strange to you, Julia, but when I agreed to marry Edward something in me realized that while I do want a home and family, I don't wish to settle. I don't want a lukewarm marriage with someone I cannot speak to above the day's comings and goings and the weather. I think... I think I shall be happier with Evan. I know I will."

Julia threw her hands in the air. "Now I know you're raving."

Fleur shook her head. "No," she laughed. "Listen to me, please. With Evan, I can be myself. I'll be able to run the house the way I want. I'll be able to raise and perhaps even school my own children before they need tutors or go off to school. There will be fewer appearances to keep up and fewer social calls to make. As the wife of a viscount and future earl I'd have all sorts of obligations, but as Evan's wife I'm so much more... free. Free to have a loud and boisterous home in the country and not have to be watched at every move. Evan hates society as much as I do."

"Oh," said Julia.

"And Julia, it's Evan, my Evan. I know he can be horrible, but, he's just... Evan. The boy that once carried me home because I fell and scraped my knee. The young man that once went shop to shop in the freezing rain all to acquire a book in town that he knew I wanted. I do not know why you have never acknowledged him, or how can I convince you of it? He can be very giving too."

"No, I think you have been quite convincing," Julia said, a bit put out. "My, my, Fleur, careful, or you will find your-self very much in love with your husband, which isn't the thing at all."

Fleur grabbed a cushion from the settee and pitched it at Julia, who stared, wide-eyed and shocked.

"See, he is a bad influence already."

They laughed as they waited for the others to arrive. Fleur was nervous but also excited. She did not know what life would be like as a wife, but the thought still excited her.

———

Evan and Nathan arrived at Lord Norfield's home and were ushered inside to the drawing room. Evan paced the floor, his nerves on edge. "What is taking so long?"

"In a hurry to be leg-shackled?" Nathan teased.

Evan stopped in his tracks and leveled Nathan with a glare. "It is just strange, is all. Why was not one person here to greet us? Why are we being shuffled away in here?"

"Who knows? We are earlier than the others, which is only natural seeing as you are the groom. I'm sure your family will be here soon."

"I do not like waiting," Evan groused.

Nathan rubbed his temples. "You do not *like* anything."

Evan threw his hand in the air, his other already in his hair as he made his way to the door.

Alarmed, Nathan followed him. "Where are you going?"

"To see what is happening out there," Evan said slowly

as if talking to a child. He opened the double doors and walked outside, Nathan close behind.

"Evan," he tried to whisper but was ignored. "Evan, we should not be —"

"Do you hear voices coming from that room over there?" he asked, walking on.

"Perhaps," Nathan said, saying nothing else, not wanting to further encourage his friend.

"Who do you think is in there?" Evan eyed the room like he wanted to storm it.

"Probably just the servants, setting up for the guests, you know. Evan?" Nathan jolted when Evan started walking towards the room. "Get back here!" He tried to shout, but it came out in a strangled whisper.

Evan stopped short of the door a few yards and whipped around, annoyed. "What is the matter with you?"

Nathan looked at Evan. His friend really was unbelievable. "What is the matter with me is that I am not accustomed to sneaking around other people's homes."

"Sneaking? We're not sneaking, just trying to find out where everyone is, and lower your voice."

He started walking again only to be nearly knocked over by a maid exiting the room hastily.

"Oh! I'm sorry, sir."

"That is quite all right," Nathan said, trying to put the nervous girl at ease. "We were standing in the doorway, precarious place to be, is it not?"

She laughed and nodded. "May I be of service to you?"

"No," Nathan said.

"Yes," Evan corrected.

The maid looked from Nathan to Evan, her mouth opening and then closing. "We heard voices," Evan supplied. "From this room, we wondered if the other guests had arrived?"

"Oh, I see. That would only be Lady Fleur and Lady Julia, sir. As far as I know, you are the only guests to arrive. Begging your pardon, sirs, if I seem too bold, but are you guests of the groom?"

"Yes, we are, ah... cousins of his," Evan said. "We will just go back to the library and wait for the rest of the party to arrive."

The maid curtsied and bustled off upstairs. Nathan stared at Evan until he started to shuffle uncomfortably under his gaze. "Why did you lie to the girl?"

Evan sighed heavily. "Because if she knew I was the groom she would have insisted on either announcing me to Lady Fleur or would have continued on with her questions. She looked like a prattler, that one."

"Hmm," was all Nathan said while Evan walked slowly, edging closer to the room.

"Do I even want to know what we are doing now?" Nathan asked wearily.

"Shush," he said, waving his hand at Nathan and moving his head closer to the door.

"Oh no, I will not stand here while you eavesdrop on their conversation. It is completely —"

"Nathan, be quiet," Evan whispered.

"This is completely immoral, not to mention ungentle-manly and —"

Evan clapped a hand over Nathan's mouth. The two struggled, one to keep his hold, the other to shrug him off. Nathan won when Evan whipped his wet hand away, wiping it on his pants hastily.

"You disgust me, Carter," Evan whispered angrily.

Nathan waggled his eyebrows with a grin. Both stiffened when they heard voices inside.

"Yes, but, this is all so sudden. And he is so disagreeable. I cannot like him..."

Evan blanched. "Is that —"

"That was Julia, Evan. I would know that bite anywhere."

Evan nodded. "Perhaps we should go," he whispered.

"Yes," Nathan agreed.

Neither of them moved.

"I wish it were Edward, your life with him would have been so much easier."

"Yes, it would have been ..."

Evan slowly moved his head from the doorway.

"Evan..." Nathan faltered, unsure of what he wanted to say.

"Well that is an unfortunate bit of... news." Evan looked about the room, looking anywhere but his friend. "Besides, I'm sure I am quite difficult to live with," he laughed, trying to hide his hurt. "My mother has said so for many years."

Evan felt the full effect of embarrassment come over him as he remembered his actions and feelings earlier that morning. He could not believe he had become so carried away.

"Come on, let us return and wait for the others," said Nathan, not wanting to watch his friend flounder in the hallway any longer. "All she needs is time, my friend. Marriage is an adjustment for all, not just men you know."

Evan nodded and followed Nathan to the library, not quite as optimistic as he had been that morning. Any hope he had of Fleur returning his feelings, even in some small way, at this point was lost to him. He felt like any and all visions he had ever conjured of the future, both when he was young and now, were cast out of his reach once more.

———

EVAN STOOD at the end of the music room with Nathan. There he waited, leaning upon the fireplace mantle with his chin in his hand, wondering where his mother had taken Fleur and her father, sure she was hiding them from his sight until the moment of their vows.

He then looked over and saw Julia, standing to his left, waiting to attend her sister, and maybe even more impatient than he. Their eyes connected, and she smirked, turning her head towards the door to ignore him completely. *The little imp*, he thought.

He shook his head while rubbing his jaw, then raised off the fireplace. "What could be keeping them?" he asked Nathan. "The vicar looks restless. Half an hour has passed since he arrived."

Nathan took the watch out of his pocket and glanced at the time. "Nonsense, a quarter at most, stop fidgeting."

"I most certainly am *not* fidgeting."

"Quite right," said Nathan. "It is only your wedding day, why would you fidget?"

"One day it will be your turn, then I will ..."

Evan trailed off and quickly turned when he heard the door. "Is it she? Are they here?" he asked, his posture stiffening.

His mother walked in and silently closed the door behind her, she glided up the provisional aisle and took her seat next to his father.

"No, not fidgety at all," Nathan teased.

"I heartily dislike you."

"You adore me. Look, the door is opening, I think it is they."

Evan held his breath as the door creaked open. A footman passed through to open the double doors and soft music, he did not know — nor care — whence it came, played.

Then he saw her, on the arm of her father in a dress of soft blue with a deep cerulean ribbon in her hair. She looked so content next to him, so lovely. He knew that, somehow, he finally attained the one happiness he thought forever beyond his reach, and in that moment, he was utterly terrified.

Somehow by some random chance of what some would call a disaster, he was going to finally marry her, and he promised her father that he would make her happy. Only he did not know how he was to accomplish it. Surely she would not welcome his attentions, after the way he acted towards her.

He scarcely noted the vicar moving into place as she made her way toward him, and when she stopped and looked at him, her own smile slightly faltering as she looked him in the eyes, he drew a shaky breath.

The vicar cleared his throat, and the room quieted. "Dearly beloved, we are gathered together here in the sight of God, and in the face of this congregation, to join together this Man and this Woman in holy Matrimony..."

———

FLEUR LISTENED to the droning voice of the vicar and found it soothing, all she had to do was concentrate on his voice, not the stone-faced look Evan was giving her that very moment. She expected to be nervous or even a bit frightened, but she felt a sort calm settle within her.

Her father was there, beside her, and Madeleine and Julia. Most everyone she had ever cared for or loved as family was there with them and she was happy for it.

"Evander Charles Woolf, wilt thou have this woman to thy wedded wife, to live together after God's ordinance in the holy estate of Matrimony? Wilt thou love her, comfort her, honour, and keep her in sickness and in health; and, forsaking all others, keep thee only unto her, so long as ye both shall live?"

He looked at her, never removing his eyes from her own, a stare so intense it took her breath as his gaze never once wavered.

"I will," he vowed.

"Fleur Marianne Osborne, wilt thou have this man to thy wedded husband, to live together after God's ordinance in the holy estate of Matrimony? Wilt thou obey him, and serve him, love, honour, and keep him in sickness and in health; and, forsaking all others, keep thee only unto him, so long as ye both shall live?"

Her father rubbed the back of her hand with his thumb, a small reassuring gesture that the others may not have seen, but that she felt fully, and she loved him for it.

"I will," she answered.

"Who giveth this woman to be married to this man?"

Julian handed her forward, the vicar taking her hand and placing it inside of Evan's, holding them there, together. She listened as he spoke his vows to her, waiting to vow herself to him in return.

"I, Evander Charles Woolf, take thee, Fleur Marianne Osborne, to my wedded wife, to have and to hold from this day forward, for better, for worse, for richer, for poorer, in sickness and in health, to love and to cherish, till death us do part, according to God's holy ordinance; and thereto I plight thee my troth."

They released each other for a moment and then she took his hand again, this time holding onto him. She felt him trace his thumb down the back of her hand, the same gesture her father had made only moments before, but one that felt so different. She gathered the courage to look up at him, into those same dark eyes she'd always known, and she held them there as she spoke to him.

"I, Fleur Marianne Osborne, take thee, Evander Charles Woolf, to my wedded husband, to have and to hold from this day forward, for better, for worse, for richer, for poorer, in sickness and in health, to love, cherish, and to obey, till death us do part, according to God's holy ordinance; and thereto I give thee my troth."

She watched as the vicar handed him the ring, and she felt him take her left hand into his, placing the ring on her fingertip and holding it there gently, as he spoke to her.

"With this ring I thee wed, with my body I thee worship, and with all my worldly goods I thee endow: In the Name of the Father, and of the Son, and of the Holy Ghost. Amen."

He slid the ring down her finger, ever so slowly and she watched him watch her. Coming out of her trance as he placed his hand at her elbow, she felt him brace her as they turned and knelt, reluctantly breaking their gaze.

"Let us pray." The room collectively bowed their heads in prayer. She listened with her heart as the ceremony concluded, and when it was over, she stood in front of the marriage register and silently signed her name for the last time— Fleur Marianne Osborne.

13

BROKEN CARRIAGES
& MARRIAGES

Her new mother-in-law told her the wedding had been beautiful. Her sister said it was a farce, and everyone else applauded them as if they had done something heroic or worthy of praise. Fleur was just relieved it was over.

She watched the flurry of activity around her as they waited to leave. Soon they would be on their way to her husband's family country seat.

Her husband.

The thought made her dizzy both with excitement and a healthy dose of fear, fear of the unknown. She knew how to run a household, balance the accounts, tend to the menu and the weekly meetings with the housekeeper, but she knew nothing of being a wife. It was times like these she really missed her mother. She would have known how to soothe her. Instead, *she* was soothing her sister.

"I do not see why Fleur cannot ride in our carriage, Papa." Julia stood rigid, her arms folded, her dark brown gloves standing out against her pale yellow dress. "We will discuss this later, Julia," Julian hissed.

Fleur felt her cheeks heat, and she was glad most of the party had already made its way out-of-doors so they could not hear. Unfortunately, that did not include her husband.

Evan stood next to her, starring at the ceiling with his hands clasped tightly behind his back. "I am standing right here, little sister; therefore, I am able to hear you."

Julia glared, and Fleur sighed, knowing her sister would not be persuaded. She relaxed when the footman announced their carriage had arrived.

She watched her father escort her sister outside and suddenly she was acutely aware that they were alone. Fleur brought the back of her hand to her cheek, feeling relief at the touch of her cooled skin.

Evan looked around, a slight frown on his face. "Where is your lady's maid?"

Surprised at the question, Fleur looked around as well. "Is something wrong?"

Fleur felt her chest tighten when Evan ran his hand through his hair and grumbled.

"I had thought you would be chaperoned, but I guess that was silly of me."

Fleur followed his eyes with her own, his landing on the new gold band gracing her finger. She covered it with her other hand quickly and looked outside.

They stood in the entryway, she not knowing how to respond as she fiddled with her gloves, pulling them on one by one, and he, staring at the opposite wall with his hands still clasped behind his back.

"Perhaps it would be more appropriate for you to ride with your father and sister..."

His suggestion at first confused her, but then she realized he did not want them to be alone.

"I've only just remembered that... the wheel..."

Fleur waited for him to continue, a small feeling of disappointment creeping upon her at his obvious ploy to not be near her.

"The wheel," she prompted.

"Yes, the wheel, it's a bit shaky and with all that has happened over the last few days it completely slipped my mind. Not safe for you I'm afraid, no, not safe at all."

He walked towards her as he rambled and took her by the elbow, escorting her outside and over to her father's carriage before he flung open the door, startling everyone inside. "Lady Fleur is going with you," he said, slightly out of breath.

"Is there a problem?" Julian asked, confused as Evan helped Fleur into the carriage.

"Shifty wheel, not safe," he barked.

Making a hasty retreat, Evan was relieved when Lord Norfield nodded and did not stop him to ask questions. He moved quickly over to his own carriage, which he now could not ride in for appearances' sake, and cursed his own stupidity. He could ride with his brother, but Edward would be with Felix and Dom, and he didn't fancy explaining to them why he had just run away from his wife, so that left only Nathan.

When he walked over to Nathan's carriage he reached to knock on the window, only to lower his hand. He stood there, feeling like a fool, and just when he was about to gather his courage and knock, Nathan pushed the door open.

"What in the devil are you doing?" Nathan asked, leaning through the open door and looking about outside.

"I am, ah, riding with you."

Nathan leaned back into his seat. "With me? Whatever for? Where is your wife?"

"She wanted to ride with her sister, is that so strange? It's a long drive, and I did not want to deprive her of her sister for company," Evan explained.

"Then why are you not riding in your own carriage?"

Evan gritted his teeth and moved over to the farthest corner of the box. Not knowing what to say, he blurted the first thing that came into his mind. "I didn't want to be alone."

"Didn't want to be alone?" Nathan asked, clearing his throat in that way that Evan knew indicated he was trying not to laugh.

Yes," Evan ground out, shoving his hand in his pocket to fiddle with the metal object inside.

Nathan smiled. "You're lying."

"Lying?" asked Evan, his eyes bulging.

"Yes, lying. You always touch whatever it is in your pocket when you lie or feel anxious, don't think I haven't noticed. Even so, I'd still know you were lying, 'didn't want to be alone,' indeed."

Evan whipped his hand from his pocket and leaned into the carriage wall, closing his eyes.

Nathan laughed but thankfully let the matter drop and started speaking about Oliver and when he and the other guests might arrive the next day.

Evan settled in for a very long and very chatty drive as he blocked out the noise inside and outside of the carriage. The silence in his mind opened feelings and memories he did not bid and could not ignore.

Perhaps she did not care for him as she had in the past, but his own feelings remained ever constant. It was then he decided he would do everything within his power to make her happy, even if that was to lessen his presence around her and give her the solitude and ease of life she so desired. Certainly then, things between them would become easier.

———

THINGS DID NOT BECOME EASIER.

As soon as Evan stepped out of the carriage behind Nathan, his mother accosted him, bringing him aside and away from the others.

"I have just had the most wonderful idea," she said, her green eyes sparkling.

Evan blinked hard, trying to wake his tired eyes and wanting nothing more than a good stretch after being cooped up in a box for hours on end. "And what might that be?"

"The dower house."

Evan smiled as his mother practically bounced with excitement. "What about it? Weren't you having repairs made while we were in town?"

"Yes, but they were completed, and the house sits empty now, though it is ready for use. Why don't you and Fleur stay there during the next few weeks? It could be like a honeymoon! Of course you will have to arrange to visit the main house every day for activities, but that should not be a problem, it's only a ten-minute walk or quick carriage ride —"

"Mother."

"This will give you some privacy. Time to get to know each other as man and wife —"

Evan slumped. "Mother, I don't think —"

"It's perfect. I can't believe I didn't think of it before and don't slouch like that, darling. Oh! I shall have to inform the servants —"

"Mother!"

Madeleine jumped and looked around to see that the others had stopped and were now looking at them curiously.

"You don't need to shout, dearest," she said, a wobble in her voice.

Evan was horrified. "Mother, no, forgive me, please don't be distraught." He took her by the shoulders and pulled her to him, patting her slightly on the back as he whispered. "I do not think it a good idea. Lady Fleur still has not had time to accustom herself to all these rapid changes, and I think it may be prudent for you to have a talk with her about... about what to expect."

"Expect?" she asked.

Evan could feel his face flaming. "Expect of marriage, and all that entails," he said slowly, trying barely to move his lips as there were still onlookers.

Realization dawned on his mother's face, and she grinned. Embarrassed and in disbelief, Evan wished he had not said anything at all but knew he must. Shrugging his shoulders, he went on. "Her mother passed before she could fulfill that role, and this all did happen rather suddenly. I doubt anyone thought to discuss it with her, and yesterday Lord Norfield made it perfectly clear Fleur will want children." Evan wanted to sink into the ground at his mother's expression. "Not that we need to have them right away," he added quickly. "Mother, please stop staring at me like that."

"You are right, of course," she agreed as he watched her try to wipe the smile from her lips. "Oh, how could I have forgotten? And her father would not have, surely. Not to worry, darling, I will handle everything."

She smiled beautifully and stood up on the tip of her

toes to kiss his cheek. "I will tell Hayward to put you in the white room in the east wing. He will be vexed with the last minute change, but it is a larger room and has a sitting area that you could use to give each other some space. You won't mind roughing it for a few days on the settee while she becomes accustomed to your presence, do you? If I put you in separate rooms, people will talk."

Evan thought that, yes, he rather did mind the thought of sleeping on a hard sofa, but the alternative was too unthinkable right now. "Of course not. Please convey to the lady that I do not wish for her to feel pressured." Evan paused. "But do not let her know I said so, do not let her know I said *anything*, just handle it, please, Mother.

She brought her hand to his face, her eyes bright. "You are going to be such a wonderful husband to her. I know it."

Evan smiled as she turned with a whoosh of her skirts and walked towards Hayward, who was standing on the steps, waiting for her. He followed and wondered if Fleur would feel relieved as he for the option of space.

She was an innocent, to be sure, but she would know that something was wrong if he immediately settled into the sitting room. He shook his head and jogged up to the stairs and then bounded up. He would worry about all that later, he decided, for now he would let her behavior be his guide.

14

BILLIARDS &
WEDDING NIGHTS

D inner was a quiet affair, Madeleine having declared that dressing for dinner after such a long journey was not to be done, especially when it was just close friends and family.

Fleur was thankful for the respite as she and Julia joined her mother-in-law in her private rooms for dinner while the men had gone elsewhere to take theirs.

Madeleine shifted in her chair. "Oh, I ate too much, and I really should be doing more than sitting after that long drive, but I'm too tired to do anything else."

"I won't tell anyone if you won't," Fleur teased, looking over to Julia, who had fallen asleep, her head resting on the side of the large wingback. "Look at her. She's gone completely." Fleur smiled and nodded her head towards her sister before taking a sip of her wine.

"Poor girl, she really should be tucked away in bed. Your father said she was quite the nuisance on the drive out of town."

Fleur laughed. "She was. Julia does not handle travel

well, and she and Papa argued about everything from the weather to the state of the roads, and she even accused him of taking the most comfortable side of the carriage. They almost knocked me to the floor switching sides."

Madeleine laughed, brow raised. "Oh? Were you in their carriage? Now that I think of it you were not with Evan when I found him earlier, how did I not notice?"

Fleur looked away, unsure what to say. Could she tell her mother-in-law that her son practically fell over himself to rid himself of her?

"He said that his carriage had a faulty wheel, and it was not safe for travel.

Madeleine gave her a confused look. "Who said?"

"Mr. Woolf," answered Fleur, feeling the awkward formality of his address.

Madeleine's face relaxed, and she smiled, her voice gentle and quiet. "Mr. Woolf?"

Fleur winced, her uncertainty making her feel nervous. "I feel silly, referring to him by his surname, to you especially, it is my name too, after all. Though I know I must as convention calls for it, we are not children anymore are we?"

"My dearest, you must never feel silly when it comes to your new role in his life, and you don't have to refer to him as such, not to me. You have both been thrown into an impossible situation and forced to make the best of it. Even the most acquainted couple will feel out of sorts during the early days, and I would wager you have scarcely said two words to one another since we arrived."

"No, we have not. I went to our room to freshen up, and I assumed he was with the men, but then we separated for dinner."

"Give yourself time. It is perfectly understandable for

you to feel unsure about each other just now. Evan is also very abrasive — trust me in this, Fleur, I do know my own son. He does not mean to be harsh, but he tends to be more so with those he cares for. You will have to teach him."

"Teach him?"

"Yes, teach him how a proper gentleman should act. Lord knows I have tried and failed. Do not let him run roughshod over you. He will if left to his own devices. It is how he copes with situations in which he does not feel confident."

Fleur nodded. She could understand that, except she retreated when she felt that way, as she did not want to bring attention to herself. Could she help someone else feel comfortable when she herself had such a hard time in those situations?

"You look worried, my dear, and you need not be. You will prematurely gray, you know," said Madeleine, winking.

Fleur laughed and couldn't help but feel more at ease. Madeleine had always had that effect on her.

"What would you know about graying prematurely? Papa says you have not aged a day since he met you."

"Your father was always bad at giving compliments. I most certainly have aged, and I resent being compared to the ninny girl I once was," she joked. "Oh, how I have missed having someone to talk to, someone to let my guard down with. I have my family, and I love my sons and nephews dearly, but I finally have a daughter I can dote upon, someone to share things with."

Fleur looked over to Julia, her breath slow and steady as she slept on. "It has always been just Julia, father, and I. Perhaps having more than one motherly figure in Julia's life will also help."

Madeleine nodded. "You have done a wonderful job

with her, Fleur, but Julia is a free spirit. I, for one, admire that in her."

"I worry for her; she can be very forceful. What if she runs into trouble and I am not there to help her?"

"We will not allow it, dearest. Frankly, I'm more concerned about you."

Fleur's head snapped up from the wine she was about to sip. "Me? Have I done something wrong?"

"Nothing at all, I just meant you are a new wife now, and there are plenty of things that come along with that role."

"Oh, I see. I've long kept the accounts for Papa—"

Madeleine chuckled. "No, dear, that is not quite what I meant."

She trailed off when Julia stirred, opening her eyes in surprise. Fleur was glad of the distraction, which took the focus off her acute embarrassment when it dawned on her what Madeleine had been referring to.

"Did you have a good nap?" Madeleine teased.

Julia tried to hide her yawn. "If I had fallen asleep any sooner, I would have dived straight into my dinner."

"Now that would have been a sight to behold, but you must be tired still. Fleur, you and Julia go on up to bed, we will see each other again in the morning."

Both girls nodded and kissed Madeleine on the cheek before saying good-night. Making their way up through the dark wood walls of the hallway, Fleur gazed at the paintings of what had to be every Earl of Blackburn for the past several generations. It had been a very long time since she'd seen them and as she walked by the earl's father, Evan's grandfather, she smiled at her memories of him and greeted him in her mind as she passed.

Julia paused in front of her door and Fleur woke from her woolgathering at her small voice. "Everything is going to change now, is it not? If you had not married, we would be staying together, and we could stay up and talk like we always do."

Fleur smiled. "You mean you would stay up and talk whilst I would try to sleep."

Julia's chin quivered, her voice thin. "I do not have anyone now."

"Julia." Fleur stood in the hallway, dismayed. Julia was always so strong, so vivacious. She had no idea how badly her marriage had affected her, and Fleur felt guilt press upon her. "Come, let us go inside."

Fleur opened the door and laid her hand on Julia's back, ushering her into the dark room. She lit the candles on the bedside table from the candle in her hand, and they sat upon the bed.

"Now, what is this about you not having anyone? You will have father and Prudence. I'm sure she could come stay with you for an extended period of time. In fact, she would benefit from it next season."

"I know, and I love Prudence, I truly do, but it is not the same," she said, looking at Fleur with her bright blue eyes misted over.

"And I will not be far away, just a two-day ride for a visit, and during in the spring we will be minutes away from each other during the season if we are both in town," said Fleur, faltering. Would she be in town during the season? She had no idea what Evan even did for a living. It frightened her, how little she knew him now.

"And I will write to you, often. I am not going anywhere, Julia."

Julia nodded and sank onto Fleur's shoulder, tears falling on her neck.

"Besides, one day, some dashing young man is going to come and sweep you off of your feet, and you will have a family of your own."

Julia snorted, laughing through her tears. "I do not want to be married, not ever, not if it means I have to leave behind everyone I love."

Fleur reached up and started to unpin Julia's hair. "You would not be leaving your family, Julia, you would be adding to it, giving me a brother and Papa a son he could spend time with, another cousin for Andrew."

Julia sighed and sat up from Fleur's shoulder. "I've ruined your dress. Now it's all snotty."

Fleur laughed. "I have been in a carriage most the day, so I'm not sure it matters, but how do you feel? Better? You know I am just a short walk away if you need me."

"Short? Blackburn Hall is monstrous. It may take me a week to find you."

They laughed together. "You are overtired and need to get some rest. Undress and prepare for bed properly, or I will send Lucy in here after you, and do not leave your candle burning."

"I will. Goodnight, Fleur."

Fleur stood and looked down on her sister lying upon the bed, already nodding off in her clothes. She sighed as soft light twinkled onto Julia's alabaster face from the window.

She walked to the door and turned the knob before looking back. "Goodnight, Julia."

She left the room and closed the door gently and made her way to her own assigned rooms, thinking it was time for her also to let go. Her little sister was grown now, and as

Madeleine had said before, she was a free spirit, and free spirits needed to fly.

———

Evan sat around the room with the men feeling drained. He was just about to stand to serve himself a cool drink when his mother flung open the doors to his father's billiard room.

"I figured you boys would be playing billiards, seeing how we are all still on town hours, but here you all are, sat around the room and looking maudlin."

"Actually, we are all worn out, the young and the old," his father said amidst laughter. "Where are the girls?"

"I sent them to bed nearly half an hour ago. Poor Julia was nodding off into her dinner, and Fleur was not far behind. I just came in to say a quick goodnight before I retire as well."

The earl stood and held out his arm for her to take. "I think I am for bed as well. Julian, shall the old folk retire and leave it to the youth?"

"If we are to tour your lands in the morning with your steward then I better sleep now. It has been quite some time since I spent more than an hour on horseback. Good night boys," he said, nodding to them all. He walked towards the door and stopped, looking back to Evan. It looked as if he were about to say something but thought better of it, and shook his head before walking out the door.

"You boys behave," the earl said, escorting Madeleine out of the library.

The boys sat in silence, most having the good grace not to stare at Evan.

All but Felix, that was. "Well?" he asked.

Evan nearly jumped at the break in silence. "Well, what?" he asked, irritation replacing alarm.

"*Well, what,* he asks. Should you not be upstairs with your wife? Evan, it's your wedding night."

Evan glared at his cousin, ready to let him have it. "Leave him be, Felix," Edward intervened. "I think it is time we all went to bed."

Felix, Dom, and Nathan all took that for the dismissal that it was and followed each other out of the room, Nathan giving Evan a long look before he trailed after.

Evan and Edward could still hear Felix as they trailed out of the room, Dom behind him telling him to be quiet, while Evan was sure Nathan was trying not to laugh.

"Ignore Felix, you know how he is," Edward said, trying to soothe Evan's annoyance.

"I'm not angry with Felix, not really. I should probably be grateful he held his tongue this long and did not pop off in front of her father."

Edward moved forward and grasped Evan's shoulder. He watched his younger brother fidget, certain that something was bothering him, and certain that *something* was a pretty, shy young woman with dark hair and blue eyes. One who was, at that very moment, waiting in Evan's bedchamber.

"So you are not angry with Felix, but you have been surly all evening, barely saying a word."

Evan snorted. "Am I not always so?"

Edward smiled. "Yes, but usually you are not so quiet in front of the family, and I know you find comfort in Nathan's presence, however much you try to deny it. So tell me what is troubling you."

Evan looked up at Edward, a slow smile edging onto his face. "You know it still bothers me that you are taller?"

"It is fitting for the elder brother. Now stop stalling, Evan."

Evan sighed and walked across the room, his brother's hand falling off his shoulder. He paced and his thoughts raced. How could he explain?

'Fleur..." he said abruptly.

"Yes?" Edward prompted.

Evan spun on his heel, his pacing grinding to a halt. "She's my wife."

Edward chuckled. "Yes, I'm aware."

Evan gave him a look. "What I mean is she's my *wife* and I don't know how to speak to her. Hell, I don't even know how to be in the same carriage as her. What if I do something wrong? Say something idiotic? Again? I always show my worst side to Lady Fleur, which is probably no more than I deserve, seeing how I broke her heart so many years ago. Now all of a sudden she's my wife? Edward, I can barely look her in the eye. Perhaps God is punishing me for my past."

Edward stared at Evan, thinking it might be the longest speech he'd ever heard Evan utter. "God is punishing you? I didn't know you were so devout."

Evan glared. "That is beside the point."

Edward leaned against the wall, one long leg crossing over the other, raising one finger to push the spectacles back onto his nose. "Evan, listen to me. You have been married for approximately, what? Fourteen hours? And to a woman you have not spoken to or seen since she was sixteen."

"Yes, and I was horrible to her when we saw each other last, I can't deny it."

"The point is you are now both adults. She does not know *you* any more than you know *her*, so why not show her the real you? Get to know one another again, slowly, there is no rush you know. We both know you still care for her."

Evan bristled. "It is only natural —"

"I am not accusing you, Evan, or poking fun. Unlike most men I do not think it a burden to be married, or it a weakness to love one's wife. How could I, after seeing mother and father? They're absolutely revolting."

Evan smiled but felt very tired, remembering what he overheard earlier that day. "Still, I have it on good authority she would rather it have been you. Her life with you would have been easier after all."

Edward cuffed Evan on the back of the head.

"Edward! That smarts!" shouted Evan.

"Keep talking nonsense, and I'll do it again," said Edward, straightening his cuffs and coat. "She's probably up there right now, terrified and wondering why it is taking you so long to come to her."

Evan sighed. "I wish Mother had put us in separate rooms."

"That would hardly be appropriate."

Evan reached down and slammed the cue ball into the corner pocket. "Damn what is appropriate."

"And that too is your problem. Evan, I am quite sure Lady Fleur cares, as much as you do not. You have to take into account both of your needs now, not just your own. She might be shy, but keep in mind she will want for friends in her new home. You need to help her ease into her new life and meet those around her, and perhaps in return, she can do the same for you."

"What is that supposed to mean?" Evan asked, perplexed.

Edward sighed. "Not a thing. Let's retire. Just remember, if you are feeling unsure, then do not you think she probably is as well?"

Evan nodded and led the way from the room towards the stairs. What Edward said made sense, and he wanted to become the man that she could rely on to settle into her new life as his wife, but he also hoped and prayed that life would be kind to him, and that Lady Fleur would be asleep when he arrived at their room.

————

FLEUR LAY IN BED, listening for any sign of Evan. She had heard the other men pass by her room more than half an hour before, and she wondered what kept him.

Leaning up, she strained to hear but heard nothing but the hum of quiet. She peeked around the room and felt foolish, so she rolled over onto her back with a huff. She knew Evan was avoiding her earlier that day and while it did bother her, if she was truthful with herself, she was also relieved.

What would we say to one another? She wondered.

It was almost if they had to start anew, as if it would have been better had they never met before marrying, yet they had known each other, knew each other well in fact, and now she was suddenly his wife, laying in bed waiting for him.

What if he expected ... but of course he would. She knew more than Madeleine suspected. Madeleine spent her formative years in Paris, but Fleur grew up on a farming estate with plenty of horses and livestock. She knew exactly what to expect. Well, maybe not *exactly*, but definitely in theory.

She covered her eyes with her hands and shook her head back and forth, her hair wildly whipping about.

"I'm definitely not ready," she said to the empty room.

Raising up quickly, she flung her legs over the bed and picked up the candle she had left burning for Evan on her bedside table. She stood and crept toward the door, feeling silly, but she could not stand the anticipation any longer.

She placed the candle down on the dresser by the door and leaned forward, placing the flat of her ear against the cool wood, her hair falling in a curtain of dark around her face. Irritated, she pushed it behind her ear.

Hearing nothing, she eyed the door handle, wondering if she dared open it just a crack, just so she could hear something, anything. Taking a deep breath, she slowly reached for the handle, and that is when she heard it. Footsteps, heavy booted steps getting louder, coming closer and closer. Fleur stood in place holding her breath, scared to move when the booted feet stopped directly in front of her door.

She should have run when she first heard the footsteps, but now she was frozen. If she ran now he would surely hear her, so she waited and waited until she wondered if she imagined it, but then she finally heard him.

"Just open the door, you great idiot," she heard Evan say.

Fleur's eyes widened, and her hand flew to her mouth as she ran for it. Flinging herself on top of the bed, covers and all, she closed her eyes feigning sleep just as the door opened. Her hair was splayed around her, covering her face, and she was thankful it hid her small nervous smile.

She heard Evan walk around the bed and felt him work the cover out from under her feet and then carefully slide it over and up to her shoulders. There he stood looking at her, and she could almost feel his gaze as she wondered what he was thinking.

She felt the edge of the bed dip slightly, and she knew he was kneeling in front of her, his elbows placed upon the bed as he leaned, his breath not very far from her own as it stirred the hair covering her face.

Then she felt it, the roughness of his hand as one lone finger slipped under her hair and caressed her face as he moved her hair backward, tucking it behind her ear.

She heard him sigh. "What am I to do, Fleur?" he whispered. "After everything we have been through, you are still the one constant in my past that has made me want to do better, to *be* better. You have ever been my driving force, even after I left you behind. Yet, I do not know you as I did before, and you do not know me. It is difficult... to say these words to you even though I know you won't remember them when you awake. I really am a coward, Fleur."

She heard him stand and walk away, and the urge to grasp onto him and make him stay warred within her. Tears threatened to spill from her eyes, no matter how tightly shut. She listened, hearing the rustle of fabric, and she dared a peek as she saw him shrug out of his overcoat and waistcoat then remove the cufflinks from his shirtsleeves. She squeezed her eyes shut, feeling like an intruder, but then she heard him lay down onto the chaise at the end of the bed and groan.

Within minutes she heard soft snoring, and feeling brave, she leaned up ever so quietly, and scooted towards the end of the bed to look at Evan. She marveled at how his features softened in his sleep. Though he needed a shave, he looked handsome and young.

His coat was draped over him, sliding halfway to the

floor, so she took her robe that was folded across the edge of the bed and slowly lowered it down on top of him.

As she moved back up, she lay her head down on her pillow and sighed, the stress of the long day ebbing from her. No matter what they were to each other in the past or what they would be in the future, she now knew for certain that he cared for her still, and the thought calmed her fears and warmed her heart.

15
LADIES & NON-EXISTANT EARLS

Fleur awoke to the soft sound of birds chirping outside her window. It was quite bright in her room, so she knew it was close to noon and she should rise, but she could not resist closing her eyes once more.

She wondered where everyone was and if Evan had yet to start his day. Suddenly, remembering her married state, her eyes popped open, and she quickly rose to see if he was still in the room, laid upon the chaise. Noting he was gone, she didn't know whether to be disappointed or grateful.

She settled on grateful, as she wasn't sure she was quite ready to face their first real discussion in years, in a bedchamber of all places. She laughed, covering her mouth, and knew she was acting like one of those silly girls Julia despised, but she couldn't help herself. It all still felt like one, long, convoluted dream.

Pushing the covers off her lap, she rose and rang the bell for her lady's maid and readied herself to make her way down to the breakfast room. Once outside the room, she heard voices and smiled.

"But Fleur is married now, how would she ever get away to visit us?" Julia whined.

Madeleine laughed. "My dear, you make it sound as if Evan has your sister locked in a dungeon somewhere. I assure you that won't be the case. Evan is all bark and no bite, just like his father. Fleur will be able to go wherever, whenever she pleases, provided she is not with child, even then she will only need to restrict her travel."

Julia dropped her fork onto her plate, the loud crash sounding in time with a gasp from the doorway. Fleur stood there, face flaming, wondering if it was possible for her to actually die from an overdose of embarrassment.

Taking pity, Madeleine rose to pull Fleur into the dining room and ushered her towards the sideboard. "You look lovely today, Fleur, don't you and Julia make a vision, you in lavender, and she in her blue. Your father must rejoice in the beauty that you two bring to his life."

Fleur smiled and reached over to kiss her mother-in-law good morning and gave Julia a nod as she filled her plate. "Where are the others? Surely I'm not the last to rise?"

"The boys are touring the estate with our steward," said Madeleine. "They will be gone most of the day, so it will be up to the three of us to welcome the remaining guests if they have not returned."

"Who is arriving?" Julia asked.

"Let us see," Madeleine said as she raised a hand and counted off each remaining member of the party. "There is a Mr. Mason. He, Nathan, and Evan went to Cambridge together, and then there are your three girls. Prudence, Phoebe, and also Charity, along with Phoebe's mother and Prudence's aunt.

"When do you think they will arrive?" asked Julia,

"I expect they will arrive between two and four. What shall we do until then, girls?"

Julia leaned back in her chair and laid her napkin beside her plate. "A walk please, maybe into town? I need some exercise after the breakfast I devoured."

"That can be arranged, and perhaps we will even run into the boys," said Madeleine, her eyes sparkling as she watched Fleur flush and tuck back into her breakfast.

———

Evan sat on his horse with the others in the middle of a field of tall rolling grass. He had questioned his father's steward on everything he knew about running an estate as he gave his father an update on Blackburn Hall. Edward, being the heir, had been given the education he needed to run the land, but he, being the spare, had not.

One thing was clear from his abrupt education: he had his work cut out for his new country home.

"What are you thinking about?" Nathan asked, shouldering his horse up next to Evan's.

"The property I just acquired. It's apparent even to me that I will need staff to run a place of its size and loathe as I am to lose my privacy, it must be done."

Nathan balked. "Staff? You will need *considerable* staff, Evan, that place is ramshackle. Everything needs repair, and all the rooms need outfitting from the walls to the furniture. Lady Fleur can help you there."

Evan nodded, glad to have someone to help with the finer details. "I have kept on the old steward, though he wishes to retire as soon as possible. He has been a great help and says he has a nephew who is keen on taking his place."

"That old place has a steward?" Nathan asked skeptically.

Evan laughed. "The man is almost seventy years old, Nathan. He did what he could considering the previous owners refused to hire on and let the place go to ruin. She will be beautiful once I am done, though. "

Nathan nodded and greeted Edward, Dom, and Felix as they rode up along side of them and the duke and the earl continued to converse with the steward.

"What are you two doing hiding back here?" asked Felix.

"I was just asking Evan about his new estate."

Evan, knowing Felix would pounce, stiffened and wished Nathan had never brought it up.

"Oh, you bought a country home? Why have I not heard of this? Did you know, Dom?"

"Yes, Edward told me," Dom smiled, happy to duck the blame as long as Felix left him out of it.

Sensing Edward's discomfort and knowing his brother kept his purchase a secret for his benefit, Evan took the focus. "It is nothing, Felix. I purchased an old estate about ten miles west of here."

"When can we see it? What's it called?"

Evan cleared his throat. "When it is ready, and it doesn't have a name."

Murmurs swept from Felix to a surprised Nathan. "Of course it has a name. What did the previous owners call it?"

"They called it nothing. The place was built decades ago and never occupied. The owners just left it sitting there."

Edward shook his head as Felix's eyes lit up bright as a school boy's. "Then we shall have to name her. How about Wolfham Hall or HighWolf Turret?"

"Those are horrid names, Felix," said Dom, his nose

wrinkled in disgust. "And it doesn't have a turret. It's Palladian."

Evan smirked at Felix's sour face. "I think I will wait to name her until after she is restored to her former glory."

Nathan nodded in agreement and pulled out his pocket watch. "Half past four; we were out here longer than I expected."

"And longer than my wife will care for," said the earl, riding up with the duke at his side. "Let us head back to the house before she sends out a search party."

They rode back to the house and all the while Felix spouted off ridiculous names. Evan laughed at his antics but would not be taking his advice anytime soon.

———

CHARITY SAT in the carriage listening to the chaperones chatter on. She felt thankful her aunt had invited Prudence and Ms. Wilson along as Prudence kept Phoebe occupied while she contemplated the marriage announcement they had all awoken to yesterday morning.

Fleur was married... to Mr. Evander Woolf!

"I do believe we are getting close," said her aunt. "We've been swaying away in this carriage for hours. Surely we are nearly there."

All eyes turned to the window when they saw a young footman running and then jumping on to the side of the moving carriage. "We are nearly there, ma'am, we can see the house now."

"Thank you, Adam," said Mrs. Simmons. The boy nodded and jumped down to rejoin the other servants in the carriages that held their belongings.

"Thank goodness," Phoebe said. "I long to take a turn

around the gardens, hopefully with a nice breeze. My legs need a good stretch."

Prudence slipped her arm through her aunt's. "We all need a good stretch. I am not at all sure I can feel my toes anymore."

Phoebe laughed. "If yours are numb, dear Prudence, just think of how your aunt and my mother feel."

Suddenly the carriage stopped, and sighs of relief made their way around. When the door opened, and a footmen set a step in front of her and reached inside to help her down, Charity looked up to see Julia practically bouncing next to Fleur and Lady Blackburn.

Once everyone was set down, she turned to Phoebe and Prudence and whispered while the chaperones talked. "Right. So how are we going to go about this?"

"I for one want to talk to Julia and Fleur as soon as possible about this marriage announcement nonsense," Prudence said, waving the marriage announcement from *The Times* in her hand.

Charity shook her head. "Why are you still carrying that around? And how do you suppose we will be able to do that? We will immediately be taken to our rooms and expected to rest until dinner."

Prudence closed her eyes, and Charity knew she was praying for patience. "Then we will have to be very careful and very quiet. I am sure my aunt will be asleep within minutes. I'll sneak into the hall and claim I needed to stretch my legs if I am seen and wait for you two there. But do try to hurry, I'm not sure how long I can wait in the hall without looking suspicious to the servants passing by."

"And then what?" asked Charity.

Prudence, becoming irritated, spoke sharply. "We will sneak into Fleur's room, of course."

"And what if her husband is in there with her?"

Prudence's eyes flew wide. "O-oh, well... I did not think of that."

Charity smiled and shook her head. "Good heavens, you are really terrible at this, you know."

"You will have to forgive me if I am not as well-versed in manipulation as you."

"Have someone show you to my rooms," said Charity. "My rank will certainly assure me private quarters where we can talk. I'll send a note off with a maid to both Fleur and Julia to meet us there."

The other girls nodded and Charity looked again to the vestibule of the large home. Julia was already speaking rapidly to Phoebe, who had made her way up the stairs. Her shoulders relaxed, and she smiled, glad to be reunited with her best friend once again, but she was going to find out about this marriage business even if it took her the entire stay to do so.

Evan and Nathan stood outdoors to the side of the house, hidden from his mother and the girls who stood outside waiting to greet the other women.

They watched three very different carriages drive up to the front of the house. The first was elegant, carrying three young ladies, two dressed in the latest fashions and one equally pretty but not as expensively coiffed, Evan noticed.

The next two to exit were older ladies, the chaperones, he gathered. Guards of young maids' virtues and match-makers alike, at least he would be spared their notice. Being married, he was now unimportant in the eyes of mamas everywhere.

The next carriage was a fine specimen but plain, carrying servants that were now bustling around with his family's own, preparing to pull the carriages around the back of the home to unload.

The third and final carriage, the finest of them all, brought a smile to his face; though its occupant had yet to leave its confines. Evan elbowed Nathan and nodded his head toward the carriage. Nathan smirked.

"Oliver," they said in unison.

Noticing how his mother was now greeting the girls and making their way indoors, Evan deemed it safe to reveal himself. He tapped Nathan's arm, and they walked towards Oliver's carriage. When he reached the door, he yanked it open, threw his head back and laughed.

There was Oliver, sitting in the very corner of the cabin, his feet stretched across the seats while his face was pressed against the side of the wall. He was sleeping soundly.

"Typical Oliver," Nathan said, shaking his head.

"How should we wake him? Pull his boots off?"

Nathan laughed. "There is a danger he would be too lazy to put them back on, and he'd greet your mother in naught but his stockings."

"Classic round of ear flicking?"

"Did it, last year of Cambridge."

"We could always smack him in his fool head since a fool he is to fall asleep anywhere within a stone's throw of us."

"As much as I would love to continue our game, I don't fancy the conversation we would likely have with your mother if we awakened the Earl of Stonewick with a smack."

"Hmm, you may be right, but now that you mention it, I don't think I ever addressed him as such in her presence."

Nathan laughed. "You mean to tell me your mother invited 'Mr. Mason' to her house party? Evan, she's going to murder you when she realizes—"

"And who says she needs to?" asked a raspy voice.

"Ollie! Good to see you, and awake, what a rarity."

"You have a bloody loud mouth, Carter, and it would please me greatly if we could just leave off on the earl business. Much less fuss that way."

Evan smirked. "You mean much less harassment by well-meaning mamas trying to lay their claws in you."

"Quite right," said the non-existent earl.

"Don't worry, your secret is safe with us, for now," said Evan. "But don't think, even for a moment, the ladies, including my mother, don't have the peerage memorized cover to cover. No one is safe, even elusive earls who inherited when they were babies."

Oliver yawned. "Hmm, perhaps, perhaps not."

"Well, come out of there, my mother is waiting with the others inside."

Oliver leaned forward, rubbing his blue eyes. He reached up and tried to tame his chestnut curls but soon gave up when it proved too much trouble.

He scooted down the seat and jumped out of the carriage. "Let us go then, shouldn't keep ladies waiting, especially ones as enchanting as your mother."

Evan scowled. "You have never met my mother."

"True, but Nathan says —"

"Never you mind what Nathan says," Evan said sourly. The others laughed while they made their way towards the house. Evan smiled, damned if he wasn't looking forward to a few days with his family and friends. Surprised with himself he had not realized just how much he'd missed them all after years of shuttering himself away from everyone.

He took a deep breath and exhaled slowly, wondering if perhaps it was time to forgive himself, time to make amends and repair damage done. Yes, he did believe it was time for just that.

16

GOOD FRIENDS

Fleur sat in her bedchamber reading by the window when a knock came at the door. She looked up and then closed her book, one of her fingers marking her place. "Come in."

A maid peeked into the room, waiting for her nod of approval, and walked forward. "I'm sorry to disturb you, milady, but I was asked to deliver this to you."

"Thank you," Fleur said, taking the letter and flipping it over, thinking it strange nothing was written on the outside. She looked up to ask the maid who penned the missive, but she had already excused herself.

"How odd," she muttered. She held the letter tightly and wondered if it was from Evan. She nervously fingered the edge of the paper, working up the nerve, and after counting to three in her head, she broke the seal and was surprised to see Charity's elegant scrawl.

She skimmed the invite requesting her to come to Charity's room immediately and crumpled it in her hand while slowly lowering it to her lap. She could not deny that she was slightly discouraged it was not from Evan. She had thought for a moment that he had written to her. Inviting her on a walk or perhaps exposed some sense of his feelings that were so hard for him to convey in person, but she was wrong.

She sighed and laid her book on a side table before walking outside into the hall. Spotting a maid, she quickened her pace to catch her. "Excuse me, but in which room is Lady Charity installed?"

"I was just about to ask the same thing."

Fleur was surprised to find Julia there, a note in hand. "Julia, were you asked to come to Charity's room as well?"

"I have been summoned," she said, waving the note in the air. "Though I cannot think of why," Julia continued. "She never talks to me unless it is with you. I'm relieved you are to be there."

"If you would just make more of an effort with her —"

"Oh, don't start, Fleur. I am still recovering from Madeleine's shopping excursion this morning, and I don't feel accommodating in the slightest."

Fleur cleared her throat and looked toward the maid. "Could you point us to Lady Charity's quarters?"

"Of course, Madam, it is just down the hall, fourth door on the right."

Fleur thanked her over Julia's giggles. "Madam?"

"We best hurry, we're late already," said Fleur, trying not to look Julia in the eyes as they walked.

"Yes, Madam."

They both laughed, and Fleur took Julia's arm. "I am a married woman now; it is only proper."

Julia cringed. "But it sounds so odd, though I suppose not so odd as Lady Fleur Woolf. I may expire from shock the first time I hear you announced formally."

"Just Mrs. Woolf will do, thank you very much."

"Oh? Abandoning 'Lady Fleur' are we?"

"Yes, most definitely," she said with a grin, stopping in front of Charity's door.

"Whatever for? Afraid plain *Mister* Woolf will feel slighted?"

Fleur dropped Julia's arm. "It is my choice how I am to be addressed, now I am free to do so, and you know as well as I do that Evan has never cared for situation nor titles."

Julia brought her hand up to her face and looked at her fingernails. "I suppose that's true, but neither does Edward, and he *has* one."

Fleur looked up and down the hallway, relieved they were alone. "That was a very stuck-up remark, Julia, even for you. Why are you bringing this up again? What is the matter with you?"

"Do you really want to talk about this now? In the hallway when we're already late?"

Fleur's eyes darted about again, and, no, she didn't like the thought of it, but she could not stop herself. "Yes, yes, I do want to talk about it, so let us hear it, Julia."

"It is only that... I think you would be happier as Edward's wife —"

"Well, I don't," said Fleur, her eyes flashing and her jaw set.

Julia stared, her eyes blinking slowly and her mouth trying to form words. "I... I'm sorry. You don't need to be angry."

"Don't I? From the start you've done nothing but show your disapproval. Julia, I realize that to everyone, it was always meant to be Edward, a perfect match on parchment, but for me, it was always meant to be Evan."

"But... why?" Julia asked, nose scrunched and brows furrowed.

Fleur laughed, exasperated. "Has not he already shown he's not the monster you think."

"I did not say he was a *monster*..." Julia's shoulders stiffened along with her demeanor. "...oh, God, you already love him. Did you ever stop?"

Fleur smiled and shrugged.

"You are completely daft."

Fleur scoffed. "I thank you for your support."

"Oh, you have it. If you tell me that you truly will be happier with him than anyone else, including the handsome, kind and perfect Viscount Ravenbrook —"

"Julia."

"Then I will love him as my only brother, and never say a word against him again, to you, that is. I reserve the right to complain to others."

Fleur laughed and gathered Julia into her arms. "Thank you, now should we actually knock?"

"Let's," Julia replied, rapping on the heavy wood door, taking Fleur's hand in hers. "Let's enter the lioness' den."

The door swung open, and they were pulled inside.

———

PHOEBE AND PRUDENCE sat on the chaise positioned at the end of Charity's bed while the latter paced before them.

"Did you send the notes?" asked Phoebe.

Charity answered with a look.

"Then what is taking them so long?"

Prudence stood as well. "Phoebe, it has only been five minutes, let us give them a moment to arrive."

"It is just that one of us married! It's so shocking."

"Well, try not to be so shocked, if you please," said Charity, patting Phoebe on the head as she walked past.

"Because what does that say about the rest of us if you're shocked about Fleur?"

Prudence could only agree with a nod. "It is true. I never imagined she would be unattached for so many seasons. She's the kindest of us all, not to mention stunning —"

She stopped talking and stood still. "Do you hear that?"

"Hear what?" Charity asked, stopping to listen.

"Why ever for? Afraid plain Mr. Woolf will feel slighted?"

"That! Did you hear that?"

Charity nodded and ran to the door, Prudence and Phoebe not far behind. "Shh," mouthed Charity, a finger across her lips to signal silence.

"I just feel..."

"From the start you've done nothing but show your disapproval ..."

Charity gasped, clapping her hand to her mouth, while Prudence and Phoebe looked at each other, eyes wide, jaws slack.

"Thank you, now should we actually knock?"

All three girls reeled backward a step, and, once Fleur and Julia knocked, Prudence opened the door, pulling them both inside before slamming it shut. "You are married!" shouted Prudence.

Charity rushed forward, grasping Fleur's hands. "To Mr. Woolf?"

Fleur laughed, though it sounded more like strangulation than merriment. "Um, surprise?"

Tired of the topic, Julia walked over to the bed and sat upon it, leaning against the poster and watching Fleur flounder with amusement.

As Fleur explained the particulars, Julia watched her sister and wondered if she knew how she sparkled when she spoke of her wedding, or how she smiled when she said his name.

Definitely in love with the devil, thought Julia as she conceded. It was time for her to stop being selfish and thinking only about her own feelings, to stop disparaging her new brother-in-law because all it did was cause Fleur pain. Above all the most important thing was for Fleur to be happy, and there was no denying that she was well on her way.

———

FLEUR SET her wine down upon the dining room table and fiddled with her wedding band, her thumb spinning it around over and over. She was still not used to its constant presence, but the sight of it pleased her.

She looked across the table as Evan chatted with his friends. They had not spoken during dinner, but that was expected as it would be rude to shout across the table, though it seemed like all were doing so.

Dinner had been a relaxed affair. Madeleine always had a way of making formal situations seem informal with her easy manners and relaxed atmosphere. Prudence and Julia were laughing, and Phoebe was shushing them, though she was clearly amused. Charity was in a conversation with Prudence's aunt and seemed content.

Her favorite thing to do, though, was watch Evan. He was so different. Changed from the young boy he once was. Being surrounded by his friends softened him she thought, and it was something new. She'd never seen him interact with his university friends before, and she was fascinated.

Suddenly Evan caught her eye, and a smile lingered on his face like it was meant for her. She quickly took a long sip of her wine, trying to hide her unease at being caught staring.

She wondered if tonight would be the night they could finally talk. Would he come to her or would they keep dancing around one another? She admitted to herself that she tired of the avoidance and the anticipation. She wanted him to come to her, like he had done before, to hold her hand as he did on the day they married and ... suddenly she felt warm and decided she'd had too much wine.

The sound of chairs being moved across the wood floor as everyone stood caught her attention. Madeleine signaled the end of dinner by ushering the ladies to the drawing-room. The men would follow soon after, and maybe then they could spend some time in each other's company.

———

EVAN WATCHED FLEUR ALL EVENING. It was the only time — since everything began — that he was able to sit in her company and regard her. She seemed happy enough sitting between Mrs. Simmons and Lady Charity, easily conversing with them both.

Their eyes met, no more than a glance, but her movements turned wooden and her demeanor apprehensive. He felt hopeless in that moment, her composure revealing his worst fears, his regrets. He knew not how to reach her.

His mind elsewhere, he did not hear his mother bring dinner to a close and when the ladies rose to leave he stood, the action so practiced it did not require his attention. He saw nothing but her as she walked away in her dark plum evening dress, gold embroidery gleamed in the soft candlelight when she moved, her raven hair shimmering, beautiful on its own with no need for adornment.

Nathan nudged him when he failed to notice the men were also exiting to the billiard room. It would be another hour at least before he saw her again, such was the after-dinner custom. He did not much feel like joining the men for drinks and cards or one more bloody round of billiards.

He clapped Nathan on the shoulder and waited for him to turn. "I think I will go for a walk, clear my head."

"I will join you if you don't mind the company."

Evan nodded in agreement and made his way outdoors, Nathan behind him. He stood on the vestibule and took a deep breath, looked over the grounds, and smiled. It had been too long since he came to his childhood home and took in the air. Always was he running, busy with some plan or another, but this reminded him of his youth, of simpler days, and it calmed him.

Nathan walked up beside him. "The moon and stars are so bright we do not even need a lantern."

"Country moonlight. One cannot see near as much in London, even with a lamp on every corner."

Evan slipped his hand into his pocket, feeling the cool metal against his warm fingers, knowing exactly where he wanted to be. "Coming?" he asked before he walked down the stairs, his stride long and with purpose.

"Evan, slow down," Nathan shouted, trying to keep up with his brisk pace.

Evan slowed and stopped, standing in front of the stables. He pushed the wide doors open and walked inside. Darkness filled the room to every corner, the moonlight unable to reach.

"Stay here," said Evan, running into the stable.

Nathan carefully stepped inside and shouted. "Evan, what are you doing..." He trailed off as moonlight flooded the room.

He saw Evan run from one side of the loft to the other, throwing open another window. He walked back to the center of the loft and looked down on Nathan. "Coming up?"

Nathan grimaced. He hated heights.

He took a deep breath and climbed, not wanting to think about how he would get down again, and once his feet landed on the floor, he sighed. He walked over to the window, wishing Evan would stop leaning out of the godforsaken thing. He peeked out of the window himself and decided it would be safer to turn around and lean against the wall.

"I have always loved it up here, but it has been almost eight years since I last came," said Evan.

Nathan smiled. "It is just the sort of place you would love. I can see it now, you with a book in hand, hiding away up here, basking in your solitude. I bet Edward had to come fetch you for dinner."

Evan laughed. "Of course. I devoted so much time to sitting up here, Fleur too, when we were younger."

"I bet her father loved that."

"He didn't mind. We were but little things then."

"Is there a reason we are here now?" asked Nathan, daring to peek out the window once more.

Evan's fond memories faded along with his smile. "I just wanted to see the old place again."

"I think it's more than that."

Evan's head swung around, staring Nathan down. "I don't know what you mean."

"You do, you only have to discover it for yourself, but let us start with the fact you have been avoiding your wife for the past two days."

Evan snorted. "Have you been speaking to Edward? He said the same thing to me last evening."

"No, but it is not hard to see. I can understand, you know, it must be hard to be thrown together with someone you were not previously courting, but you and Lady Fleur have so much history. Why is it that you run from her?"

"It's not so simple. We have history, yes, but that does not make it any easier, I assure you. If anything, it makes it harder."

Nathan shook his head. "I don't understand."

Evan looked out of the window once more, not sure he could help Nathan to understand but decided to try.

"The first time I knew I was in love with Fleur I was standing right here, much as we are now. She was taking a walk with her sister, and I was sulking, having wanted to walk to town with her like we always had before, but that time my mother had forbidden it. I was seventeen at the time and Fleur fifteen, and I suppose she was right, it had become rather inappropriate for me to escort her around alone and unchaperoned."

Nathan laughed. "I should say."

"I know, but at the time I thought my mother was raving, because who could ever suspect something between myself and Fleur? We were friends, nothing more. But that day I secluded myself up here, and when I heard voices below I stood and looked out of the window, and I could see her. I still remember it so clearly. She was laughing at something Julia had said, wearing a lavender walking dress. I even remember the ribbon in her bonnet was white."

"Ah, you were definitely smitten."

Evan nodded. "Then Edward came upon them, and she took his arm, as she had done many times before, mind you, but I was so angry and full of... jealousy I suppose. I could not speak to why I felt so bitter in that moment but I also could not stand seeing them together. As the days passed I realized that I loved her. I definitely didn't know how to handle those emotions with any type of grace."

"Did you ever confess to her?"

"I tried once."

Nathan gave Evan a look. "Perhaps you could elaborate?"

Evan smirked. "Fine, but you won't like it. It was little more than a year later, and I was home for the holidays. It was Fleur's birthday, and I had prepared a gift for her." Evan Laughed, remembering how nervous he had been. "I thought I was so clever, but really I was still too immature and did not think things through.

I was going to tell her that night that I loved her and propose marriage, she was but sixteen and I nearly as young. I knew we would have to be patient to actually exchange our vows, but I could not wait to ask her. It would had been wiser if I had."

"My God, she refused you?" Nathan asked.

"I did not give her the chance. I asked her to meet me here that night, and I waited so long for her to come, but she never did. It was freezing, and I became worried, so I walked back to the house. I could see her through the windows with Edward, and he was kissing her under the mistletoe, innocently enough on the forehead, but everyone around them was laughing and making a fuss, and they were smiling at one another."

Nathan nodded, knowing that seeing such a thing as a love-sick youth would be soul crushing.

"What did you do?"

"I did what I always do. I became angry and we quarreled. I said horrible things to her, Nathan, and then I shut myself up in my rooms. The next morning, I saddled my horse and went back to university. I did not see her or talk to her again till the night of the Brockhursts' ball."

Nathan's brow furrowed and he paused, letting calm take him over lest he shout at Evan that he was a damned fool. "That was cold, even for you. Just think how devastated she must have been."

"You have to understand that from the moment Fleur was born our families had intended her for Edward. I couldn't stand it anymore, and I finally just... gave up. Now you know why our past complicates things."

Nathan clucked and slapped Evan in the arm. "Are you finished?"

Confused, Evan looked to Nathan. "What?"

"You said you came up here to sulk when you were younger, and now look at you, are you finished sulking yet?"

Evan shook his head, irritated. "Not quite. What would you have me do?"

"Woo her, you fatwit! You have to show her that she still means everything to you. She does, does she not?"

Evan gave a curt nod. "I would not know where to start."

"You start my friend, where everyone else does, from the beginning. Do you think everyone else magically knows how to woo the one they love?"

Evan huffed and whipped his head back towards the window. "It's impossible. She could never forget how horrible I was."

"It sounds to me like you are the one holding onto the past. Your negativity does neither you nor Lady Fleur credit. She is gentleness itself, and no one could ever lead me to believe she is capable of holding a grudge. I am not telling you she won't be angry — you deserve it, mind you — but she will forgive you. I'm certain."

"So I am just supposed to take her on drives, bring her flowers, and confess my undying love and devotion? She'd think I'd gone mad."

Nathan sighed. "If you had never met the lady before, what would you do?"

Evan thought long. He did not have any experience wooing ladies or the like as he only knew what other men did.

"Perhaps... perhaps this evening I could ask her if she would like to walk in the gallery? Away from the others?"

Nathan smiled. "There, you see? A beginning."

Evan laughed and put his head in his hands, embarrassed. "I suppose it is."

"I am curious, though, the birthday gift you brought her so many years ago, what was it?"

Evan placed his hand in his coat, pulling out a small silver pocket watch, handing it to Nathan. The edge was tarnished, and the colors dulled with age, but Nathan could see that the watch doubled as a miniature portrait of Evan himself, as he was when they went to school together.

"From the day I meet you, you have always fiddled with something in your pocket, and it was this all along?"

Evan nodded. "When I left for university, Fleur was quite upset. I had it commissioned while at Cambridge from one of the artists. Took nearly my whole damn allowance for the year."

Nathan laughed, his shoulders shaking, his smile wide, as he handed the watch back to Evan.

He groaned holding the watch once more. "Don't, it's too embarrassing. I don't know what I was thinking and I probably would have never worked up the courage to give it to her."

"Forgive me, it's just the fact that you have carried around a miniature of *yourself* for the past eight years."

Evan laughed and placed the watch back in his pocket. He looked over the grounds once more and felt more content than he had in a long time.

Nathan was right. There had to not only be a beginning between them, but something new. Something that would not erase the past but help them remember the fond memories and not only the ones that held pain.

17
WOOING A WIFE

Fleur took a turn around the room with Charity while the others talked about the following day's plan to ride across the grounds to picnic in the woods in excitement.

She reached out to take Charity's arm in her own when she saw her friend blanch. "We do not have to go if you would rather stay. I can invent some excuse and you can say you do not wish to leave me alone."

Charity smiled but shook her head. "No, it really is silly. Who ever heard of an Englishman, or an Englishwoman for that matter, being afraid of horses?"

Fleur stopped and turned to her friend, grasping both of her hands in her own. "It makes perfect sense to me."

"That is because you love me without question, no matter my faults or disagreeable temper."

Fleur laughed at Charity's mischievous smirk as they walked towards the far window in the drawing room. "You aren't disagreeable, not to me."

"Yes, well you and Julia have known me since we were children, though your sister despises me —"

"She does not, Charity. She just doesn't know you as I do."

"Fine, then Prudence hates me. Don't deny it we both know she does. And I know it is horrible, but I don't care one fig about what Prudence Wilson thinks of me. I don't have time to coddle her hurt feelings when I'm already five and twenty and no sign of a husband on the horizon."

"You have plenty of time—"

"Time is the one thing I don't have. Fleur, my father is ill, and the doctors say it is only a matter of one year, perhaps two before..."

Charity swallowed hard, blinking swiftly, and Fleur sat them down upon the window seat. "I didn't know, I'm sorry."

"Nobody knows. My father doesn't want to appear weak, but he is fading. I must find some sense of security before then, before my cousin inherits."

"But surely your cousin will provide for you. It's his responsibility —"

Charity laughed, a bitter sound caught in the back of her throat. "My cousin has, in a few short years, squandered his own inheritance gambling and racking up more debt than the estate can handle. He will ruin the estate and finally the family line. The Earldom will become penniless and along with it myself. Even my inheritance is in danger should he decide not to honor it. He knows I would not drag the family name through the mud with a suit."

"Oh." Fleur didn't know what else to say, shocked at Charity's misfortune. To lose her father when not even two years had passed since she lost her elder brother to a riding accident. It was too cruel.

"Prudence would laugh if she knew. I'll be worse off than she is in a few scant years. At least she can find work as a governess if the need calls for it, but who is going to hire an earl's daughter with no references or work experience? I will be a laughingstock."

"You do her an unkindness. Prudence would never laugh at someone's misfortune. Besides, I would never let you suffer such a fate, and neither would Julia, Phoebe, or even Prudence."

"You must not tell them, Fleur, promise me?" Charity said quickly, looking around the room as the men made their way inside. "My aunt doesn't know, she already has so much to worry about with Phoebe and her brother's."

Fleur gripped her shaking hands. "I promise."

Charity put on a smile for the room, straightening her shoulders and looking around, her stiff and haughty protection back in place, her fan out and waving between herself and the rest of the room.

It was then Fleur understood how tired Charity must feel. First losing her mother then her brother and now her father. In that moment, Fleur felt lucky despite her own loss in life and love.

"So how is married life?" asked Charity, wanting to lift the concerned look Fleur was giving her.

"It has only been two days, so I cannot rightly say. I haven't even really had a chance to talk to him."

Charity's brow arched, her smile sharp. "As his wife, he will have to talk to you eventually. You know I always thought you might marry into this family, though of course then I figured it would be to the elder brother."

Fleur thought to herself that her friend didn't know how close that came to becoming reality.

Charity looked over at the viscount and saw him watching them. Her breath quickened, and she fanned the heat from her face. Finally able to tear her eyes from his, she turned fully towards Fleur. "Look alive now, here comes your beloved, Mr. Carter, and one of his cousins. Which Woolf is that?"

"Felix," said Fleur, her heart quickening.

"And is he eligible?"

Fleur laughed. "You're terrible."

"What? Time is of the essence, remember? Not everyone has a pool of male childhood friends to choose from." Charity put on her most flirtatious smile and closed her fan. She knew she looked ravishing in her blue silk.

Felix walked straight to Fleur. "Ah, cousin, may I call you that?" He asked, not even pausing for an answer. "It is a bit dull in here isn't it? Perhaps you could astound us with a song? All ladies sing well, don't they? Or maybe play a jig for us, a dance seems agreeable."

Fleur sat frozen. "Oh, no, I don't sing at all, Mr. Woolf, nor play."

Felix waved her off. "Nonsense, of course you do."

Fleur flushed. She really wouldn't have to make a spectacle of herself in front of all, would she?

"Felix," Evan said, his face pinched. "Leave her alone, would you? Fleur, you look a little warm, would you care to —"

"What if the lady joined you for a duet? Would that be more agreeable?"

Charity, taking pity on her dear friend, intervened. "Mr. Woolf, I would be happy to play for you if the room agrees. Might I inquire if you have any musical talents of your own?"

"I have been known to sing a tune or two. Shall we entertain these poor clods?" he asked, holding his arm out for Charity to take.

She took his arm and stood. "Yes, let us do. Lead on, Mr. Woolf.

"Call me Felix, please," he smiled as he lead her away.

"I certainly will not. You are very impertinent, Mr. Woolf, and are you not aware, sir, that you horrified poor Fleur back there? She did not even have a moment to make our introductions, as such we should not even be speaking."

Felix laughed. "I was trying to incite Evan's protective feelings for the lady, lest they dance around each other the rest of the summer. A little interference won't go astray."

"Unless the interference is interfering itself, again you are not aware, but he was trying to ask her for a walk. A private one."

Felix stopped walking. "Really?" he asked, looking back at his cousin, who was standing with his hands behind his back, looking anywhere but his wife. "That does not seem likely. Look at them. Perhaps we should go back, give him a nudge."

Charity huffed and held tighter to his arm when he made to turn. "Of course it doesn't seem likely *now*, he's lost his nerve, poor man. I beg of you not to try to help in the future. You are not very talented at matchmaking, Mr. Woolf."

Felix looked affronted. "I'll have you know I am the one who brought the happy couple together. I'm brilliant at it, the best. Name two people in this room, and I will have them swooning over each other within a fortnight."

Charity laughed. She liked this man. "Absolutely not, I wouldn't put anyone in this room through such scrutiny. You must be fearsome when on a mission."

Felix drew himself up and preened. "But of course, will

you set your cap at me now, or maybe you would benefit from my scheming?"

Charity reared back and scoffed. "How absurd! You are in no danger from me, Mr. Woolf, I assure you, you are much too..."

"Much too what?" he asked, grinning madly. He had not had this much fun with a woman in ages.

"Much too silly, you are a very silly man, and frankly, you are not the type of man I am inclined towards."

"You wound me," he said dramatically, palming his chest. "And pray tell, which man is the lady's type, if one may know?"

"Hmm, tall," she said and laughed when Felix drew himself up higher.

"With dark hair, I think."

He palmed his own light brown hair and faked a frown. "A hit, my lady."

Charity brought her free hand up to her mouth and tapped her bottom lip. "Reading, he must be a great reader."

"Reading?" asked Felix, wrinkling his nose. "You're right. We would never suit. Our amore was short lived, but we will always cherish these moments, won't we?"

Charity threw her hand to her mouth and tried not to bring attention to herself laughing in such a boisterous manner. Oh, how she was having fun!

"You and I are just not meant to be," he shook his head sadly.

"Friends then?" she asked. "I could use one more at this party."

"Friends it will be, my lady."

"Please, call me Charity. We are friends now, are we not?" she asked, mirth in her eyes.

"Of course, Lady Charity! Shall we find my aunt and put that duet into her mind?"

"Yes," she said, happy to have made a friend that she didn't have to trick or trap into marriage. Felix Woolf, she knew, would have made a great catch but she didn't want to spoil it, not the one thing that had made her laugh heartily for the first time in more years than she could count.

———

EVAN WATCHED as Felix charmed Lady Charity to the point of hysterics. The idiot. He damned his own inelegance in speaking to others and looked out the window.

Fleur cleared her throat. "Has it been long since you've been back at Blackburn Hall, Eva...Mr. Woolf?"

Evan stiffened. "Mr. Woolf?" he asked, trying not to let his astonishment show. "We are alone, madam, one would think you could call me by my given name."

"I'm sorry ... Evan. I'm not used to this, please forgive me."

Evan winced. "Don't apologize. It should be me who begs your pardon. After all these years you know I'm not gifted with easy speech, not like Felix," he said, nodding towards his cousin, who still had the lady in a fit of giggles.

"I haven't seen Charity that relaxed and happy in a long time," she said absently, enjoying the sight of her friend being carefree.

Evan coughed. Somehow his simple plan to ask her for a walk had derailed horribly.

Fleur fanned herself lightly, feeling the room heat up from all the activity. "It is a bit warm tonight, don't you agree?"

Evan, seeing his chance, charged at it. "Yes, it is. Would you maybe care to walk in the gallery? It is sure to be cooler, and I don't think anyone would miss us."

Fleur looked around and saw everyone deep in conversation. Julia was still speaking to Prudence and Phoebe, and Charity and Mr. Woolf now spoke to Madeleine, Lord Blackburn, and her father. "Yes, I believe you are right." She looked over to him. "I'd love to, Evan."

He tried not to grin like an idiot, he really did, but he knew he failed when he saw Nathan, Oliver, Dom and his own traitor brother looking at him and laughing together. Had they nothing better to do?

"Shall we?" he asked, holding out his arm.

Relieved they would finally be able to have a conversation, Fleur slipped her arm through his and he led her towards the door, only to be stopped by her father and Lord Backburn.

The duke nodded in greeting. "Fleur, Evan, Lady Charity and Mr. Woolf are going to grace us with a few performances for the evening, will you not come and join us?"

Evan opened his mouth and then shut it. How was he supposed to tell his father-in-law he wanted to be alone in a dark gallery with his daughter?

The earl walked behind them, placing his hand on their backs, pressing them forward. "Yes, you two go ahead to the music room, and we will be along in a moment."

Evan looked at Fleur and they both resigned themselves as he led her out of the drawing room, though not towards the gallery. His mother, Lady Charity, and Felix followed.

"There now," said the earl once they were gone. "They will have to sit beside each other for a full hour at least."

The duke shook his head in worry. "They did not say

one word to each other this afternoon or throughout dinner."

"We will just have to keep an eye on them, Julian, make sure they have plenty of opportunities to be together."

The duke agreed and walked towards the door to make his way to the music room with the earl, all without knowing they had thwarted the very thing they were trying to accomplish.

18

INTERVENTIONS

The following morning, Fleur laughed along with the other ladies while Madeleine regaled them with anecdotes of when her boys and nephews were young. They would be properly put out if they knew, which just made the whole thing more laughable.

The night before had been lovely, even if she and Evan were never able to speak. The men all left for the card room again after a bout of music and charades. The ladies talked until they retired. Exhausted, she did not even hear Evan come in, and when she woke, he was gone again.

The ladies had risen by ten that morning, with the men once again rising early, this time to go shooting. After breakfast, they had retired into the morning room and were now waiting for them to return so they could all ride out together for an afternoon picnic.

She looked over at Charity, again talking with Prudence's aunt. She worried for her friend. Would it be good for her to seat a horse again? Surely they would give her a docile mount.

"Where have you gone off to?" Julia asked, tapping her sister on the temple.

Fleur looked over, smiling. "Just woolgathering. I'm concerned about the picnic as we will all be riding before-hand and Charity does not do well with riding these days."

Julia nodded, instantly knowing what Fleur was refer-ring to. She was much too young to have known Charity's older brother, but she could imagine losing her cousin, Andrew, to the war. It was a fear she lived with every day.

"Charity scared of horses?" asked Prudence. "I always thought that one was scared of nothing."

"Think, Prudence," said Phoebe. "If you take a moment you will remember why she might be frightened."

Prudence looked from one to another and then it dawned on her, and she felt ashamed. "Oh."

"Don't look like that, I have told you over and over not to worry where Charity is concerned, she's not herself late-ly," said Phoebe.

"She has never warmed to me, not the way you three have. I know I haven't known all of you as long since I met you only last year during my come out, but you have all been so kind to me." Especially Julia, she added to herself. "You know, it's just occurred to me that my aunt and your mother, Phoebe, will have to ride out in a carriage with Lady Blackburn. My aunt is not able to mount a horse at her age."

Phoebe nodded and looked over to Charity. "That is true, maybe you and I could convince her to go with them. She seems fond of your aunt; they've been talking all morning."

"You and I? Convince her?" Prudence asked, her jaw having yet recovered from astonishment. "Are you mad? She'll throw me from her room before I get a word out."

"Don't be silly," said Julia. "Madeleine will call for us to go up and change soon, and afterwards we can all meet in Fleur's room to go together. Between the four of us she'll have to relent, though don't expect it to be easy. She is proud and won't want to lose face."

Fleur nodded. "She will want to make a good impression too. We can remind her that she would be in danger of doing just the opposite."

Julia laughed. "You mean she won't want to be dumped on her backside in front of all those marriage prospects."

"Julia!" Fleur scolded but lost when the others laughed. She shook her head and smiled.

————

FLEUR LOOKED at herself in the mirror, adjusting the matching hat to her riding habit when a knock came at the door. At her nod, the maid let in Julia, Phoebe, and Prudence.

"Don't you and Julia look smashing in your matching greys," said Phoebe.

Fleur sighed happily and looked everyone over through the mirror. She remembered the day she and her sister had chosen the same thick cotton for their habits, though the styles were different. Julia's was more military-influenced and Fleur's was less severe, but they did make a pair just the same.

Phoebe was also in a lighter cotton, a sapphire that matched her dark blue eyes, but Fleur noticed Prudence was pulling at her sleeve cuffs self-consciously. She was in an older style made from brown wool, something more suited for winter. It had little to no decoration besides the frog clasps that lined her front.

Fleur walked over, hugged Prudence to her, and asked the room, "Are we ready to go to war?"

"I am dressed for it," joked Julia, pretending to be in good humor, but not looking forward to the confrontation at hand.

They left Fleur's room and walked slowly to Charity's. "Maybe I should wait downstairs," said Prudence.

Julia clicked her tongue. "Nonsense, everyone knows Charity is harmless, just quite rude when it suits her."

Fleur cleared her throat in warning as she stopped in front of Charity's door. She knocked.

When the maid opened the door, Fleur could see Charity inside. She was pacing and wringing her hands, her golden hair lovely next to her burgundy habit.

"Charity?" Fleur said, trying to catch her attention, but her friend did not hear her.

"She's been like that for the last half-hour, madam," whispered the maid, her brow furrowed with worry.

Fleur smiled and nodded in understanding. "What is your name?"

"Clara, milady. I don't know what to do, and she's been in a right state —"

"It's all right, Clara. Would you run down for a fresh pitcher of cool water and cloths?"

"Of course, milady."

Fleur watched the harassed maid curtsey before she ran from the room. Charity was now sitting down upon the bed fanning her face.

"Charity..." Fleur said, though she didn't stir.

She walked over and placed her hand on her shoulder, regretting the action when Charity jumped. "Forgive me. I did not mean to startle you."

Charity nodded, and when she caught sight of the

others, she stood with her back ramrod straight, her chin lifted. "Is it time to go?"

"No, not yet. We, the four of us I mean, we would like to speak to you about today's picnic."

Charity frowned. "What of it?"

Fleur cleared her throat and pushed forward. "We were talking, and we realized that Phoebe's mother and Prudence's aunt would be riding out in the carriage with Lady Blackburn. There will be room for a fourth, and we wondered if you would not like to join them?"

Charity was dumbfounded. "And miss the ride? Whatever could you be thinking?"

"You won't miss much," said Phoebe, trying to soothe her.

"I will miss everything! How am I supposed to go about... making new friends if I cannot interact with them?"

Prudence shook her head at Charity's stubbornness. "Don't you mean catching a husband?"

Charity glowered, her face red and her hands unsteady. "How dare you? Are you not the same as I? As any woman in our position?"

"Of course I am, I just don't feel the need to go about it as you do. We are not all as pragmatic as you about finding love."

Charity stood silent for a moment, then with a shaky voice spoke directly to Prudence. "Love? Is that what you hope for? And how, may I ask, should I go about finding love? I can ill afford to prioritize such things as romantic love." Charity spat, "You think because my father is titled that I have every opportunity in the world? You, who know nothing of what I suffer. You, who thinks I am no better than a fortune hunter. Yes, I admit it, I will hunt, and I will scheme. I will laugh at every joke that a man makes, though I may not find it amusing, and I will compliment when it is not in my opinion to do so, and I will say yes to the best and wealthiest man who offers for me, if he is able to provide protection and a comfortable life for me and mine. I will do all of those things because I need to survive. It is the only way I can, society has made it so, not I, so do not judge me, Prudence Wilson, lest someday you find yourself in my position."

Prudence looked down to the ground, following the wood grain with her eyes. She knew not what to say, only that Charity was right, she knew nothing of her life or what problems might come with being an earl's daughter. Not all of the upper echelon were well off or had an abundance of family to support them.

Fleur stepped forward. "Ladies, please, we didn't come together to argue. Charity, dearest, please listen. The point we all came here to make, Prudence included, is that we are frightened for you. You have not ridden in almost two years and are anxious to do so. Don't you think now is not the best time to re-acquaint yourself with riding?"

Charity shook her head. " I... I have been riding since I was —"

"Charity, think of it this way," interrupted Julia, "You are very unlikely to make a good impression upon any of the men if you make a fool out of yourself on horseback. Do you really want to put yourself in such a vulnerable position?"

Charity looked away. "But it is so silly, fearing something you have done practically your whole life."

Fleur felt slightly guilty for bringing Prudence and Julia. Their words were harsh but it was the truth — only a fool would put themselves in such a precarious position when only one's best foot forward would do. Then she thought of her own fears.

"People," she said to her surprise.

Charity broke her gaze at the wall and turned to Fleur. "I beg your pardon?"

"Yes, people, I am terrified of them," she said, then took a deep breath. "I hate balls and the theatre. I can't even enjoy the gardens at Vauxhall because of the crowds. Is it silly? Yes, sometimes I feel it is. Like you, it is something I have done many times and still yet, it is something I dread."

Charity relaxed and reached for Fleur's hand. "I had no idea it affected you so greatly."

"Heights," added Julia. "Terrified of them. Never visited The Tower for that very reason."

"Spiders for me," offered Phoebe. "I can't even bring myself to kill the smallest one, and of course my wretched brothers were always using them to frighten me."

Everyone laughed and looked expectantly at Prudence. "Oh all right," she said. "Boats. Not small row boats but large ocean-crossing ships. Just looking up at such a monstrous object from the ground is enough to make my stomach turn, and I hope I never step foot on one."

Charity stared hard at Prudence and bowed her head slightly. Charity could recognize a concession when she saw one.

"All right, you have won, but what am I to say? What reason will I give?"

Julia stepped up to Charity in three long strides and stopped. "I've already thought of that." She reached up and grasped the delicate edging of Charity's sleeve and ripped the whole of it from her arm in one quick sweep.

The room was silent.

Fleur's hand slowly dropped from her mouth as she

looked at her sister, beaming as if proud. "Julia Miette Osborne! I cannot believe you just did that!"

Charity, recovered from her surprise, laughed. "Can you really not, Fleur? This is Julia we are speaking of, and besides, it is the perfect excuse, somehow my habit was torn and I had nothing suitable to ride in."

"We could have just *said* it was ruined," Prudence protested, hating to see such a beautiful frock ruined.

Fleur, her eyes still locked on Julia, wondered what on earth she was to do with her sister now she wouldn't be able to keep an eye on her. She shook her head, clearing her worry. Julia was no longer her responsibility, she was a young woman now, and Fleur needed to learn to let go.

Charity fiddled with the edging of her sleeve and shoulder, no doubt seeing if it could be mended later. "I will need to change back into an afternoon dress. Fleur, would you mind ringing for the maid on your way out?"

"Of course," she said, ushering the group out. Things had gone well, considering Charity had unveiled her unstoppable temper, but she had not been offended too greatly. Overall, she would say it was a roaring success.

19
GOOD INTENTIONS

Evan stood waiting with the rest of the party as they watched for the ladies to come down. The horses had been brought around, and the carriages were packed. All that was left was to find his wife.

Needing to put his thoughts in order, he was actually glad they had not come down as of yet. He was definitely looking forward to the ride, knowing he could steal a few moments of her time today, but the previous night had been a bloody failure. They were stuck in the music room for hours, not a situation conducive to talking when one was meant to be listening.

He heard chatter from above and saw the ladies descending the stairs. His eyes searched and settled on the one he was looking for, and for a moment he was stunned.

Beautiful, he thought.

The grey brought out the lightness of her eyes and the pink of her cheeks. She looked happy, and he hoped he would manage to keep that smile upon her face the whole day.

"Shall we depart?" his father asked, his mother taking his arm to be led outside and put up in their carriage.

He turned and offered his own to Fleur, and she did not hesitate to take it as she smiled. He tried to smile in return but felt like a fool. He walked her outside, stopping in front of her mount. Placing his hand on her elbow he steadied her as she stepped onto the wood box, then moving to grasp her waist, he helped set her down upon her side-saddle.

Evan looked over the saddle and thought the thing looked dangerous and unsteady and was glad he never had to sit upon one, but that was soon forgotten as he realized his hands were still upon her waist.

His hands lingered there, his fingers moving with the motion of her breath, the warmth of her skin reaching him from underneath her habit.

He raised his eyes and was startled to discover she was still looking at him. He quickly removed his hands, and after restraining his urge to run his fingers through his hair, he asked if she was well situated. She said she was, so he walked away and mounted his own mare.

He looked down at his reins, vaguely hearing the conversation around him. Oliver telling Nathan that he hoped there was a decent tree to nap under. Edward talking to his father about the best place to find shade while they lunched. His mother inquiring after why the Preston girl was not riding with the others, the answer something about torn habits and he knew not what, nor did he care. These were nothing but distractions to keep him from making a fool of himself and staring at Fleur until it was time to ride on.

When the time came, his horse shouldered hers while they walked on behind his family.

"I'm sorry we missed our walk last night."

Surprised she had started the conversation, he eagerly replied. "Should we try again? Tonight?"

She smiled, the simple gesture making his stomach flip. "Yes, provided there are no impromptu concerts this evening, we should be able to get away."

"Lord, I hope not. Felix has not the talent for singing he thinks he has," Evan shuddered.

She laughed. "That is unkind. I especially enjoyed the performance when he kept switching the tempo and Charity had to rush along to catch up."

Evan shook his head. Only Felix would do such a thing. "She must have been so vexed with him."

"I think it was quite the opposite. That is the most enjoyment I have seen her have in ages. I think they could be great friends."

"A man and woman, friends? Is there such a thing?"

She looked at him, a small knowing look. "You know there is, yet you say you disagree?"

"In most cases, I would tend to disagree, but in Felix's case? No, he makes friends almost instantly and keeps them just as easily. I have often envied his talent for charm and conversation, though I must confess, I am not one for clubs and parties and keeping up appearances. As you know."

Fleur tightened her grip on her reins when the party veered left and led her horse to follow. "That is me as well. I'm much more at ease at home in the country. Town is so harrying it becomes exhausting."

"Exactly. Nathan is always rushing me off to do something or another or he tries anyway. I just want some peace and quiet, and he's dragging me off to the theatre or some other thing."

Fleur grinned at the thought of Evan being led around

by Nathan. "You don't like the theatre then? I guess I should not expect to see many plays from now on unless I accompany Julia or your mother. I had no idea I was to be so cloistered."

Evan's eyes widened. "That's not... I did not mean to imply you could not —"

"I was only teasing, Evan, I owe you from years past, you know," she said, her eyes shining.

He was again surprised. Fleur teasing him? Things had definitely changed.

"You are different," he said, just as the party was stopping at their destination.

"I should hope so." She smiled brightly, and he wondered if she had any idea how much it affected him to see her so unguarded, so open to him.

He wondered what else about her had changed, what her life had been like these past years. He wanted and needed to know her again, and he vowed he would listen to every detail of every day he had missed with her.

———

The Duke of Norfield sat with the earl, scrutinizing every move his daughter and new son-in-law made. *Was she content?* he wondered. She did not look unhappy, sitting on the blanket, her parasol shading her from the harsh summer sun. He thought they might have gone with the others to walk along the path by the pond, but they had stayed. It worried him greatly. The young did not tend stay with the old at these things. Why did they not want to go and frolic with the others?

He needed to find a way to spark their interest in one another, and fast, because at the end of a few scant weeks he would have to let her go, to say goodbye, and he would no longer be able to help her.

"Do they look happy?" he leaned over and quietly asked the earl. "They seem relaxed, but I cannot tell."

"They look... content. They are at least speaking to one another now."

"Content," he mumbled. "That's not good enough, a newly married couple should be more than content. We're running out of time."

"Julian, we have a fortnight to make sure all is as it should be. Why don't you relax as well?"

"I cannot."

"Why in God's name not? We're at a picnic. The entire point is to relax."

"Because, *Lord Blackburn*," he whispered through clenched teeth. "When we had the idea of our children marrying long ago, they were to be betrothed before marriage. They were to court. Do not you think they might just be the smallest bit uncomfortable with one another?"

Charles laughed, his head held back and his hand upon his chest, drawing the curious gaze of his wife. "Of course they are. Just as they would be even if they had a lengthy betrothal. Come now, tell me you were not terrified of your wife the first days of your own marriage."

Julian smiled at the memories. "You have a point, but this is Fleur and Evan, she is not trying to gain his attentions, and he's —"

The duke stopped, catching a warning eye from the earl. "Also shy," he continued. "Should not we help them along? They need to be alone so they can talk freely. We both know romance cannot blossom under the watchful gaze of your parents."

Charles stood swiftly from his seat on the ground. "Come then. I may have a plan."

Julian jumped up and made to follow, grasping the earl's shoulder to stop him. "A plan? What plan?"

"Don't worry, just follow my lead."

"Absolutely not, the last time you said that I ended up leg-shackled!"

"And later you thanked me for it, and you have two beautiful daughters to show for it, so shut it, and come along."

Julian snuck a look at Madeleine, who sat with an exasperated look on her face. He looked up to the sky, praying for patience. This could not end well.

———

EVAN LOOKED at his father and became suspicious when he and the duke asked if they would join them for a walk.

"The old become stiff when idle, so we must stretch our legs." He raised his leg as if to demonstrate his infirmity.

"The others are down by the water," the duke added. "Why don't we join them?"

Evan rose to help Fleur to her feet, and they walked between the two older men.

"Evan, have you told Fleur about the pretty little estate you bought last winter?" his father asked.

Evan looked at Fleur, her face open and curious. "Oh, is it near Blackburn Hall?"

"It's about half an hour by carriage, quarter of an hour or less if you're on horseback and moving swiftly."

"That close? Then we shall be able to meet your family often."

"Yes, you and my mother —"

Evan stopped talking and raised a brow when his father started shouting. "OH! Oh, my leg!"

His father hopped on one foot and held the duke's shoulder to keep from falling, all while wailing loud enough for Prinny himself to hear all the way in London. Evan eyed his father's dramatics while Fleur tried to help steady him from his other side.

"Did you turn your ankle?" Evan asked, knowing damned well he didn't.

"No, no, just a leg spasm, it will pass. Norfield here can walk me back. Why don't you go on without us and show Fleur the gardens before joining the others, won't you, Evan?"

"But you should have someone hold your other side," Fleur protested as the earl pushed her forward towards Evan.

She walked over, and Evan's eyes widened when he saw his father wink and point at his leg while her back was turned.

Evan walked towards her and took her shoulders in his hands, keeping her facing toward him while the duke shooed them away with his free hand.

"Unbelievable," he mouthed to them, eyes narrowed, before he turned her direction and offered his arm. "He will be all right, Fleur, it is only a leg spasm."

She nodded as they moved onward. He could hear the two featherbrains talking and laughing as they walked away. They thought they were so clever.

"You realize that my father is fine, don't you? And that was all just a ploy to get us alone?"

Fleur's head jerked towards him. "And last night as well? Arranging for us to sit together during the musical performances?"

"So you noticed too?" He asked.

Fleur laughed. "Yes, but to go as far as to fake a leg injury. I had no idea your father was such a performer."

"Or that yours could play along so well?" Evan shook his head. He had to admit he was surprised at the duke.

"Oh, no, that is not surprising at all, really. I have seen my father act quite silly when it comes to Julia."

"For example?"

He watched as she tilted her head, the sun low in the sky, setting the dark strands escaping her bonnet to flame.

"I once saw my father wade into a pig pen and help the servants clean out the troughs."

Evan laughed. "*His grace?* Why on earth?"

"Because Julia had been causing trouble for the maids. She was very opinionated, even as a young child — you must remember. It was her opinion that since we had servants, she could paint all over the walls in our nursery, after all, the maids would wash it away. My father told her it was very unkind to create extra work for the servants and exceptionally rude to draw on the walls, and that it looked like we now lived in a pigsty. Julia said, 'Speaking of pigs, you create more work for the servants by keeping them at all.'"

Evan laughed. "Sounds like Julia.

Fleur nodded with a smile. "My father was, of course, baffled as to how to reply. Julia reasoned he could keep more chickens or any other animal and that pigs were the dirtiest, therefore, created more work. My father marched outside and dove right in to help clean. Afterward, he told Julia that even a person of rank and wealth has their duty to others, and that includes respecting and taking care of the people who serve us daily."

"I'm surprised."

She grinned. "That my father would get his hands dirty?"

"No, at your sister. She is very headstrong, yet I'd have never thought she'd torture servants."

"Oh, she didn't, not really, but people do things that are mean and hurtful when they are young, before they understand that it is wrong and that they will come to regret their actions." She avoided his eyes, her words too close.

Evan stopped walking and turned towards Fleur. He let her arm slide from his and grasped both of her hands in his own. "Like myself?"

She looked into his eyes, slightly hooded from the glare of the sun. "Do you regret it?"

He leaned down, his face so close to her own that she could no longer make out his features. She felt his breath upon her lips as he answered. "Every single day."

He slowly leaned into her, his lips barely brushing hers, when he stopped suddenly, hearing the pounding of hooves and the whine of a horse. He looked up to see a great Byerley Turk, the horse black as night and its rider wearing the dark blues of a naval uniform, the gold trim glistening like flames from the sun.

His hair was dark, his brows knitted together in anger, the scar on lip prominent as he came barreling towards them. Evan pulled Fleur behind him as the man came to an abrupt stop, yanking his reins and throwing grass and dirt at their feet when the horse dug in its hooves.

Evan looked up, and his mouth almost dropped as he stared into the very angry eyes of Andrew Osborne, Fleur's cousin. *Oh hell,* Evan thought, as he watched the man dismount and come striding towards them in all his military glory.

"Andy!" Shouted Fleur, surprise and elation lighting her

face as she ran to him. Evan tried his best not to look displeased when he lifted and spun her around.

"What are you doing here?" she asked. "I thought you could not come." She reached up, wiping the dirt of the road from his face with her hands, dirtying her white gloves.

"What have I told you about calling me Andy?" he asked as he laughed, not really vexed with her. "I was in London and saw the marriage announcement, not that it was needed. You are the talk of the town, Fleur."

He smiled down at her, and Evan was struck by how a man he considered to be a loose cannon could be so loving towards his cousins.

"Oh," Fleur cringed. "I suppose we did leave a bit of an uproar behind."

"Everyone is just bitter they missed all the delicious details, myself included," he added. Evan shrank back a bit at the cold look he was receiving, then gripped his overcoat, yanked it down, and tried to stand taller. Osborne had two good inches on him, but what of it?

"Where were you two off to before I arrived?"

"Walking down to the pond to meet the rest of the party. Oh, Andy! Julia will be so happy to see you," she said, "would you care to join us?"

Osborne looked around. "How far away is this pond?"

Fleur looked to him to answer, and Evan sighed. "It's just a few more minutes, you can see it just over that way," he pointed, and sure enough they could make out the water and their friends sitting on blankets laid upon the ground.

Osborne nodded. "Fleur, why don't you go and join them? I wish to have a word with your husband."

Fleur hesitated, the disdain evident in Andrew's voice.

Evan felt his stomach drop as she looked him in the eyes. "No. I think I would prefer to stay here," she answered.

Evan nearly laughed at the shocked look on Osborne's face. He could tell he was not accustomed to disobedience, being a military man and the heir to her father's title. Not to mention he would head her family one day.

"No?" Osborne asked.

He felt proud when Fleur didn't back down. Apparently, she was not half as afraid of him as he himself was.

"That is right. Do you really think I don't know what is going to happen the moment I walk away?"

"Fine," he conceded, "what if I promise not to punch him in the nose?"

Fleur looked skeptical, and Evan almost wanted her to stay, though she did not need to be witness to this conversation.

Evan gave him a stiff smile. "I'll be fine, Fleur. We're just going to have a chat, right, Osborne?"

"Of course," The other man agreed, his own false friendliness unnerving.

She looked again between them and sighed. "Fine, I will go, but don't think I won't send the other men back here as soon as I meet them, so you have roughly five minutes for your foolishness."

Evan watched the grey of her dress twist as she abruptly turned and walked swiftly away. At that pace they would be lucky to have two minutes.

Evan looked at Osborne, who was now walking towards him. "So get on with it, tell me how much you hate the fact I married her —"

Evan crumpled around the fist that drove deep into his stomach and sent him doubling over. Andrew stepped back, giving him a moment. He grasped his knees and spat onto the ground, breathing slowly in and out through his nose, trying to regain his breath. "That was foul play, Osborne. Breaking your promises to Fleur already?"

"That is Captain Osborne to you, and I only promised not to pop you in the nose," Andrew sneered.

Evan stood up straight and leveled him with a stare. "Well, luckily," he said, swinging high and hitting Osborne right across his face. "I didn't make the same promise."

His fist came down swiftly and he felt his knuckles crack and his skin tear, but he didn't have time to look at the damage before Osborne, crazy man that he was, started laughing of all things. "I knew you would fight dirty, Woolf. Too bad you didn't come into the military like a good little spare, we could use men like you. Unfortunately, the Crown will have to make do, because I'm going to obliterate you." He growled and ran at him full speed.

Evan sidestepped but was caught around the waist and nearly lost his balance, but he leaned over Osborne's back and grasped him around the waist. "It seems we are evenly matched. What should we do?" He asked.

"You could stand there and let me pummel you. You know you deserve it, you bastard.

"Yes, no doubt I do, but I'm not going to let you. For one, my mother is going to be very upset if she finds out about this, so please show some restraint, and two, how will Fleur feel if she sees we've been fighting?"

"Too late for that! I'm already bleeding from the nose."

"Oh?" asked Evan, "all's fair then." He yanked Osborne down to the ground, and they rolled, dust and dirt flying all around them. He felt himself land on his back with Andrew on top of him. He gripped the other man's fist just in time as it came towards his face.

Next thing he knew, he was being gripped by the shoulders and hauled up, with Nathan and Oliver holding his arms. He blinked, trying to clear the dirt from his eyes as they watered. He could barely see Osborne being held in a similar fashion by Dom and his brother.

"Don't touch him again, Osborne," he heard Edward say in that damned calm voice of his, the frames of his glasses glinting. "Or I'll be the next one you go rounds with."

Osborne laughed deeply, and unpleasant sound, and held up his hands. "You are ridiculously tall as ever, Raven-brook, so pardon me if I decline. Woolf and I were just having a moment."

"And you could not talk it out rationally, could you?" Edward asked. "Lady Fleur has already married Osborne, so what do you hope to accomplish?"

Evan caught his breath and shrugged out of Nathan's and Oliver's hold.

Oliver cleared his throat, brushing away the dirt that holding Evan had transferred onto his superfine. "Excuse me if I seem a tad slow, but who is married to whom? And why are we unhappy about it?"

"Do try to keep up, Oliver," said Nathan, shaking his head. "Evan married Lady Fleur Osborne before we quit London. How can you not know this, you've been here for two days."

Oliver shrugged. "I am never in town, so all the good news escapes me," he defended, then looked at Evan as if his head had rolled off his shoulders. "You really are *married*?"

"Quite married," he responded.

"Good Lord." Oliver blinked, still digesting the news.

Andrew huffed. "While this is very diverting, I still need a word with Woolf here."

"A word is all you'll have, Osborne," Edward said,

letting go of his arm, "we will stand away but do not try anything. I won't let you touch him again."

He looked to Edward and nodded. "Agreed."

Osborne grinned as the others walked away. "Big brother is still quite protective of you."

Evan's face burned. "No more than you are of Fleur and Lady Julia."

"Why her, Woolf? Of all the women in England, why did it have to be her?"

Evan thought for one heart-stopping moment that maybe Osborne was in love with her, but quickly discarded the thought. He has always been like that with the girls, even when they were children.

"What's happened to you, Osborne? We used to be friends, remember?"

"That was before."

"Before what?" Evan asked, genuinely confused.

"Before everything!" Osborne shouted. "Before you tore her heart out and carelessly waltzed all over it. Why would I trust you with it now?" He stopped and ran his hand over his jaw. "Why did you leave? I never understood, and neither did Fleur."

Evan shifted his stance, stalling for time. Every time he explained his reasoning for leaving, the weaker the excuse felt to him. "I was just a fool child, for God's sake, Andrew," he implored. "I'm not going to treat her that way now, you know. We're adults."

"Won't you? I will have your word on that or I'll end you. Do we understand one another?"

"Yes, I swear I will take care of her the way she deserves, or I will put my own face in range of your bloody fist, all right?"

"My pistols damn you. I'll not bother with fisticuffs if you hurt her. Mind you keep that close to your heart."

Evan swallowed and nodded.

"I heard of your heroics at the ball. I guess I should be thankful you saved her from being injured... so, thank you."

Evan laughed, not able to help it. It was all just so absurd, the whole of it.

Andrew looked at him hard. "Do you love her?"

Evan stopped laughing, his smile fading from his face. "What?"

"I asked, do you love my cousin?" Evan squirmed at his interrogation.

"That is a bit personal, don't you think?"

Andrew shook his head. "I still don't like you."

Evan watched him walk towards the other men, irritated with himself for being slightly in awe of how Osborne did not seem the least bit intimidated to walk over there, considering everyone was either Evan's own family or close friend.

He looked down at his hand. Now that the urgency of the moment was over it was starting to ache, though the blood had dried. He wondered how on Earth he was ever supposed to spend time alone with his wife now that one more obstacle, a very large one, stood in their path.

20

HOUSE WITHOUT A NAME

Evan stood alone in the corner and watched his father's cue ball drive into Julian's red, sinking a perfect hazard play. The duke had lost once again, and Evan wondered if he'd ever learn. His father lived and breathed the game in winter, and he'd yet to meet anyone who could best him.

"What are you thinking about?"

Evan turned towards Nathan. "Hmm, just wondering why anyone bets against my father when they know he never loses."

"Come now," Nathan scoffed. "You've been off over here on your own for half an hour. Tell me what you're really thinking."

"Osborne's an unsocial bastard, isn't he?"

Nathan looked to the opposite corner of the room where the officer stood off alone.

"No more than you. Why? Afraid he might ask you for another dance?"

Evan's smiled. "No, it is just with everything and everyone, I'm lucky to spend ten minutes alone a day with Fleur.

I didn't talk to her at all during dinner and after everyone was playing whist. How does one ever find a match at these things? No one is ever alone."

"I see your dilemma. Why don't you just speak to her at night when no one else is around?"

Evan looked skyward. "Oh, yes, I'll just accost her in her sleep and ask her what her favorite color is. She won't be alarmed at all."

"She's already asleep, then, when you come round?"

"Yes, though even if she wasn't, it would be awkward at best. What if she thinks I'm about to..." Evan waved his hand around.

"Ah, I see, but well, someday you will have to..." Nathan said, repeating the gesture.

Evan laughed. "Yes, but not now. I'd like to at least have one conversation longer than ten minutes before..."

"Yes, before..." Nathan agreed.

"There is only one solution then. You must take her away from here. Go honeymoon somewhere."

"Who is honeymooning where?" asked Felix, walking over with Edward and Dom.

Nathan looked around. "Where is Oliver?"

"He felt sorry for the captain standing off on his own, so he went to make conversation."

Evan looked over and nearly winced when he saw an irritated Osborne and a cowed Oliver. "Poor bastard," said Evan.

"He has never met him before, so he wasn't to know," defended Nathan.

Evan snorted. "Yes, because making an entrance by pummeling one of the guests give off a friendly air. Amiable the man is not."

Everyone laughed.

"I'm still waiting to hear about this honeymoon," Felix interrupted.

"I'm trying to convince Romeo here," Nathan said as he backhanded Evan in the chest, "to run off with his bride so they can get a moment's peace."

Edward nodded. "It is a good idea, what with her father and now cousin in residence. Not a very romantic setting, is it?"

"I tried asking her to accompany me in the solarium, nearly made it too until Captain Chucklehead showed up. He actually wedged himself between us on the settee."

Edward shook his head, smirking. "You're not very good at this wooing business are you, Evan?"

"Says the man who swore at her during his own proposal of marriage." Evan snickered when Nathan, Dom, and Felix again laughed.

Felix wiped a tear from his eye. "Oh, God, did you really?"

Edward flushed, cleared his throat and looked away, his long hair swinging under its ribbon. "Yes, well, we're not discussing me, are we? What are you going to do, Evan?"

Evan smiled, taking pity on Edward's plight, and took the change of subject in stride. "I guess I can take her to the new estate. It *is* close."

"Are you mad?" Nathan asked his face a perfect picture of disbelief. "You can't take her there."

"Why ever not?"

"Because it's a catastrophe. The walls need plastering, and you've no furnishings whatsoever. Where will you eat? Who will even make the food?"

"It is not so bad. Besides, I had a letter this morning from my steward. At my request, he has found a housekeeper, a cook, and a few servants. They have been there for a fortnight already."

Nathan stood and stared in astonishment. "Tell him, Edward. Tell him it would be completely inappropriate to take the lady there."

Edward looked between the two. "I have yet to visit. Is it that awful?"

"Yes," said Nathan.

"No, it is not," Evan countered. "The matter is settled. I will go up early and speak to her about it, and we will leave in the morning if she agrees.

"What will you tell mother?" asked Edward.

"I'll tell her they needed me on some urgent business. It's time I stayed and oversaw the renovations, and Fleur should be part of those decisions."

Nathan rubbed his forehead before throwing his hands in the air. "God save me from fools and stubborn brothers. This is a terrible idea I tell you."

Evan looked at Nathan. "Yes, but when did I ever listen to you?"

Nathan shook his head. "It's your marriage."

Evan nodded. Settling his plans for tomorrow in his mind, he turned to leave when Oliver walked up.

"The captain's not a very agreeable sort of fellow, is he?" he asked, looking relieved to have escaped.

Evan laughed all the way out the door and until he reached the stairs. Not very agreeable, indeed.

———

Fleur tossed and turned in bed, wishing she could read her book, but she had already blown out her bedside candle, and her thoughts were making her restless.

She reached up and touched her lips, trying to replicate the gentle brush Evan had given them earlier. At the thought, she rolled around in the bed, hugging her pillow, landing on her stomach, her face full of her own hair, muffling her giggles.

He had tried to kiss her today, and he would have if not for Andrew. But things had been easier between them, and they had spent some time alone together before Andrew's arrival. The smile slipped from her face, and she turned her head and slammed it down on her pillow as she huffed. She knew her cousin would never leave them alone. Evan would be lucky if he weren't black-and-blue before they left.

She tossed again, sitting up before gathering her hair in her hand, twisting it to throw it behind her head. Looking at the door, she counted to five. If he came in before she was finished, she would wait up for him, and if not she would just feign sleep as she had done before.

One, she thought. He was probably still drinking and playing cards with the others. *Two*. The ladies had left for bed more than an hour ago. *Three*, she wondered what the men talked about when ladies weren't present. *Four*, did they gossip? Surely they did. *And five*, he hadn't come.

She sighed and lay back down. Just as she reached down to pull her blanket up higher, she heard the door. Lying still, she held her eyes closed, her breathing slow and steady, motionless.

She heard him walk up to the bed, much as he did that first night. "Fleur," he whispered.

She lay there frozen. What should she do?

"Fleur, are you awake? I need to speak to you."

Her eyes popped open, and he was standing right in front of her. She raised her eyes to his, and she scooted upwards, sitting up and propping herself up on her pillow to listen.

She waited, and when he looked like he regretted rousing her, she gave him a small smile, hoping it would urge him to speak, but he remained silent.

"What is it?" she finally asked.

He reached out a hand to steady himself as he sat on the end of the bed, and when he felt her foot, he whipped his hand away and sprang from his seat. "Forgive me, I ..."

She tucked her feet up under her and leaned forward. "Please sit; tell me what's on your mind."

He sat down again and rubbed his chin, where a small shadow of a beard showed. She thought it handsome.

"You know when we were children, it was so easy to find ways to escape everyone, except maybe Julia. She had a talent for finding us wherever we were, did she not?" He chuckled at the memory as Fleur smiled. She could not deny it was true. "It's different now, of course. We have not had a very easy time finding ways to be alone, have we?"

She laughed. "With Andy in residence, we should not expect that to change anytime soon."

"My thoughts precisely. What if we were to leave here? We could go to my estate, our estate. It is not far, as I told you."

She stared into his eyes, surprised, and said nothing.

"Of course, we don't have to leave," he said, looking more uncomfortable by the moment. "I just thought maybe we could..."

She watched him struggle for words, and at that moment she knew she would say yes, that she would follow him anywhere.

"Forget I said anything, really," he smiled, but she saw

hurt in his eyes, and when he went to stand, she reached forward and laid her hand on his arm, stopping him.

"When should I be ready?" she asked. When he didn't answer right away, she gently shook his arm. "Evan?"

"Oh, in the morning? Say about eleven? Everyone should be up and about by then so we can say our goodbyes."

She nodded. "I will be ready."

He slid his hand over hers, grasping it before letting go, allowing her hand to slip from his arm. He stood and walked over towards the other side of the room to ready himself for bed as she slid back down under the covers, once again pushing her hair behind her head.

She wished she were brave enough to ask him to stay, but she was nowhere near that bold. She flushed thinking about their almost-kiss earlier and wondered if one day she would ever be so bold as to kiss him first.

She raised the covers over her lips to hide her smile. She felt silly for thinking such things, but she knew she wanted to finally be kissed by someone, and for that someone to be Evan.

———

FLEUR HUGGED JULIA, already having said goodbye to the other girls. Phoebe told her to be sure to write, while Prudence told her to look after her health. Charity held on a bit too tight and a bit too long, and Fleur felt a moment's regret at leaving her alone.

Julia held her closer. "I feel like I'll never see you again."

"We will see each other for Christmas if not before."

"It is not the same," whispered Julia.

Fleur backed away and placed her gloved hands on

Julia's face. "I know. Be good to Papa. Make sure he doesn't eat too many sweets throughout the day. You will be in charge of the accounts and the house now. Also, make sure he does not stay up too late only to get up at dawn."

"I will, I promise."

"Write to me often, and promise me something?"

Julia reached up and placed her hands on top of Fleur's. "Anything, just name it."

"Stop picking on poor Mr. Carter," Fleur smiled when Julia flushed.

Julia leaned forward and kissed her cheek. "Oh, off with you, Papa is waiting."

"Goodbye, Julia," she said, returning the kiss.

She walked over towards the carriage. Evan was already there, shaking her father's hand.

"I will, I swear it," she heard him say before turning to look at her. He nodded at her father and then stepped up into the carriage, giving them privacy.

Julian held out his hands for hers and grasped them lightly when she placed them into his palms. "I knew this day would come, but I find myself shamefully unprepared."

"Papa," she simply said, at a loss of what to say.

"I don't know how Julia and I will get on without you. We might murder one another within a fortnight."

Fleur laughed. "You will be here for another two weeks, so I give it a month."

He pulled her forward and hugged her tight. "Be safe and write often. Madeleine has already invited us for Christmas, so it won't be long before we see each other again."

"Yes." It was all she could say, afraid the tears she held may fall.

She kissed him on the cheek, and then he helped her into the carriage.

"Madeleine asked me to inform you that she is sending one of her maids to attend you until you can make arrangements for your own," he said, closing the box door.

She leaned forward out of the window, taking his hand once more.

"Tell her thank you, and tell Julia I love her."

"I will."

"I love you, Papa," she said before leaning back into the carriage. Evan leaned forward, tilting his head to the duke.

Her father let go of her hand and rapped on the side of the carriage, and she knew she did not imagine it when his voice was just a little bit rough when he said, "drive on."

———

At first, the ride had been blessedly silent because she knew if she spoke, she would weep. She would miss them terribly, but she did not want Evan to feel responsible for her tears.

Though now she was starting to feel a bit anxious, and she wished he would just say something, anything. She took a deep breath and decided to take the situation into her own hands. "How long have you had ownership of ... oh, you never told me what the estate is called."

Evan who had spent the majority of the trip looking out of the window straightened and turned towards her. "It doesn't have a name."

She blinked. "But... of course it has a name."

Evan laughed. "It was built in 1718, and the owners never took residence, so it was closed up and left to ruin.

The family kept a steward on, and he did what he could, like his father before him."

"But why would someone build a grand house only to let it sit unoccupied?"

"New money, I suppose, wanting to impress? Almost a hundred years later it is old money now, is it not? They probably even have a title by now."

"Only a hundred years?"

"Why, Fleur, I had no idea you were such a nob."

She laughed. "But how will we bear the shame of living in such a home?"

He grinned.

"But really, it must have a name or else we will never receive the mail. What do you call your London home?"

"I call it *My London Home*."

Her breath quickened at the smirk he was giving her. "You are going to make this difficult, aren't you?"

"Probably."

He scratched his whiskers and relented at the flat look she was giving him. "Oh all right, if we must," he said, secretly having the time of his life. "How about Wolfham Hall?" repeating one of the horrid names Felix had mentioned to him earlier.

She curled her lips inward trying not to smile. "Evan, that's horrid."

"Is it? How about HighWolf Turret?"

"No, absolutely not."

"Then you try. It's not as easy as it looks."

She pulled on the tips of her gloves, pulling them off one finger at a time. After all, one could not think with gloves on. "How about Wolffert Lodge?"

He laughed, throwing back his head, and she smiled at him. Making him laugh felt wonderful.

"I didn't know you had it in you," he said.

She grinned. "I have my moments."

"You really are not very good at this. Keep it up, and I won't let you have any say in naming our children."

Her eyes widened slightly, and he cleared his throat.

"In all seriousness," he said, quickly changing the subject, "we probably should come up with a proper name, but let us wait until you see it."

Fleur nodded. "How much longer, do you suppose?"

Evan leaned forward and looked outside as they took a turn. "Look... right about... now."

She bent forward, placing her hands upon the box window, and exhaled. The house sat atop a perfectly situated hill, with large trees that lined the drive in invitation. The house itself was a red-brick Palladian, and while it must once have been stark white, the trim had become muted with time. There were three stories, though the house was not overly grand. *It was just perfect*, she thought, and it was her very own. "It's breathtaking," she said.

He agreed, but it was not the house that held his attentions, but her wide blue eyes and the look of wonder on her face. It was a sight to behold, and he considered himself lucky he would be able to see her grow older and more beautiful with age. *By some miracle*, he thought, *life started now.*

21

THE WEASEL

It was mid-afternoon when they arrived, and Evan was famished and ached for a fresh bowl of cool water to wash his overly warm face.

As the carriage rolled to a stop, Evan opened the door and jumped down, turning to help Fleur down the steps a young boy brought forward.

Evan watched as the boy stood back and watched in wonderment as Fleur descended.

He probably has never seen a lady before, not with all the trimmings, Evan thought.

"And what is your name?" he asked.

"Thomas, sir, but they call me Little Thomas 'cause I'm named after me father."

"I see, and where is Big Thomas?"

"Here, Mr. Woolf, Thomas Briggs," he introduced himself, nodding at first Evan and then Fleur. He was a large man, his shoulders square, his face tanned and freckled, his red hair slightly receding.

"Forgive me for not making it in time to greet you, but

we was all in a tizzy trying to make ready for your arrival. We had little notice, sir."

Evan detected a bit of pique, but Thomas would soon learn that was just his way. Evan cared not if he was waited upon at his door, but then he remembered he was a married man now and that kind of thinking would no longer suit.

"Yes, my apologies for that, Briggs, but my wife and I had need to come early. This is she, Lady —"

"Mrs. Woolf please, I would prefer to be called Mrs. Woolf," she interrupted. Thomas and his son bowed as Fleur smiled at them both.

Evan wondered why that made his stomach do a little waltz.

"As you please, madam."

"I was told my mother-in-law sent a maid this morning, has she arrived?"

Briggs nodded. "She was also accompanied by a Mr. Stewart. He said he was an under-butler at Blackburn Hall and was to help you set up house."

Evan should have known his mother would sneak in one more servant. "Yes, that sounds like my mother. I think I might just keep him on. It will serve her right for meddling and will save me the trouble of finding a new man."

"Evan," Fleur scolded behind a smile.

He turned towards her. "She should have known better. In fact, I bet she hoped I would. Are the others inside?"

He ushered Fleur towards the front entryway, and Big Thomas followed.

"Yes, my wife is currently at the cottage making it ready for your arrival and my mother is inside the kitchen, taking on the duties of cook as well as head housekeeper for the moment."

"The cottage was opened? What on earth for?"

"The house, sir, we only arrived a fortnight ago and have barely had time to make repairs on the servant floor. It seemed appropriate to make those a priority so we could staff the house while other renovations are being made."

"Yes, makes sense, but what about my quarters? The upstairs sitting rooms?"

"None of it has been touched yet, sir. We figured you would want a say in how it was remade." Thomas cleared his throat before continuing. "The cottage has been well-maintained, sir, and has many rooms you can make use of while we start the major repairs. It has two sitting rooms. No proper dining room, but it does have a small breakfast room."

Evan nodded and took Fleur all the way inside the home. He watched as she marveled at the beautiful wall coverings that had been left to ruin and peel from the plaster. Evan took in his surroundings, and finally, with Fleur standing in the middle of all the dilapidation, he could he see what Nathan has been trying to tell him.

He coughed, the dust in the air tickling his nose. "The cottage is fine, I am sure, Briggs. Thank you for having the foresight I lacked. I underestimated what needed to be done here."

Thomas nodded and held his arm out towards the door. "Would you prefer to drive to the cottage or to walk?"

"Oh, please, let us walk," Fleur interrupted. "I don't know if my legs can stand another minute in the carriage."

"Seems like we are walking," said Evan.

Fleur looked over the grounds and fell in love for the second time. The house, while in disarray now, would be wonderful when finished, and the grounds themselves were lush and green. She could see a pond with beautiful willow trees reaching towards the water, and she felt the urge to run there and sit in the shade.

The cottage itself was quaint, red brick matching the large home, green shutters framing the windows covered in mature vines. Thomas opened the white gate that closed in the small courtyard surrounding the cottage. She loved it, all of it. She could easily imagine raising a family here, inviting her father and sister over for holidays and christenings. Life was going to be peaceful here. She knew it.

———

THAT NIGHT FLEUR sat in the morning room of the cottage, finally feeling rested. She lifted her warm tea to her lips and was thankful to finally have a moment to breathe as she knew the next several weeks would be chaotic.

After they had arrived at the cottage, Thomas had left them to freshen up but then he returned with the layout and plans of the main home. He and Evan poured over them for hours while she had a small nap.

Over dinner, Evan had told her what he and Thomas discussed and asked her opinions. They were going to share the responsibility he told her. He would take on the structure and outside of the home, and she, the interior.

She thought when they married, that she would come here and fade into the background of his life, but he was determined to include her. She wouldn't just be running the house; it was to be someplace she could feel at home.

She took another sip of tea and looked over to him asleep in a large wingback chair. His head had fallen to the side, leaning against the patterned fabric.

She stood and walked over to him. Touching his brow,

she pushed his dark hair up and behind his ear. "You must be so exhausted," she said. "Evan? Evan, wake up."

When he did not stir, she sighed, and decided not to wake him. He would only move from this chair to another in their room, so what was the use? She pulled a knitted throw from the sidearm of the matching chair beside him and draped it over him.

Fleur was grateful for the courtesy he was showing her, but tomorrow, she decided, tomorrow when they retired, she would ask him to stay, to sleep beside her in their bed.

She walked around the room blowing out candles and leaving one to light her way upstairs. "Goodnight, Evan," she said, leaning down to kiss the corner of his lips before taking the candle and making her way to the bedroom before what she had just done could really dawn on her.

FLEUR LOOKED IN THE MIRROR, fiddling with the loose tendrils of hair escaping the braids placed in her hair by her new maid. She then smoothed down her pink muslin dress, while wondering if Evan was having breakfast or if he had gone to start the day.

She left the room and made her way downstairs to the breakfast room, and she was glad to see him there. He had finished eating and was leaning back in his chair with his eyes closed, and his hands folded on his chest.

She wondered if he was asleep. "Evan?"

His eyes slowly opened halfway and he smiled, slowly, up at her. She flushed as he just sat and stared, then she started as he frowned and popped out of his chair suddenly. She laughed.

"I don't require you stand upon my arrival to breakfast,

especially if you're going to make a habit of sleeping at the table."

He smiled and rubbed the back of his head. "Forgive me. I did not sleep well."

"I did try to wake you before I went up."

"Yes, I noticed the blanket. Thank you."

She looked down and away from his piercing dark eyes, then nodded. "Will you be at home this morning or..." She waved her hand in the air.

"I will be with Briggs, we're going to survey the damage to the eastern wall while the sun is still in our favor, then there are plenty of other things. What are your plans today?"

She loaded her plate from the sideboard then sat down, disappointed she would not see him until dinner. "I think I will walk the grounds then later come into the main house and take notes of furnishings we will need. We don't need to do everything now, but the downstairs living areas and at least three of the bedchambers should be done immediately so we can have guests. The rest can be done at a more sedate pace."

Evan nodded. "Agreed."

He walked around the table to her, and she thought for the briefest moment he was going to lean down to kiss her cheek. She waited, but in the end, he placed his hand on her shoulder and patted her before rushing towards the door.

"I was thinking," he said, hesitating at the doorway. "I won't be with Briggs all day, and I am willing to wager there are some interesting things in the attic we could use. Care to go hunting later?"

Her eyes widened. "What do you think could be in there?"

"No way to know. The house was never lived in, but was

fully furnished at one time. I bet we find a treasure trove up there."

Her spirits were raised as she quickly accepted. She smiled at him when he nodded to her before leaving the room and thought, *Perhaps the day will not be so dull after all.*

———

FLEUR WALKED around the big house taking note of needs and wants for each room, hoping they could fill many of those needs with things from the attic as there was a very long list. She finally made her way upstairs, past the servant's floor, and stopped in front of the attic.

She had intended to wait for Evan, she really did, but curiosity won out, and she swung open the door.

Fleur gasped. There were hundreds of items scattered all around all covered in dusty white linen. Paintings, mirrors, furniture, and who knew what else.

She ran her hand over what looked to be a covered round table, landing on a small lamp. She lifted it, trying to see the maker's mark, excitement running through her. "I wonder why they didn't take all this when they cleared the bottom floors to sell."

"Who knows," said Evan, giving Fleur the fright of her life.

She clutched her chest and breathed slowly through her nose, trying not to lose her wits. "Good heavens, Evan, I nearly threw this at you."

He laughed, and she slammed the lamp down on a nearby wooden crate.

Evan looked around, taking it all in. "All this must be decades old, maybe even as old has the house."

"Possibly older if they purchased antiques," Fleur said.

"Shall we?" she asked, motioning to the table she was eyeing before.

Evan nodded and grasped the large linen covering, flinging the fabric off. Fleur stared.

It was a painstakingly crafted table with hundreds of diamond-shaped marble inlays covering the surface and the sides. The legs were carved ornately out of a beautiful dark mahogany. It might have been beautiful, but it was not. Dozens of colors clashed with each other, the inlays on top seemed to be made from every possible marble one could think of, and the grains were unmatched. It was, in short, hideous.

Fleur swallowed. "Have you ever seen anything like it?"

Evan stared, unsure what to say about the offending table in case Fleur genuinely liked it. "No. No, I cannot say that I have."

"The craftsmanship is stunning."

"That is true," was all Evan could bring himself to say.

"You hate it, don't you?" she asked, praying he said yes.

"I... well ..."

"Oh, please say you hate it, Evan."

"I can honestly say I have never hated a table so much in my life."

She laughed and looked around, her once-excited dreams of finding beautiful furnishings turning into fear. "What if it's all like this? How will we ever get rid of it?"

"There is only one way to find out." Fleur held her breath as Evan walked over to another piece and ripped the linen away. She breathed. It was a dining room sideboard, a perfectly normal sideboard.

"Well, that will be useful," said Evan. "I bet there are other dining room pieces around in here somewhere to match it."

Fleur was about to agree when she heard a thumping noise coming from inside the sideboard. "What was that?"

Evan walked over and grasped Fleur's arm. "I do not know, but maybe we should leave it be."

Fleur laughed. "Don't tell me you are frightened?"

"Of course not, but you know these old homes — what if there are bats in here?" he asked, looking around the ceiling as if a bat were ready to dive at him any moment.

Fleur gave him a skeptical look. "In the sideboard? It's probably only a mouse."

"Must be one enormous mouse," he muttered.

She walked towards the sideboard, and he stopped her. "I will go."

He slowly walked over, kneeling down, preparing to open the doors of the cabinet. "Step back a bit," he said.

He took a few quick, short breaths and quickly opened the door, only to quickly slam it shut again. "It's a weasel."

"A weasel?" she exclaimed. "How on earth does a weasel find its way into an attic?"

"No idea, perhaps it—"

Evan trailed off as another thump sounded, this one larger and more urgent. He looked at the sideboard door as it shuddered before settling back again.

Just as he was about to again suggest they leave, the weasel burst forth through the door further to the end and shot towards him with a loud screech.

Evan stood and ran towards Fleur, his arms flailing wildly. Once he reached her, he flung her over his shoulder without so much as a by-your-leave and ran through the attic door before slamming it shut.

Breathing hard, he leaned his shoulder into the wall while Fleur tried to orient herself while remaining upside down which was hard to do when wheezing in laughter.

"Evan?" she asked, trying to crane her neck around to see while collecting herself. "I think you can put me down now."

He leaned forward slightly and allowed her body to slide down his own, slowly and carefully until he heard her feet touch the floor. They stayed like that for a moment, his hand on her waist, and she looked up at him, amused.

He cleared his throat, and took a step backward as if to see her better. "I'll have it cleared out, and the rest of the attic opened and checked, along with all the rooms."

"They won't hurt it, will they?"

"By no means, but I don't want you up here alone until the men go over it."

Fleur smiled and then giggled, trying her best not to cackle, but she lost and laughed madly. "Forgive me, Evan, but you should have seen your face."

Evan smiled at her then laughed along. "I suppose I did look rather silly."

She nodded, grin still in place.

"Well, I'm famished, how about you? I would say some dinner is in order as the sun is starting to set."

The thought of the setting sun made her nervous since the time to retire approached, but she vowed not to cower when Evan came to their room. Tonight she would ask him to join her, and while she felt a little anxious at the thought, the appeal of him holding her, maybe even kissing her, let her know that she was ready.

———

"You seem tired," Evan said to her as he shuffled papers around on the end tables the servants had shoved together, providing him a makeshift desk so he would not have to keep clearing their breakfast table after insisting Fleur make use of the one writing desk in the morning room.

Fleur sat in a chair with her book closed on her lap. She opened her eyes and blinked. "I am. I don't normally stand on my feet for hours cataloging. I had fun going through all the rooms, but who knew it would be so draining."

He walked over and grasped her hand in his own, an affectionate overture they had become comfortable with. "Why don't you go up to bed? I won't be much longer."

She nodded and walked through the room to leave. As she reached the stairs, she wondered what he would do while she readied herself for bed. *Have a drink?* She wondered. She wished she could have one, her nerves tightening with the thought of what she would ask him that evening.

When she reached their room, she slipped inside and closed the door softly, ringing for her maid as she walked further into the room. She couldn't wait to slide into bed and relieve her aching feet.

She slipped out of her shoes and sat upon her bed, lifting her skirts to unfasten her stockings. She heard her maid come in and she silently stood to undress. As she was worked out of her dress and stays, she thought about Evan. How he would come upstairs into their room when he thought she was already asleep, and how he would slip into the chair by the window. Tonight that would change.

She raised her arms as the maid slipped her nightgown over her head, and she turned to be tied. She thanked and dismissed her before sitting down to brush out her hair and wash her hands and face, taking her time and hoping Evan would come up soon if she dawdled.

She felt somewhat silly delaying any longer, so she

climbed into bed, rubbing the soles of her feet on the cool soft sheets, trying to soothe the ache.

It had felt like hours before she heard the turning of the doorknob, and when she did she held her breath, closed her eyes and then exhaled before sitting up and looking at him.

He stopped in the middle of the room and shrugged out of his coat, and when he turned to see her sitting there awake, he stared into her eyes, surprised. Embarrassed, she looked down at her lap and played with the sleeve of her gown.

"I thought you would be asleep by now," he said, reaching for his cravat.

"My feet ache," she said simply, "and I wanted to ask you something."

He slid the scarf from his neck and threw it on the chair with the coat. "Oh?" he asked, walking towards her.

He sat down at the foot of the bed, reaching to push the covers up. Before she could protest, he grabbed one of her feet and brought it to his lap.

"W-what are you doing?" she asked. "You don't have to—"

"Allow me," he said as he slowly kneaded the arch of her foot. "What was it you wanted to discuss?" He moved down to her heel, rotating his thumb and applying slight pressure.

She swallowed and gripped her hands in her lap. How was she going to ask him to stay now? When he was touching her like that?

"Give me your other foot," he said, breaking into her thoughts.

"What?"

"The other one, this one feels better now, does it not?"

She flexed her foot, rolling it from side to side. "Oh, yes

it does." They looked at each other as she brought her other foot around and placed it in his hands.

She watched as he first gently touched the bottom of each of her toes, moving down to the arch of her foot, rubbing upwards before again rubbing her heel.

"You were saying?" he prompted.

"I was thinking... Evan, I want you to stay here tonight."

He looked at her, confused, and she waited patiently for him to understand. When he did, his hands stopped. "Are you certain?"

She nodded. "We are going to spend our lives together, there is nothing untoward about..."

She could not bring herself to finish, and she hated that she sounded so missish. "I trust you," she said softly.

He looked at her for a moment before standing, while she slipped down further into bed and settled on her side as he blew out the candle, the room going dark.

She heard the rustling sound of cloth, and as her eyes accustomed themselves to the moonlight, she caught sight of him. He was wearing his trousers and his white shirt, loosened, as he had done since the first night, but this time she looked her fill, as he leaned towards her, slipping into the bed on his knee as he sat slowly. He raised the blanket and slid underneath.

She had not realized how close he would be, how small the bed became once they both were inside. They lay there, she facing him and he on his back. Suddenly he rolled to his side, and she saw he was surprised at how close their faces were.

"Hello, there," he said.

She laughed. The tension in her stiffened shoulders eased.

She raised her eyes to his when she felt him reach across

and take her hand in his own. She watched as he twined their fingers together, moving his thumb in small circles over the soft inside of her palm before moving down to her wrist.

He raised her arm slowly, bringing it towards him, and he laid a delicate kiss to the inside of her wrist.

Her breath hitched ever so slightly, and looking into his eyes she felt him move their hands down between them, laid next to his chest. She tucked her head further down under his chin, closing her eyes and squeezing his hand gently as she made herself comfortable.

They fell asleep that way, her hand in his, as they finally faced one another.

22

THE CHICKEN

Evan's eyes were closed, but he could feel the first signs of the sun beaming into the room to wake him. He felt warm, much warmer than usual. He blinked, trying to open his eyes fully as he stirred, but he did not get far. His arms were full, one pinned and the other clinging as his cheek rested upon something soft that was definitely not his pillow.

He moved his hand down and felt the curve of her soft waist, and as his hand moved further he followed the trail of an arm to a hand that clutched his own chest, clasped tightly onto his shirt. His eyes flew wide, and he calmed when he remembered he was sharing a bed with Fleur.

Sometime during the night they had become entangled with one another. His arms wrapped about her waist and her head tucked under his chin as she held onto him.

He knew she would be frightfully embarrassed if she woke and discovered their positions, but part of him wanted her to wake so he could see her blush prettily, see how she would react to his touch.

He knew he wanted her, to make love to her, wanted to

woo her, but that was not entirely true either. What he really wanted was to tell her that he loved her. That he was happy he had married her, and that having the honor of spending his life with her meant everything to him, and he wanted to tell her now.

He wondered if it was time, and he knew the answer was yes, he only needed the proper time and setting. Tonight he would confess his feelings to her.

He closed his eyes, willing his own state of need to abate. He heard her take a deep breath and sigh, having no idea how the heat of her breath on his chest affected him.

Knowing it was time to leave, he reached up and uncurled her fingers from his shirt and slid his arm from beneath her. She shivered slightly, the loss of his warmth obvious to her even in her sleep.

He pulled the blankets higher to cover her, lingering for a moment longer before dressing for the day. He had to hurry if he wanted to breakfast. He still had a lot of work to accomplish, and now a romantic evening to plan.

———

FLEUR OPENED HER EYES, hunger slowly waking her, and the first thing she realized was that Evan was gone. She could not help but think back to their first night together when she had awakened alone. She wondered if they were back to square one when he would run away anytime something changed between them, and she hoped she was wrong.

She rolled to her side and saw a letter resting atop Evan's pillow. Thinking it odd, she picked up the letter and turned it over in her hand. The front said only *Fleur*.

Forgetting her hunger, she ripped into the missive, smiling when she saw it was Evan's handwriting.

•   •   •

My lady,

By now you are awake and probably cross with me. Please know I did not want to leave you this morning, but I had urgent business with Briggs.

I would like to invite you to join me this evening for dinner. It is very fine out, as you will have noticed, and I have asked the staff to provide us a light dinner of your choosing that we can take out-of-doors. I will be waiting for you by the willow trees looking over the pond. Shall we say sunset?

Forever yours,

Evan

SHE FOLDED the note again and held it in her hand, sliding it under her pillow. She smiled; Evan was trying to woo her, and the thought made her giddy. She knew she should probably try to fall asleep again, but she also knew she would never be able to. Excitement filled her, and she pulled the letter out and read it twice more, smiling at his closing, before readying herself for the day.

Later that afternoon, she sat in the morning room reading. It was a little past noon, and Evan was off somewhere with Mr. Briggs, plotting the land for new rent homes to be built next spring.

She had tried thinking about decor for the big house, tried writing letters, and now she tried reading. In short, she was bored, but no, it was more than that. She was excited about her outing with Evan later that night and could not sit still.

She closed her book and stood to return it to its place on the small low shelves that lined the room on both sides of the fireplace. She slid the book into place and then huffed, standing there turning and looking at the clutter of Evan's papers.

What was she to do now? She was so used the bustle of servants, to Julia prattling in her ear, and even her father. She missed them, that was certain, but mostly she needed to find something to occupy herself.

She could take a walk to town, but that would take up too much of the afternoon, and she wanted to take her time dressing tonight, for him she realized. She wanted him to find her beautiful, to know she had taken special care.

She walked over to the window and stared outside into the front garden when it dawned on her. Pudding. She had completely forgotten to add it to the menu. She walked to the back of the cottage and made her way into the kitchen and smiled, running her hand along the wood table in the middle of the room.

When she was younger, before her mother passed, they would spend time in the kitchen. Her mother was never what one would call a conventional English lady, being from France, and Fleur laughed thinking how much Julia resembled her, in looks and in manner.

"Can I help you, milady?" Cook asked as she rolled and crushed fresh strawberries.

Her hair was white and her smiling face was open and friendly, and Fleur remembered that she was Briggs' mother.

"Mrs. Briggs, how are you getting along? Adjusting well?"

"Of course, milady, though I will be happier once we're all in the big house. This kitchen is small, the fire smokes something fierce, and the windows are too high for me to open properly, but I get along all right."

Fleur smiled at the woman's forthright manner and instantly liked her. She reminded her of Mrs. Davis back at Norfield. "I'm glad to hear it. I came down to ask about supper. It seems as if I completely forgot about dessert. Is there anything that can be done? Nothing fancy, but maybe you have some tarts or something lying about?"

Cook smiled. "Don't you worry about that, milady, I've planned to prepare some berry tarts, perfect for handling outdoors, they are. And Mr. Woolf said they were your favorite, he did. I was just on my way out for some more eggs to start them when you came in."

Fleur wondered when Evan had spoken to Mrs. Briggs about her affinity for strawberries and realized he must have sneakily told cook this morning to prepare them for her. "That is perfect, thank you for thinking of it. Though let me go and fetch the eggs, you are so busy." Fleur turned to walk outside but faltered at the cook's shocked face.

"I can't be sending you out to fetch and carry for me, milady!"

"I assure you it's fine, I always did at home when I was younger, and I am well familiar with a chicken coop."

"That's different. A child is a child, and a lady is a lady, and it would not be fitting..."

Cook trailed off at the disappointed look on Fleur's face.

"Oh, please, Mrs. Briggs, I am going absolutely mad with nothing to do."

Cook sighed and nodded. "Very well, but mind you be careful. It won't do for you to slip and dirty your dress."

Fleur beamed. "I will, I promise."

She picked up a basket next to the outer door and walked outside. Glad of something to do, she practically skipped down to the barn.

She took her time, looking around the property with a

leisurely walk, but came to a stop when she heard voices and loud banging coming from the stables.

"We will need more wood before we can mend the other stall, Briggs. Hold this like so, would you, Little Thomas?"

Fleur hid behind the large doors as she looked inside and watched Evan hammering on a stable door. His shirt was loose with no cravat, coat, or waistcoat in sight. His sleeves were pushed up to his elbows, rolled to stay in place.

She had seen Evan several times now in the same state of undress, but she had never seen him like *this*.

His brow glistened with sweat, the muscles of his forearm flexed as he lifted a long heavy board, helping Little Thomas hold it steady while he grasped the hammer and affixed it into place.

She moved forward slightly to have a better look, and the gravel under her feet sounded her arrival.

Evan looked up away from his work and saw her. "Fleur? What are you doing down here?"

He set down the hammer and jogged towards her, wiping his brow as he stopped in front of her.

"I was on my way to gather some eggs for Mrs. Briggs when I heard the noise."

Mr. Briggs stepped forward. "My mother sent you for eggs? Please accept my apologies—"

"No, please, I offered. Truth be told, I'm going a bit mad shut up in the cottage."

"Still, it is a strange thing," said Evan. "A duke's daughter fetching eggs," he teased.

"Sort of like an earl's son mending stable doors?"

Evan laughed. "Touché."

He turned around to address both Thomases. "Briggs,

we're done here for now. I don't think that mare will be able to escape again. Make note of the lumber we need to mend the other stalls, won't you? I'll escort Mrs. Woolf to the coop and find you later."

"Of course, sir."

Evan walked Fleur out of the stable as he heard Big Thomas ask Little Thomas how many pieces of lumber they had left in storage. As a steward, Mr. Briggs has been a Godsend. He was well educated in all matters of running an estate, but he was not above getting his hands dirty while they were short staffed. Evan liked that about him.

"How are things coming along?" asked Fleur.

"Slowly, but we are making progress. You will be happy to know that we now have enough stables in repair to stop the horses from fleeing, and we have more staff coming this weekend for you to interview, and a slew of carpenters, plasterers, and others will be here Monday to begin the real work. You won't have time for idleness then, I'm afraid."

She laughed, and then pretended offense. "I have not been idle. What is one to do until the work begins?"

Evan nodded. "Fetch eggs, I suppose. I think Mrs. Briggs may be in for a scolding from her son later."

Fleur sighed. "I really did force her, you know," she said as she reached forward to open the wooden door to the chicken coop.

"Allow me," said Evan. He swung the gate open as he looked at her face. Her hair was in loose curls on top of her head, a single white ribbon giving the illusion of holding it all in place.

Suddenly the gate lurched as a chicken burst out of the door and into the open yard. Coming to his senses, he quickly closed the gate.

"Oh, dear, how will we ever catch it?" asked Fleur.

The hen walked slowly after fluttering around on the ground, obviously pleased with her escape.

Evan looked at Fleur, a confident smile gracing his face as he handed back the basket he had taken earlier. "It's not a problem. I can handle one measly chicken, surely."

Fleur crossed her arms, a brow climbing her face as she watched. *At least I am no longer bored*, she mused.

Evan crouched and walked slow and quiet. He lunged and the chicken fluttered away, barely escaping his grasp.

This went on for five minutes, Fleur trying not to laugh, and Evan becoming less concerned that his wife was in earshot of every expletive he uttered.

Finally, he cornered the hen near the pigs, and with one great leap his arms latched around her. He smiled in triumph, only for the hen to flap her wings, knocking him off balance, straight through the pen and into the mud below.

Fleur gasped, hand flying to her mouth as she dropped the basket and ran towards him.

The chicken escaped, again, and Evan, not caring one whit, propped himself up with his hands, breathing hard.

Fleur looked him over, and he seemed to be fine, besides the thunderous look he was wearing. She tried, she really did, but laughter bubbled within her, and he gave her a scathing look.

She bit her lip, giggles abating as she cleared her throat. "I am sorry, Evan, truly, but..." She dissolved into a fit of giggles again.

He remained sitting, too tired to move yet, and also not entirely sure how he was going to stand in all the sticky mud without falling straight over again.

"Are you going to come out of there?" she asked.

He grinned. "No, I quite like it in here. You know I have

it on very good authority that dukes love spending their time in here. What's good enough for a duke..."

He trailed off, waving his hand in the air.

She laughed and shook her head at his antics. "Even dukes must listen to their wives sometimes, so come out of there."

He laughed and rose forward, standing on unsteady legs. He sloshed through the mud and straw, surveying the damage he caused. He would have to get someone to mend the fence immediately.

As he moved forward, she took a step backward, her nose crinkling.

Then the most devious grin Fleur had ever seen slanted across his face, and she quickly backed further away, pointing at him in warning.

"Evan? Don't. You. Dare."

"Dare what?" he asked, as he lunged forward to catch her. She squealed and dodged him, though barely, and ran towards the cottage laughing.

He followed, trying to reach her as she ran in circles, hiding behind trees, doing everything she could to avoid him.

In the kitchen, Cook looked at the time and wondered where Fleur had gone off to with her eggs.

23
A MATTER OF TIME

Fleur gazed at her reflection in the mirror and flushed. The dress was simple, elegant even, as silver netting cascaded down the most emerald of greens. It was *the* dress. The one Julia had persuaded her into, but never dared wear, not until now. She knew it was vanity, but she could not help but own she felt beautiful.

She leaned forward to smooth her chignon, catching a glimpse of the swell of her breasts in the mirror. She leaned back, hastily, covering herself and wondering if she should not wear a chemisette after all. She had never wanted it before, to have men gaze at her, though it was not lost on her that she *wanted* Evan to gaze upon her, to want her and to think her as beautiful as she felt.

Seeing the sky grow dim with the warmth of the setting sun, she knew it was time. Excitement thrilled through her at imagining him waiting for her. She had no idea what he had planned for them this evening, but she could no longer wait to go to him.

Making her way out of the cottage; she walked down the clearing towards the road that lead to the main house.

The pond was not far, so visitors would see the water and the sweeping willow trees on its banks as they arrived.

She walked towards the trees, not seeing Evan but catching a glimpse of light shining from under the canopy. She moved forward, separating the willows with her hand, and as she stepped inside, she gasped.

Lanterns twinkled, made brighter from the darkness of the branch cover. They sat strategically placed around within, and hung from branches galore. She saw a small round table, chairs arranged on either side adorned with linens, wine, and table settings. It was like a painted scene from Vauxhall Gardens, shimmering with light.

Walking further into the secluded area she saw him, standing by the water's edge, looking out over the horizon, his hands clasped behind his back. He was wearing what she had come to think of as his customary browns, his pantaloons showing every line of his muscled legs, his figure making a dark silhouette against the soft glow of the remaining sunlight.

"Evan," she spoke, barely above a whisper.

He turned and saw her, and looked long, his eyes roaming over her just as she imagined, exactly how she wanted. She walked over to him, joining him by the water, turning to look up at him.

"This is beyond anything I imagined, Evan. Did you do all this yourself?

He gave her a brisk nod. "Most of it, though Briggs had the table brought down from the attic."

She laughed, turning back to look at it. "*The* table?"

"I covered it," he said, smirking, turning towards her. "And all has been checked for weasels, madam, you are quite safe."

"As are you," she teased, and he laughed.

"I own I may have been a bit frightened by the weasel," he admitted, "but only a tiny bit."

He escorted her to the table. She sat, and he reached under the cover, removing a basket. Opening it, he laid out different foods and wine and took the seat across from her. He motioned to her to fill her plate first, and they began to eat.

She watched him, and she could tell he was hesitant. Several times she thought he was going to speak, but then he would look down at his plate, or sip his wine, averting his eyes. Suddenly she knew that if she was going to get Evan to open his heart to her fully, she would have to first unlock it and she knew all along only she held the key.

Realizing she no longer felt hesitant to insert herself into his life, she asked about his days, the one she knew not of, wanting to know all about his university years and beyond. He asked about her debut, first jealousy and then amusement clear when she told him of her many offers, and how her father had refused every single one. He told her he would have to shake her father's hand for chasing off so many ne'er-do-wells.

But through all of this, they carefully avoided the one issue she knew would bring both of them pain. She also knew they would have to eventually speak about it, and soon, so she took the risk upon herself, along with a steadying breath.

"Evan?"

He looked up from his dinner, where he had been shuffling and bit of cheese across his plate with his fork for the last few minutes. Placing his fork down, he took one last sip of wine, looking at her over the glass. "Yes?"

She held her breath but pressed on. "Why did you leave, or rather, why did you not return?"

One never knew how Evan would react to a thing, emotions always having an inconstant and jarring effect on him. So when he abruptly stood and walked from the table, she panicked, quickly rising and grasping his arm.

"Don't go."

He turned to her, regretting his rash action leading to her distress. "I wasn't... I just needed to move, to not feel confined."

Hurt, she let her hand fall from his arm and turned from him. Cursing his inelegant tongue, he walked up behind her, placing his hands on her shoulders. "I don't mean to say that you make me feel confined, I only meant... honestly, Fleur, I don't know how to explain my feelings to you. I never have."

She started to turn, and he held her. "No, don't, I don't know if I can get through this if I see your feelings upon your face."

Nodding, she slowly turned her head back around and stood silent.

"It's one of my nightmares, you know, the way you might perceive me once I returned. The longer I stayed away, the worse my fears became, and I knew you would be angry."

"I would not have been," she argued.

"Truly? I don't believe that, and I don't believe you do either."

"Perhaps I would have been at first, but I still don't understand. How many times have we quarreled? More times than I can recall, and I know you're not afraid of my ire or my censure."

Evan closed his eyes, hands gripping her shoulders tightly. She reached up and laid her hand over his own. "Please, tell me."

He opened his eyes, focusing on the back of her head. "I didn't know how to ask your forgiveness — I still don't — and I didn't know how to come home after I had made such a spectacular arse of myself."

"Is that the only reason?" she whispered.

He swallowed. "I don't know."

Angry, Fleur whipped around to face him. "You don't know? Do you want to know what I know, Evan? Do you want to know how wretched I felt? You left without so much as a goodbye or any indication of when you might return, and if that weren't bad enough, you didn't return because you didn't know how?"

She turned and started to walk away, and he ran to her, grasping her by her waist, pulling her back into his chest as she struggled to get away.

"I did not know if I could live my life next to you, watch you become closer to Edward as our parent's wished," he said, his deep voice in her ear, and she went dead still. "How could I live my life apart from you? Unable to be yours in the most intimate of ways? I was unsure of your feelings, having barely discovered my own."

He hugged her closer, knowing what he was about to reveal would upset her. "That day was never meant to be the last time I saw you. I had intended... I was going to ask you to marry me that night, Fleur, the night of your birthday."

She turned in his arms and looked at him in astonishment. "What? I... marriage? You wanted to propose?"

He nodded. "I had it all planned for weeks before I returned home."

Fleur closed her eyes, tears welling within. "But you... all this time wasted when we could have been together. You know our parents would have approved after a bit of time."

Evan wanted to die when he saw the first tear fall, and a little more at the second. "I know," he said, unable to defend himself further.

"All you had to do was say that you were sorry!"

"I am sorry, so very sorry—"

"And I would have understood. I would have forgiven you!"

"I am asking you to now." Evan watched her carefully, knowing the fate of his entire life lay in this one moment. In her answer.

"I forgive you," she whispered, and unable to remember all the reasons he conjured for restraint, he kissed her. Her soft lips warm against his own in the cool night air. His arms brought her body against his own, and she shivered.

He rubbed her arms, his own hands shivering not from the chill in the air but from nerves. He had done it. He finally told her everything bottled within him all those years, all his feelings and his fears. And she had accepted him, fully, and without dependence upon future promises never to misstep, or false hope he would never make mistakes again. Because he knew they both would, but they would find their way together this time. Never alone again.

They stayed that way under the lighted canopy, tentatively kissing one another, until finally, the cold forced them inside. As they walked back to the cottage hand in hand neither said anything. They did not need to.

Evan opened the front door to the cottage and placed his hand on the small of her back, ushering her inside. He lit another candle from one already burning and handed it to her.

"You go on, I'll be up directly," he said, wanting to give her time and privacy to ready herself for bed.

To his surprise, she shook her head and took his hand,

and led him up the stairs into their bedchamber. Once inside, she led him to the bed, and he sat down upon it, she standing before him.

Fleur lifted her hand to run fingers through his hair. "I do not wish for you to stay away at night anymore, Evan. I want you to stay. I want you."

He looked up into her eyes as his hands moved towards her hips slowly. Worried he had mistaken her meaning, he hesitated until she nodded her approval. Then he felt the soft curve of her waist before he moved his hand around to her back, bringing her to him, resting his head on her stomach.

Turning gently, he placed a kiss just beneath her breast. Her breath quickened under his lips, giving him the courage to pull her down onto his lap. Elation coursed through him at the feeling of her wrapped in his arms, holding her as he had imagined so many times before.

He breathed in slowly, his senses clearing as he remembered himself. "We should wait. You deserve to be courted properly, Fleur," he whispered, punctuating his words with kisses to her cheeks and the curve of her ear.

"I've had enough of wooing and courting," she said, her breath heavy, hands balled into fists, crushing the shoulders of his coat.

He kissed her temple, moving down to lick the soft flesh of her lobe. "Are you certain?"

She felt his breath, a warm, soft breeze upon her neck, and unable to think or answer with words, she nodded instead.

Evan lifted her as he stood, turning to set her down gently upon the bed before stretching out beside her. He looked down upon her, leaning to kiss her fast and fiercely.

His free hand found her hair, unpinning and shaking it loose to fall in soft waves around her face.

She trembled as he moved his lips down her jaw and onto the hollow of her throat; she gasped and swiped at her hair to uncover herself, wanting more, needing to feel his lips upon her again.

As the back of his hand moved slowly down and across her décolletage, her breathed hitched, and he hesitated at the swell of her breasts. She looked into his eyes, searching his face, wondering why he had stopped.

"Fleur, I need for you to be absolutely certain. Is this what you want?"

She blinked, confused. "What? Why are you asking me questions?" she asked breathlessly as she grasped the back of his head and pulled him back down to her.

He laughed and kissed her again, winding his arms around her as he rolled until he was on his back, and she lay nearly on top of him. Fleur ran her hand down his chest and watched as he gasped for air, feeling the beat of his heart as fast as her own.

She smiled when he grasped her hand and pulled her down once more. His lips were warm on the crook of her neck, and she moved her head aside, inviting him in as he pulled the string of her laces, untying the back of her dress and stays.

Fleur felt a slight shock of connection as Evan trailed his hands up her arms before pushing her silk gown down, the front falling away to reveal her shoulders. He rose, kissing first one shoulder then the other. When he moved his mouth down she held her breath, releasing it once she felt his tongue move in between her breasts, surprised at the strength of her own excitement.

Suddenly he raised himself further, moving them both

as they stood from the bed. Her dress slipped down to her ankles, leaving her in only her shift. She watched him, heart pounding, and he gazed upon her as she stepped slowly out from her dress, the thin fabric of her shift hiding nothing. Standing before him, she felt both beautiful and exposed, apprehensive yet left wanting.

Evan looked at her long, unmoving, and when she could take no more she bravely reached up and untied his cravat with trembling hands, determined. The sound of linen swished as she slowly pulled the fabric from around his neck.

He reached up, making to remove his coat and she stopped him, sliding her own hands onto his shoulders, and like he did before, slipping his coat down his arms. She pulled his shirt from his pantaloons, and he shrugged off his remaining coat, grasping his shirt from behind and pulling it over his head before throwing it to the ground.

She reached up slowly, placing her hands on his chest before moving them onto his shoulders again, and as he stood half-naked in the moonlight, she explored him. She felt him gasp slightly when she ran a hand over his nipple and stopped, looking up at him, wondering if she had done something wrong.

"Keep going," he whispered, in no frame of mind to explain further.

She trailed her hands lower, hesitating only for a moment before she tried to undo the waist with unsteady fingers. "I don't know what I am doing."

Evan took control and rid himself of his bottoms, kicking them off to the side and out of their way.

Fleur took in the sight of him as her breath and will left her. "Oh," she gasped.

His hands wound around her waist, pulling her to him, and he touched her cheek. "Don't be afraid."

She could feel the length of him hard against her with only her shift to separate them. As he trailed his hands down, heat followed in their wake, exploding when he gathered the thin fabric in his hand and pulled it up enough to brush the bare skin of her thigh.

She sighed at the connection she'd wished for, not knowing how she'd needed him as he caressed her thigh and hip. His fingers clenched, pulling her into him hard, and he kissed her again, deeper, feverish until she gasped for breath.

Her arms raised, and he took the cue to remove the offending fabric, her body trembling; there was finally nothing between them. He walked her backward, and when he felt the back of her thighs bump the bed, he halted.

Before she could react, he placed his hands around her waist and lifted her, her legs parting and wrapping around his waist as she clutched his arms, steadying herself, pulling her to him as much as she was able. She held on, looking down into his eyes before kissing him again, this time slowly, on his lips, his neck, anywhere she could reach, her kisses no longer shy.

He climbed upon the bed, she still clinging to him, and after he laid her down, he rose and looked down at her.

"Beautiful," he muttered.

Her face burned, and his eyes settled on her, and when his hand skimmed out from under her thigh and moved down towards her knee, he fumbled uselessly with her garter.

"I suppose I don't know what I'm doing either."

She laughed, relieved at knowing they could learn together. She reached down to untie her garters slowly,

Evan watched her, and once freed, he slipped her stockings off, one by one.

Leaning down, he propped himself up between her legs and kissed her, moving his hand up her inner thigh, and she opened to him, breath held as he slowly stroked upwards. She counted the seconds until he finally touched her, his thumb sliding over her as she jolted from surprise and the sensations of his hand upon her.

He circled his thumb, and she grasped his shoulder hard as he moved against her. Cupping her, he parted her and slipped a finger inside, slowly. Unable to handle the targeted sensations alone, she pulled him to her.

"Kiss me?" she asked.

He nodded and touched her lips with his own, tentatively, slowly, much more so than he had before, and she felt his care for her as he slowed to the tune of her body.

She sighed, finding pleasure in the slow rhythm, and when she'd caught her breath, he took her hand in his and placed it gently onto himself, moving with him as her guide. When she circled her thumb around the slick head of his crown, he gasped into her mouth, and the excitement of the action thrilled her.

He slipped another finger inside, pushing into her more fully, and when she palmed him with a twist of her hand, they neither one could wait a moment longer.

He released her and laid both hands on her hips, looking down to her as he pulled her towards him. He covered her mouth with his own once again, shifting to move between her legs, spreading them wider with his hips. She felt him move slightly, guiding himself up, then down, stroking her blissfully, and her fingers flew to his neck and tangled in his hair as he pressed forward, finally meeting her.

He moaned as he slipped inside, both of them trying to breathe and failing. She was tight around him, and he waited, whispering soothing words of his love in her ear. His hand cupped her breast, thumbing her nipple, and as the sensations battled against pain, she felt the need to move against him. So she did, and he took her.

He moved deeper into her, pulling back only to take her deeper with every new movement. Her only thought was of him, and he was everywhere, gripping her hips, breath against breath, inside of her, and she wrapped her legs tighter around him, bracing herself to take him deeper, needing more of him. Needing all of him.

Her breath shallowed, her body tightened, heart beating harder with each meeting of their bodies until her neck rose off the bed with a snap, and she shattered. She cried out, realizing only then what had happened, and at the same time, she felt him let go, pushing with one final flex of his hips as he buried himself inside her, deep, gasping her name.

Leaning his head on her shoulder, she moved her hand up and down his arm as he held her, their breath still fast and wild, her legs still draped around him, he still inside her. She closed her eyes, rested her head next to his own, and sighed.

After a moment he moved from her, gently lying beside her as she turned to face him.

"Did I hurt you?" he asked, caressing her hair that cascaded down her arm and shoulders.

Smiling, she raised her head to look him in the eye. "Only for a moment."

He stroked her face as they gazed at one another for a long moment before she laid her head on his chest, closing her eyes. Knowing she was almost asleep, he woke her.

"I have something for you."

"Again?" she asked, her voice teasing.

He laughed and shook his head, kissing the top of her head before reaching over the edge of the bed and grasping his coat, bringing it over. He reached into the pocket and pulled out the small object.

She raised up, watching him, tucking the blanket under her arms so it would stay, curious to see what was in his hands.

He took her hand and turned it upwards as he placed the miniature into her palm.

She turned it over and gasped. "Oh, Evan, it's you! You look so young," she said, looking into his eyes.

He nodded. "Remember on your sixteenth birthday I came to you and told you I had a gift for you?"

She moved her thumb over the smooth enameling, the painting within detailed and accurate. The silver surround tarnished with age. "Of course, and it was this portrait? But it's an odd sort of frame, isn't it?"

Evan smiled. "That's because it's not a frame; look closer."

She turned the piece over, inspecting until she found a latch and it opened with a click. "It's a timepiece! Oh, how beautiful."

"Much like the original," said Evan, laughing when she gave him a look.

"And what is this on the inside, I cannot make it out, is it engraved?"

"Yes," he said simply.

She moved the piece towards one of the candles on the bedside table and saw that there were four dates etched within.

"What are the meanings?" she asked.

"Can you not guess?"

"Well, the first is my birthday, the third as well, though a different year, that is odd, isn't it? The second date I am unsure of, but the fourth... Evan, it is the day we were married. How did you manage this?"

He watched her face knit in confusion before reaching for her, pulling her down, her back upon his chest. He took her hand in his and brought it to his lips.

"The first date, as you noted, is your birthday, the day you entered this world and also the day we met. As you know, my mother tended to your mother's confinement, and since I was a strapping young boy of only three, I accompanied her. The fourth you guessed correctly as the day we married. I had it engraved in town after I acquired our special license."

She smiled, still turning the piece in her hands. "And the third, what does my second birthday represent?"

"That was the day I was supposed to give this to you."

Remembering that day as one of the worst in her life, she now smiled. "The day you were to propose."

"Yes," he said simply.

Fleur pulled the blankets up higher to cover her shoulders as Evan rubbed her arms, trying to warm her.

"What about the second?"

His brows knitted. "The second?"

"The engraving, the second date."

Evan took a deep breath, placing his hand on her face, his thumb moving along her jaw. "That was the day I first realized how much I loved you. I do, you know, love you, I always have. There has never been another, Fleur, not in my heart nor my bed. It was always you."

She laid her hand on top of his and smiled before leaning in to kiss him. "I love you too, Evan."

Evan glanced down at Fleur, her head upon his chest, and wondered how on earth his greatest wish had finally come true. For so long he had despaired, had felt bereft at the loss of her, and now here they were, together. He knew their history would always be there, but it could no longer create uneasiness nor pain.

Together they would not allow their past to come between them, and together nothing would stand in the way of their future happiness, love having shined its light upon every dark corner of their past.

24
EPILOGUE

Fleur stood with Evan pressed into her from behind, his arms wrapped around her waist, her eyes closed as she listened to his voice.

"Can you feel it?" he asked. He slid his hands down to her own, helping her grip and slide them over the smooth length. "Tighter... there, that's it... now swing."

She swung the bat with force, and when she heard a loud crack her eyes opened, and she cheered.

"Don't cheer woman, run!"

Evan laughed as she jumped at his words and ran to the other end of the pitch, Little Thomas awaiting her and clapping.

When she ran back towards him, eyes wide, he smiled. "That will be all, Little Thomas. Why don't you run along and see if you father needs help when he makes his run to town?"

The boy smiled, nodded, and ran off, leaving Evan and Fleur in the field.

"How does it feel?" he asked, taking her arm in his own

and walking her back to the house. "I kept my promise. I finally taught you how to play cricket."

Fleur gave him a look, still trying to catch her breath. "It was exhilarating, though don't praise yourself too hard — it did take you over a decade to get around to it."

He swung open the gate to the cottage, holding it for her to step inside the small courtyard. In the distance she could see work being done on the outer wall, the white trim of the house being restored to its former state.

They had both agreed that until all the work was completed on the main house, they would stay in their little cottage, a place both had come to cherish. There was one thing, however, they did not agree on.

"You know, if we stayed home, we could play cricket every day. There are many other games I could teach you as well," he said, wiggling his eyebrows.

Fleur laughed as she walked through the front door, removing her bonnet. "No, Evan, you promised Julia."

Evan fell into a nearby chair, laying his head back and closing his eyes. "How could I tell her no when you so obviously wanted to be the one to chaperone her this season? I can't fight you both. I haven't the strength. I don't know how your father managed it."

"Years of practice, I'm sure," she said, tying the ribbons of her bonnet before hanging it beside the door. "Besides, I haven't seen my father nor Julia since Christmas. Oh, and you will finally see Mr. Carter again!"

Evan raised his head from the chair. "Fleur, we men are different creatures. My seeing Nathan is not a priority, not one I need suffer for anyway. We will be there for weeks, and you know Nathan and Julia will be unbearable around one another. They do nothing but bicker."

Fleur crossed her arms. "More the reason for us to be there. If we don't go to escort her, there is no telling what Julia might do. It's only a few parties and balls, Evan, really."

"No. No balls, Fleur, you promised."

"We shall see," she said, smiling before walking towards him. Once she was within reach, he grabbed and pulled her into his lap.

She leaned down and kissed him. "We really shouldn't be lounging around like this, not when there is so much left to do before we away."

"It's too late now I can't feel my legs. Someone has crushed them. Can't work a bit."

She laughed and smacked him on the chest. Leaning forward, she kissed him on the nose and smirked mischievously. "Poor Evan, it must be difficult, being crushed by so many people."

Confused, Evan looked at her, but when he searched her face, filling with happiness and mirth, a great smile dawned upon his face.

"Truly?" he asked, searching her eyes, which had misted over with happy tears.

She laughed and nodded as he brought her down to hug her tightly. "I don't deserve to be this happy," he said with a sigh.

"Don't get too excited, it may be a girl you know," she teased.

He thought back to a conversation he had with her father, something that stayed with him, that having a daughter would be his privilege, and that he would one day live for her. "I hope it is a girl — a daughter — just like you," he said, meaning every word.

She smiled, looking into his eyes, leaning down to place a kiss on his warm lips, but then she remembered something and paused. "Oh, but, Evan, I just thought of something dreadful."

Worried, he sat up straight. "What is it?"

"How will we ever name our child when we can't even agree on a name for our home?"

He laughed, relaxing again. "I'm sure we will manage, though I still think 'willow' should be in the title."

"Why 'willow' specifically?" she asked.

Evan looked at her and smirked. "We first kissed under the willow trees by the pond."

Fleur smiled and melted further into his arms, knowing he was wrong but never telling him of her stolen kiss when he slept soundly in the chair they both sat in now. "All right, willow it will be. What about Willow Manor?"

Evan shook his head. "Too pretentious. What about park? Willow Park?"

The both shook their heads this time. "Hill?" she asked.

"Hmm, hill, Willow Hill?" he asked, trying it out. "You know I like it? Perhaps we've found our name."

Fleur sighed. "Finally."

Evan touched her cheek, a small caress that quickened her breath. "Finally feels like home, doesn't it?" he asked.

Fleur thought his words could not have been truer as she leaned down to kiss him.

During the last several months, she and Evan had been almost as inseparable as they were when they were children. She had, however, learned that being in love was easy, but not necessarily the same thing as living easily with a person. The latter, of which, was significantly harder.

Through it all they had quarreled, only but a little, but

they had also loved fiercely, and neither one had thought of leaving the other, their confidence in that love having grown, and their ability to convey their feelings constant. But more importantly, they knew that since they had found one another again, against all odds, they would never let one another go.

25

SECOND EPILOGUE

Opening of the Season ~ London, England, 1815

Lady Julia Osborne was frightfully bored.

He led her across the floor with effortless grace, and his manner was charming and even somewhat witty. Yet, she could not bring herself to enjoy his company. Mr. Harris was one of many suitors who could not hold her attention for more than a dance, through no real fault of his own.

Of course, he asked her all the right questions, and she gave all the appropriate answers. Practiced and rehearsed as it was, she preferred the safety and ease of such conversation when one's mind wandered, and hers was practically dashing away at present.

"Your father, he is well, I trust?" he asked for the second time. "I have yet to see him this evening."

"Yes," she said, her smile inviting enough for him to continue.

"And your sister? I noticed she was in town along with your aunt," He said while whirling her close enough to the refreshment tables that she saw Nathan Carter, her brother-in-law's closest friend, hovering upon the edge. Of course, he was smirking at her. Looking at her. It took everything in her not to look away from him, and he knew it too when she saw him raise his glass to her with a laugh.

She turned her attention back to her dance partner and somewhat succeeded at keeping annoyance from her tone. Mr. Harris didn't deserve her ire. "My entire family is well, Mr. Harris. I thank you for your concern."

He nodded, looking content, as if he had managed to impress her. She sighed as the music ebbed to an end and they bowed to one another.

She thanked him for the dance and made her way to the refreshment table, telling herself she was not disappointed when she noticed Mr. Carter had already left.

"You look like you were having the time of your life with good old Mr. Harris."

She startled and nearly spilled the contents of her glass when he appeared unexpectedly near her.

She glared up at him. "Must you sneak up on people? At least have the courtesy of making some noise when you walk up behind someone."

"There are over a hundred people in this room alone. Just how much noise would I have to make to be heard over that, I wonder?"

Julia, turning toward him, laughed. "Why are you over here by yourself? Aren't you going to hide in the card room like all the other men whose mothers aren't forcing them to dance with young ladies?"

"Young ladies," Nathan said as he shuddered visibly for her amusement, "Actually, I was looking for Evan. I see he's still guarding your sister."

Julia took a sip of her drink before setting it to the side. "Why don't you make your way over to him, then?"

"There are at least four unmarried women I don't know sitting next to your sister. You know as well as I do if I go over, there will be ten minutes of introductions alone."

Julia snorted, loud enough that her sister, if present, would have been horrified. "Are you frightened?"

"Absolutely," he readily admitted as he leaned toward her like it was a great secret. "Besides, it is nearly time for the dinner bell. I assume your next partner will be here to sweep you off onto the dance floor before being the perfect dinner guest."

Julia groaned. "Must I?" she asked, looking up into his blue eyes. They crinkled at the corners just slightly whenever he looked happy. And Nathan Carter was always happy.

"I'm afraid you must. Who is the lucky gentleman this time?"

Julia cleared her throat, trying and failing not to smile. "Mr. Harrison."

Nathan laughed. "First Mr. Harris and then Mr. Harrison. Do you not find yourself confusing one for the other?"

"It's not like it matters," she muttered.

"Pessimistic as always, I see."

Grabbing her drink once more, she huffed. "Oh, go away, won't you?"

He laughed, gave her a wink, and sauntered away toward her brother-in-law. She didn't even have time enough to be surprised before she saw Mr. Harrison walking toward her to escort her once again onto the floor.

Bracing herself for what was sure to be more of the same old conversation, she smiled at her partner as he led her out, asking about her father's health before they could make the first turn about the floor.

Trying her best to give him her full attentions, she couldn't help but lock eyes with Mr. Carter each time she twirled his way, and it wasn't lost on her that she always felt just a little more relieved when he was around. Just a little less out of sorts.

The man was the epitome of amiable. If good-natured was known by any other name, it would be Nathan Carter. It was annoying, honestly, his easy way with people. As if it had never occurred to him he could make anything other than a good impression. Still, if she had to choose between the Harrises and Harrisons of the world and the epitome of amiable to keep her company, she thought there were worse things than being annoyed by Mr. Carter.

Running from Rakes coming soon!

UPCOMING BOOKS
BY ANNE CHERIE

MEDDLESOME MATCHMAKERS SERIES

Marriage to a Mister

Running from Rakes

Capturing the Captain

Victory over the Viscount

AMERICANS IN LONDON SERIES

The Americans in London Series is a three-book spin-off of the Meddlesome Matchmakers Series and follows three siblings as they find love across the pond.

CELESTIAL COURTSHIP SERIES

The Celestial Courtship series is a four-book cozy fantasy romance set in a historic world torn apart by old magic, old traditions, and even older rivalries.

ACKNOWLEDGMENTS

To my Super Six Team, you each know who you are and what you mean to me. We may have met later in life, but better friends I could never find, not ever.

To Staci, my personal cheerleader and ball of hyperactive awesome. Without you I would have given up long ago, and would have been content to do so which was complete #BSS. Thank you for kicking me in the ass again, and again, and again, repeatedly, for three years. #LifeTwins

To my beta readers: Karla Sorensen, Zoe Streiker-Howard, Becca Mysoor, Erika King, Clea Boone, LeahKim Gannet and Kathryn Czornij. Some of you I have known for a long time, and some of you came to me as a favor from a friend, having not one clue what you were getting yourselves into. What you have done means so much to me. Thank you for helping me through this journey. Without your criticism MtaM would not be what it is today.

To Becky Slemons, my editor. Thank you for putting up with my repeated spazz. You are a miracle worker.

And last but certainly not least, to the wonderful readers. Marriage to a Mister is my debut novel and I feel honored and humbled you took the time to read my work, so thank you, from the bottom of my heart.

ABOUT ANNE CHERIE

 When Anne was a little girl she didn't want to be doctor or an astronaut, and she definitely didn't want to be a writer. She was going to be an Egyptologist, and that was that.

One day, while working as a library aide at her elementary school, Anne picked up a beat up old book called The Reluctant God by Pamela F. Service. (mostly because the cover illustration had a young modern girl with flaming red hair leaning over a mummy in a sarcophagus) The story wasn't long, but it had a time traveling Egyptian prince and a plucky strong willed girl who both came together to solve the mystery and save the day. It inspired her.

These days Anne works in the unsexy world of HR and at night she writes love stories. A far cry from being an Egyptologist but she can always revisit that plucky girl and Egyptian prince anytime she wants.

FIND ANNE @

www.annecherienovels.com